THE BROKEN SPYGLASS

Mehitable Hatch

Copyright © 2023 Mehitable Hatch

All rights reserved

The characters and events portrayed in this book are fictitious. Any similarity to real persons, living or dead, is coincidental and not intended by the author.

No part of this book may be reproduced, or stored in a retrieval system, or transmitted in any form or by any means, electronic, mechanical, photocopying, recording, or otherwise, without express written permission of the publisher.

ISBN-13: 9781234567890
ISBN-10: 1477123456

Library of Congress Control Number: 2018675309
Printed in the United States of America

CONTENTS

Title Page
Copyright
Chapter 1: Storm 1
Chapter 2: The Coffin Maker 17
Chapter 3: Flashes 32
Chapter 4: Family 52
Chapter 5: Boarded 65
Chapter 6: A Sailor and an Officer 76
Chapter 7: Justice 91
Chapter 8: The Hold 104
Chapter 9: Circle of Glass 113
Chapter 10: A Fool and a Cockerel 130
Chapter 11: Questions 144
Chapter 12: Under the Bed 156
Chapter 13: Treasure Map 167
Chapter 14: Choice 189
Chapter 15: Shot and Clubbed 201
Chapter 16: The First Breath 210
Chapter 17: Trial 223
Chapter 18: Legacy 232

Chapter 19: Home	238
Books By This Author	247

CHAPTER 1: STORM

In the year 1665, on the fifth day of June, on the gently rolling Atlantic, First Lieutenant Leopold Passy caught sight of a tiny stain of darkness on the far horizon to the southwest. The weather had been calm and obliging for days and the crew was easy, but the sight of that darkness stirred up the anxiety that had been steadily growing inside Passy for days. Since the moment he'd been told the true purpose of their voyage – which was not, in fact, to deliver the cargo of sugar in the hold - worry and stress had been his constant companions. He watched the darkness on the horizon for a time, feeling as though his skin was crawling with insects.

He tried to put it out of his mind, to carry on with his duties, but a short time later, after a turn around the deck, he happened to glance up, again, and saw that the dark stain had grown far larger as it crept closer to the ship. He took a few minutes to watch the darkness and scowled at how fast it seemed to be moving. A glance through his spyglass didn't improve his humor.

It was then, when a gust of wind blew the hat off Passy's head, that the hand in the crow's nest shouted down, "Storm brewin'!"

At once, Passy called out for all hands, and the crew appeared immediately, scurrying up from below deck and whatever nook or cranny they'd found to rest themselves in. The approaching storm was cause for action, but not for panic. Every man knew his place and knew what to do with Passy's bellowed orders. Full sail was called for, and the coxswain turned the ship just so to catch the suddenly gusting wind.

"It's going to be a strong one." Captain LeBeau came to stand at Passy's side. The heavy clouds were nearly upon them, rolling and churning in the sky as though some great hand were stirring them up from above.

"Yes, sir. It blew out of the southwest, sir. We can outrun it—it's a fair distance off and we've got the wind at our back. I think it won't take us far off course. If we are very, very fortunate, then we may even benefit from a generous push." Passy pointed upward towards the full white sails. "It's as good a headwind as we've had in days." Even as he spoke, the storm seemed to be charging upon them, roaring at their backs with such intensity that when the fullness of the wind hit them, it felt as if the ship might be carried right off the water and sail into the air like a ladies' bonnet caught in a breeze. The ship jerked forward so suddenly that even Passy, a man with years aboard ship to his credit, was nearly taken off his feet. The storm winds were strong and constant and kept them well ahead of the hurricane.

Captain LeBeau watched the men in the riggings and those scurrying about their duties on the deck with a pleased smile. "So long as the sails don't give under the strain and the storm doesn't gain on us, you may be right in this being a lucky stroke. Better than being becalmed."

"True enough, sir. A quiet voyage is all well and good, but I've no urge to linger more than necessary." He lowered his voice. "How's the cargo?"

"Well enough." Captain LeBeau said nothing further and Passy, who knew his place, dropped the subject.

Up and down on the raging, gray waves, the ship rode and, always, they managed to stay ahead of the most dangerous part of the storm and just out from under the ominous black thunderheads.

As he kept an eye on the storm behind them, Passy became aware of something small and dark on the sea and in the murkiness of the storm. He squinted and took a few steps closer to the stern of the ship, as if those few steps would help sharpen his vision. When he realized what he was seeing, the only thing that it could possibly be, he felt himself quail in horror. Again, he pulled his spyglass to his eye and found that spot tossed about on the waves.

"What do you see?" Captain LeBeau shouted over the wind.

"A small craft, sir. Not as lucky as we in outpacing the storm." He imagined he could hear the awful cries from the terrified sailors as they frantically tried to fight the hurricane. How many had been injured beyond repair? How many had been tossed overboard, lost in the gray waves?

With a deep breath though his nose, Passy let the spyglass drop away from his eye and he turned back to his own frantically working crew.

"Poor souls," Captain LeBeau muttered as he piously crossed himself.

"We can do nothing for them, sir. Consider them lost." Passy stepped away from his captain, wishing he could stop hearing the imagined screams and stop seeing that small glimpse of a near-wrecked ship. He couldn't. It was all there, flashing before his eyes and ringing in his head. It would take a true miracle for the other ship to survive.

"Someone went and got ol' Neptune's temper riled!"

Passy instantly looked at the speaker—a hand not moving fast enough for his liking—and he snarled, "Stand around like a rock and we'll all go down! Get to the hold and see that the livestock are secured!"

After the hand had gone, Passy couldn't help a look back at the other ship. The thunderheads were near black, and all of the sea had turned from sapphire blue into a murky, cold gray. *Perhaps,* he found himself thinking, *the man has struck at a vein of truth.* Passy was as Christian as any good man, but he was a sailor, too, and what sailor worth his salt didn't give due respect to that temperamental god below the waves?

Hours passed before the thunderclouds began to lighten. The fierce gale eased to a steady wind and they were once again safe, praise be. When the men had all calmed and returned to their usual activities, Passy found his attention drawn back to the ship behind them.

It seemed impossible for the storm to have cleared so quickly, but the clouds faded into nothing within the hour and left blue skies behind. The seas of the deep Atlantic had grown peaceful with enough of a breeze to fill the *Juliet's* three large sails and to slap gentle waves against her hull. The sky, uncluttered by even the most benign of clouds, was bright enough to make a man wonder if the hurricane had been anything but a dreadful illusion. The ship Passy watched, however, was proof that the storm had indeed been real and that the *Juliet* had only been lucky in escaping its full wrath.

By some miracle, some grace of God, the other ship hadn't capsized. There was enough sail left to keep it moving forward, towards the *Juliet*, at a sluggish crawl. For a long while, Passy stood stock-still on the port side of the deck of the *Juliet*, both hands tight on the railing as he stared out at the other ship. He was no coward, but something in his bones urged him to run or, better, to attack. The impulse was so strong that he started sweating as he watched the other ship. He shifted nervously from foot-to-foot and bit the inside of his cheek.

A body couldn't help but pity the wretched condition of the other ship, but storms were just one of the many dangers that so many seamen were willing to face for the wealth that the New World offered. Passy, a sailor since the age of fourteen, had seen more than a few sea battles, and he somehow had managed to survive all of them without so much as a missing toe. He knew as well as any the plentiful dangers of the sea, whether it be sickness, weather, attack, or, every sailor's most dreaded nightmare, fire. He knew the dangers and accepted the risks. He had known even as a boy that he could easily die at any moment.

Sugar, tobacco, and cocoa were only a few of the many things found in the warm, bright waters of the West Indies that had most of the European nations in a frenzy. And a frenzy it truly was. There had been much bloodshed and lives lost for the sake of those treasures, as terrible, costly wars were waged over the little islands. All the great governments desperately vied for the wealth grown there, knowing that wealth could catapult them into a position of immense power in the world. Few of those men yearning for power seemed to care that it was the poor seamen and soldiers who died for their wealth.

It was that coveted wealth that made Passy so uneasy as he watched the dilapidated ship moving slowly towards them. The *Juliet* carried some of that dangerous wealth in her hull at that very moment, wealth that was bound for the markets of France. However, the greatest treasure they carried would never be bought or sold, but hidden. . It was a treasure for all France, something that would lift the nation up to the highest pinnacle of power.

"Be at ease," Captain LeBeau stepped up beside Passy and spoke softly enough that only Passy would hear him. "I don't need a panicked, jittery crew. The men are plenty worked up enough from that storm, and now," he nodded towards the ruined ship before them, "now they see what could have happened if we'd had just a bit less luck. Looking at your stiff back isn't helping them to keep calm."

"Your pardon, Captain, but I think there may be just cause for tense nerves." Nevertheless, Passy breathed in deeply and held it. He rolled his head and then his shoulders until the muscles relaxed as much as he supposed they would under the circumstances. He still felt as if he were wound too tightly, all stiff and brittle. "No cause to be worked up, you think? After all, it's clear what's happened here; the storm took hold of that shameful-looking craft and gave her a good shake. Nothing for us to worry over, no matter how the men whisper and mutter about ghost ships and cursed voyages. But you think on it, Captain. What's that ship doing here, so far from the shipping lanes? We're a good many miles from the common routes; there's no reason for it to be here."

"It is entirely possible that they simply do not use the trade routes in order to avoid pirates. It is slower, but no less achievable. And besides that, there is no reason for us to be here, either, Mister Passy, and yet, here we are. I would hope that should we have some trouble, that a passing ship would offer aid rather than puzzling over what we were doing out here in the first place."

Passy looked sharply at his captain. "That's hardly what we should be concerned about, but rather what might happen if the crew of that ship doesn't turn out to be as friendly as you would wish them to be. We need to consider the risk we take." He sternly resisted putting a hand to his aching stomach. His gut fairly screamed at him that the other ship was trouble. "Isn't that reason enough to worry?"

Captain LeBeau looked out to the nearly ruined ship drifting such a short distance away. "It's reason for prudence, if nothing else, I'll agree. Don't mistake me—I'm not about to be too trusting." Captain LeBeau put his spyglass to his eye and looked out at the ship. "But I must insist that you control whatever misgivings you may be nursing. Caution never goes amiss, but you are an officer, sir." Captain LeBeau's voice hardened noticeably, though he didn't look away from the other ship. "You must conduct yourself as befitting one. The men look to you for reassurance, and you must show them nothing but the utmost confidence."

"Understood, sir." Passy took the spyglass from his captain when offered and held it to his eye for a better look at the other ship. It bore what Passy guessed to be a tattered English flag of red, blue, and white hanging from the mast like ribbons. The sleek sloop was skeletal with most of its sails shredded. The masts and spars stood over the ship like great long arms bereft of their rightful dressing. The rigging was a spiderweb of ropes. Passy turned his attention from the ship to the crew. Only a few souls moved on the deck of the other ship and, from what Passy could see at the distance, they were in just as deplorable a state as their ship. At the base of the mizzen mast, a small figure sat with its arms wrapped around tiny legs, head bowed low enough to hide everything but a head of bright red hair. Such a desolate image the boy made. There were a couple of other men, none of them moving all that smartly, but none standing out so much as a bearded man at the starboard of his ship as he watched the

Juliet intently. He was tall and broad, with a proud, grim face that Passy guessed must have surely been something like Death's aspect.

"The storm was rough," Lieutenant Passy admitted as he took the spyglass from his eye and handed it back to his captain. "We aren't so very far from the usual trade routes ... I suppose you're right; it's possible that they might have been blown off course."

"We were lucky to have skirted by the worst of it," Captain LeBeau said. "We didn't see its full power and can't judge how strong it might have been against a ship caught within. We've sailed a good many years together, you and I, and in those years we've been battered by storms angry enough to blow the skin off a man. From what little we saw of the edge of that tempest, I would judge that it could have easily been as wild as any squall we've ever ridden out."

They stood in silence for a time, watching the other ship, before Captain LeBeau ordered that they slow their pace. Sails were raised and the *Juliet* came to a near-dead stop. The wounded ship, meanwhile, made little headway towards them. It bobbed up and down with the rhythm of the sea like a cork but only drifted a bit closer. Passy kept his back properly stiff with his arms at his sides, but had he not been in front of the hands, he would have slouched over and leaned his elbows on the deck railing as a memory, stirred up by the other ship's plight, flared to life. He thought of the wind and rain pounding against his face and the ship dancing so wildly on the furious sea that he truly feared it would capsize. He remembered the awful terror that the dark night would be the last night he would spend on Earth. How badly he'd wanted to fall to his knees and pray for deliverance even though he had had his duty to perform and lives that depended on him.

The other ship had survived such a storm, and Passy felt foul for his suspicions. As his captain said, it was likely that they were nothing but poor souls looking for rescue ... they would die without help. He couldn't imagine what it would be like to see salvation so close at hand only to watch the other ship sail away.

Monsieur Rene Morel, the ship's navigator, slid up to Passy's left. He didn't so much as look at the other ship and, instead, watched Captain LeBeau. "Why have we stopped, Captain? There shouldn't be any reason to consider them," he jerked his head towards the other ship. "They aren't our concern; we won't gain anything by getting involved with their troubles." Such a statement was a clear example of why Monsieur Morel was not popular with the crew. To say such a cold thing and feel no shame about it was a common thing for him.

Though Captain LeBeau had always carefully kept his opinions to himself in front of the crew, as was only proper, considering his station, he couldn't help but scowl at his navigator. "A harsh view, Monsieur Morel."

With a shrug, Monsieur Morel turned to look out at the ship. He didn't care about the crew's opinion of him, nor did he care about Captain LeBeau's lack of esteem. As one of the best navigators to be had, he was quite well-aware of his own worth to the ship and the mission. He'd been serving aboard ship since they'd set sail from the port of La Rochelle in France, and in those many, many weeks, Passy had found Monsieur Morel to be petty and mean-spirited—ruthless as a starving dog. He would have been an entire waste of space aboard the ship if it hadn't been for his two redeeming qualities—his brilliant navigational skills and his devoted loyalty to France.

Even faced with Captain LeBeau's censure, Morel showed little remorse for his callous opinion. "Don't think I'm heartless, sir. I'm only thinking practically and with the best interests of our mission in mind. Not only do we have limited supplies to give, but should they get wind of the cargo ..."

Captain LeBeau made a sharp gesture with one hand and gave Monsieur Morel a thunderous glare. "Gentlemen, if I may have your company in my cabin?" Without waiting for a reply, he strode away and didn't speak again until the three of them were alone in his cabin with the door securely closed behind them. "And who would tell? Do you think myself or Passy, here, would be so slow-witted as to let our mouths run free? Or do you maybe doubt your own self-control? We three are the only aboard who know."

"Captain," Passy said. "They draw closer by the minute. What are we going to do about the ship? Sir, much as I regret suggesting it, Monsieur Morel does have a point worth considering—the cargo can't be put at risk."

"Gentlemen," Captain LeBeau smiled. "I'm well aware that we can spare very little and that our mission is of vital importance to France. However, I will remind you that God looks down on all we do, even in the midst of such a critical undertaking. His will placed us here in front of that unfortunate crew, and I cannot believe He would intend for us to simply ignore them. We cannot leave them to starve. Without sails, they will never make it to shore and as they are so far from the normal routes, it is highly unlikely that they will come across any other vessels until it is far too late for them. We can't in good conscience, leave them."

Monsieur Morel blandly replied, "Fear of God is all well and good, but you need to think of the good of your men. You are oath bound—an oath made with your hand on the Holy Book, I might remind you!—to safely deliver the cargo. Any delay, even by a few hours—"

Captain LeBeau shot Monsieur Morel a hard look. "Mind your place, sir! I will not be lectured! My memory hasn't deserted me quite yet. If the cargo is meant to be delivered, then it will be. I cannot know God's plans for it, but what I do know is that He wouldn't easily forgive anyone deliberately ignoring those in need for the sake of a treasure. Any treasure. Charity can only do our souls good."

"Captain!" Monsieur Morel hissed. "Think of security, sir. To have these people roaming the ship is unwise, at best."

"There are only a few of them. If it troubles you, may I suggest that you remain in my cabin for the duration of their visit?"

Monsieur Morel turned red, stuck a hand into the pocket of his long coat and then turned his back on his captain, looking as insulted as if the captain had suggested that he prance about the deck in a gown. There would be an accounting of his attitude, Passy knew. Such behavior was unpardonable. He was valuable, but there was protocol that all must adhere to, and the foul expression on Captain LeBeau's face clearly told that the breach of protocol would be answered for.

Passy's disquiet held firm as he watched the approach of the tiny party from the wounded ship when they finally came close enough that they were able to lower a dinghy and row over to the *Juliet*. There were five men, but his attention, at once, was fixed on only one of them. He did a fair job of schooling his features, he believed, but seeing that familiar face after so long had shocked him. As it was, he said nothing. He couldn't see how his relation with one of the storm survivors could possibly make any difference in the coming meeting. He stood with his captain, waiting to receive their guests, and watched the strangers climb aboard with trepidation. There was no visible reason for his apprehension. They were ordinary-enough men, lean from the hard sea life and a bit worse for wear, but not more so than usual, considering the storm they'd survived.

It was especially unnerving to see Raynard so cowed.

When Raynard climbed over the deck rail, Passy couldn't have been more shocked. He was thinner than the last time Passy had seen him, but that had been years ago, well before word had reached him that Raynard had been sent to prison for petty theft. The years had changed him, some. His moustache was gone and his hair had grown a good deal. The clothes he wore were, without a doubt, the most jarring change. Passy had never seen Raynard dressed in anything but the finest he could afford. To see him in patched breeches and a shirt two sizes too big with a stain of some kind down the front of it was something Passy had never imagined he would see.

Judging by the look on his face when their eyes met, Raynard was just as astonished to see Passy. He covered it, quickly, and turned to help the last of his mates up.

When the five were aboard and stood before Captain LeBeau, it was clear who their commander was by the way his fellows kept glancing towards him. The man they gave their attention to watched everyone with tightness around his eyes and a hard set to his mouth that bespoke of a man in desperate straits, but trying not to show it. Though he wore clothes that were torn and stained, he held himself like a gentleman, and when he spoke his voice was soft, belying his rough appearance. He looked around at the crew of the *Juliet* before he said something in English.

Raynard nodded and stepped forward to say, "My captain wishes me to translate as he, regrettably, does not speak French. Allow me to introduce Captain Justin Shuman." Raynard paused when Captain Shuman spoke directly to Captain LeBeau and didn't speak again until his captain had stopped. "Two weeks ago, our ship was attacked and sacked by pirates. Most everything was taken. Only a handful of our crew survived. Then, we were overtaken by the hurricane and driven here by its bluster. If you have any supplies that you are able to spare, we would be grateful beyond words: medicine, food, water—anything."

Passy knew Captain LeBeau well enough to know that the English captain's words had struck him. Captain LeBeau had always been a kind-hearted man, the type who gave to widows and orphans, who would go out of his way to feed a stray dog. Such a dignified plea for help, given by a man clearly reluctant to beg, but willing to do so for the sake of his crew, had evidently touched Captain LeBeau's generous heart.

His chest swelled and he spread his arms in a welcoming gesture. A broad smile showed off white teeth. "How could I deny so simple a request? Sir, we haven't much to spare, but what I can give, I will."

Captain Shuman, through Raynard's soft translations, gravely and humbly accepted the help. A modest amount of food stores along with enough water for a few days rations were given. There was also the gift of a big enough sail to get them moving, and needles and thread to keep the sails strong. While supplies were gathered and made ready, Captain Shuman walked the deck with Captain LeBeau. Raynard trailed just behind them and kept up a running translation and Passy walked next to him, just watching and listening.

In truth, Passy found his attention drawn more to Raynard than to the two captains, where it should have been. Raynard paid him no consideration at all as he translated for his captain. The conversation was light, almost idle, until Captain Shuman mentioned that he'd been carrying silk to the islands when pirates had come upon them and, shortly after, the hurricane had swept them well off the trade routes. He then asked what the *Juliet* was transporting.

"Sugar," Captain LeBeau answered. "A goodly haul bound for France."

Captain Shuman smiled and stopped walking, which caused Captain LeBeau to stop and face him. "Then I wish you luck in reaching your harbor. In fact," his eyes lit up as an idea seemed to hit him. "I can offer a gift for your luck. It's the least I can do. The food you gave has surely saved us. Will you accept a bottle of good palm wine?"

"Wine?" Captain LeBeau asked. "I am surprised that it hasn't been drunk, considering the state you found yourself in."

"One bottle wouldn't save a life. Now, thanks to you, I don't need to hoard it for the last dire moment. Let me show my gratitude."

Captain LeBeau smiled. "Go, then. I'll be honored by the gift."

The boy and one man were sent back to the wounded ship for the wine and the two captains continued their talk. Captain Shuman asked, "Do you not worry about pirates? Surely, using the Gulf Stream, with its steady traffic, would be a safer and faster way to get to France, rather than this desolate path. Bless me, but your ship's the first I've seen since that storm grabbed hold of us."

"And what pirate would lurk in these waters when so few ships use this way? Why would a pirate ship come out this way where the only chance they have for prey would be wandering onto a ship by pure chance? Surely, most ships will keep to the fastest routes, and the pirates will follow their prey."

"Maybe so, but sometimes we take what hunting we stumble across." Captain Shuman seized Captain LeBeau by the shoulder and pushed him to the side, forcing him against the ship's railing. The knife he pressed to Captain LeBeau's throat was long, eight inches or so, and held by a steady hand.

Raynard and the other man who'd accompanied Captain Shuman drew pistols from under their coats and whirled around to face the crew. They completely ignored the shocked and angry clamor from the men around them.

"Stop! Quiet all of you!" Passy shouted, glaring at Captain Shuman's back.

Captain LeBeau stood still as a statue. His round, good-natured face was as dark as Passy had ever seen it. He glared hatefully at Captain Shuman. "What are you about?"

Raynard translated and Captain Shuman, who had been somber a moment before, threw back his head with a howling laugh. "Your cargo, mate. I find blood an unhappy sight, and, as a naturally peaceful fellow, I must protect my crew from all unnecessary danger. I'd hate for any battle to break out, here, and keeping you close at hand will prevent one. I'm sure you feel the same. You'd not want your men to suffer any, now would you?"

Captain LeBeau's face turned red. "I take it that your name is not Shuman. May I then ask your true name, sir?"

"Not your affair. Let me warn you that any threat to my men or myself will result in blood, and yours will lead the flow."

The pirate captain—for that was what he must have been—said something to Raynard, who went to the side of the deck and shouted to their ship. Before long, men began loading into the ship's two long boats.

The raid was fast and methodical.

There was no time wasted as the pirates divided up into two bands: one searched the ship for loot, and one guarded the prisoners. Happy, gloating pirates ransacked the entire ship, taking everything from the sugar to the jackets of the officers and, considering the threat to their captain, none of the French sailors dared to offer any resistance. Grinning like fat rats, the pirates took all the arms they could find, from the crew's knives to cannonballs. The angry French crew was lined up to a man, from their young, pale-faced cabin boy to the one-armed cook with his stained apron, where they were searched.

Monsieur Morel was dragged from the captain's cabin by laughing men who'd seized him under each arm—with an assortment of vile comments about his parentage—and threw him on the deck. Give him his dues, Monsieur Morel didn't go peaceably. He struggled every step of the way until he was tossed down on the deck. One of the men, one of those who'd first come aboard with Raynard and the captain, knelt next to the navigator and began to search him. That only made Monsieur Morel fight all the more fiercely. Like a wounded animal, he not only threw punches and kicked, but he clawed and bit until the pirate searching him grew impatient. Monsieur Morel let out a yelp when the pirate took hold of his hair and slammed his head into the deck. He fell onto his back, senseless. It made the search a good deal easier. They pulled from Monsieur Morel's pockets a compass, a small spyglass, and a knife with a dainty blade no longer than a man's finger.

Through it all, Passy stood with the rest of the crew, unarmed and helpless as the pirates ransacked their ship. There was nothing to be done. Passy couldn't take his eyes from the man who'd dug through Monsieur Morel's pockets. He stared intently and only looked away when he realized how obvious he'd been. He found himself looking at his cousin, who laughed with the pirates and worked right alongside them in their looting. There had been no redemption, as Passy had hoped. Raynard was one of them.

Hours after it had begun, Captain Shuman (or whatever his

true name happened to be) ordered his crew back to their own ship. Their tattered sails were lowered and the *Juliet's* sails raised in their places. The pirates were merry, singing as they went about their work.

Passy watched from the *Juliet's* deck along with the rest of the crew. There had been surprisingly little damage of any note done to the *Juliet*. Not a single life had been taken, and only Monsieur Morel, moaning on the deck, had been seriously injured, if a rattled brain could be considered serious. Without the distraction of wounded men to tend, all of Passy's attention was focused on the other ship and on what they'd taken. He gripped the railing of the ship so hard that his knuckles turned white. "Captain—"

"I ought to shoot you where you stand, Lieutenant." The fierce anger in Captain LeBeau's voice was barely contained in his low growl. "You could have stopped them!"

"They would have killed you, sir."

"Unimportant."

"Your selfless devotion to your country is inspiring, sir, but tell me, what then? After I'd let you get killed by trying to fight for the treasure? The crew would have risen up against them for your sake—you know they would have. How many of them would you have die for it?" Passy turned and met his captain's eyes, easily. "You stopped our voyage to help people in need, people who might have died without us. You stopped because you believed that God wouldn't want people to die if there was help for it." He paused until Captain LeBeau nodded, unable to deny the truth. "Then how could you say that God would have wanted this crew to be murdered over that one little thing?"

"Damn it!" Captain LeBeau snarled. He turned his back on the pirate ship as it steadily made its way away from them. "How did they know?"

"I don't believe they did." Passy moved closer to his captain and kept his voice low. "They were nothing but scavenging rats looking for whatever they could lay hands on. I'm astonished they didn't take our boots. No. I am convinced that it was nothing more than chance that led them to us, and they used that lucky opportunity to their greatest advantage as, let us concede, any pirate would. I can't believe that something like that would have been planned—they would have had to plan the storm, and I feel certain that Neptune doesn't play to the whims of humans. No. It wasn't planned. They could have just as easily taken your teapot, but no one's hand happened to fall on it."

"We can't let happenstance ruin this mission," Captain LeBeau's fists bunched at his sides. "Get the crew organized, Lieutenant. We pursue."

"Sir, I'm afraid ..."

"This isn't a discussion! Move!"

The crew went silent and still at the uncharacteristic outburst.

"Sir," Passy pressed, insistently. "They took all our sail but that off the mizzen mast. We can move, but only slowly. We have cannons, but no cannonballs. The armory was emptied. We have some food, but not much. Sir, we are nearly defenseless. The sugar is gone—"

"Do you think I care for sugar?!" Captain LeBeau thundered, never once taking his eyes off the fleeing ship.

"Sir! The crew!"

Captain LeBeau sucked in a deep breath to calm himself, and lowered his voice. "We will pursue those dogs. At all costs, we must catch them. They took it." He looked down at Monsieur Morel. "It's too important to France."

Passy knew what he had to do and felt sick about it. He closed his eyes a moment, but it didn't help. He didn't want to do it, but he knew his duty. But Raynard ... no. He owed nothing to Raynard. They hadn't even spoken in years. Raynard had shamed the family with what he'd chosen to do with his life. Besides, Passy might just be able to keep him out of the situation altogether. Resolving himself, he told his captain, "I believe I know where we might find them."

CHAPTER 2: THE COFFIN MAKER

The morning of August 1, 1665 rose on Port Royal, Jamaica, with the tolling of the bells of St. Paul's Church, the screams of white and gray gulls, and, for Elmore Finch, a splinter in his thumb.

In his workshop, with an inch of sawdust on the floor under his feet, Elmore Finch glared at the sliver of wood under his skin, then at the wooden plank he'd been smoothing down to an even keel, before he snorted and dismissed the faint pain. He would dig it out with a needle at some point, but there was work to be done and if he stopped for every little thing, he'd never finish. He ran a hand over the plank of wood he'd been working at to test the smoothness. At five-and-a-half feet long, the plank was one of three that would, when assembled, form the lid of a coffin. The coffin body was finished and stood against a wall, waiting to be completed. Of course, it wouldn't be truly completed until the remains of a life found a home in it, but that was only a matter of time. All life was simply waiting for the end, and it was Elmore's job to house that end.

Without looking up from the wood, Elmore shouted, "Jacob! If you're late and Reverend Roberts gives you a caning, I won't listen to your whining!"

"Coming! I'm coming!" There was a flurry of footsteps rushing down the stairs before the boy rushed through the workshop and into the kitchen. "Do you need help today? I'll stay home to help."

"You offer every day and every day I tell you—no. Get yerself to school. Got yer books?"

"Right here." Jacob sprang back into the workshop with two schoolbooks under one arm and a small bucket containing some lunch in the other hand. "Someday you'll want me here and I'll just tell you, 'Too bad. I have exams today.' And then you'll wish you'd let me stay home."

"I'll regret it then. Off you go."

"Yes, sir."

The boy was lanky and over tall for his twelve years. He'd reached the unfortunate time of life when a body seemed all arms and legs, but he was bright and winsome and had a cheery smile and good humor. Elmore rather thought the boy had the face of a leprechaun. With red hair that tended towards curls and skin that tended to burn rather than tan under the strong West Indies sun, he resembled his father a great deal. There was an amount of him, however, that was entirely unlike his father. The small nose and eyes as green as a gecko's back, the somber set of his small mouth when he was upset, were traits given to him by his mother—a woman Elmore had never met.

Once alone, Elmore set back to work, pushing the heavy plane across the plank and drawing off long curls of wood that fell gently onto his workshop's floor. The floor was littered with wood shavings, like a pale carpet. The workshop was a simple large room with a table at one side, two sawhorses in the middle, which he currently worked on, and wood in various stages of work set at the edges of the room. The workshop was really only the first room of Elmore's house. The kitchen was in the back and two bedrooms upstairs, but the workshop was where he spent most of his time.

Elmore took a moment to wipe his forehead with the back of his arm, clearing away the sweat that threatened to run into his eyes. The summer was sweltering and even the breeze that blew in through the open window that faced the sea wasn't helping all that much. After grabbing his walking stick from where he'd leaned it against one of the sawhorses, Elmore limped to the door and propped it open with a block of wood he was still trying to think of a use for. While it wasn't any good for a coffin, it was too big to waste and, therefore, had become a convenient temporary doorstop. Standing in the doorway, looking out at the harbor and the ships anchored there, he brushed the sawdust off his shirt and rolled his sleeves up to his elbows.

The city was quiet, yet. Soon, all would be awake and busy. The fishermen had already set out, but there were the big frigates that would raise anchor when their captains woke and, soon, there would be dozens of people, both men and women, sitting on the docks as they mended nets or sails. Two soldiers in bright red uniforms strolled down the street in front of Elmore's home, but didn't cast him so much as a glance.

He looked up at the sign above his door, a sign he'd made and hung himself. It was nothing more than a simple cutout of a large hammer. Not for the first time, Elmore sighed at the sight of it. That hammer had the remarkable ability to depress him in an instant flat, even though it was just a painted hammer. That hammer was his life. There had been a time, long ago, when he'd harbored ambitions far beyond a hammer hanging over his door. When he'd been young …

Elmore laughed at himself for letting his mind wander. Such dreams were long ago and far away.

He stayed in his doorway, thinking old thoughts of faraway places, until he felt as refreshed as he could hope to get. Before getting back to work, Elmore walked through his workshop to the kitchen at the back where Daisy, an amiable mutt nearly as big as a small pony, slept in front of a cold stove. She was black and brown, with black eyes and long, floppy ears. As gentle a creature as one could imagine, Daisy was a block of muscle. She was brainless, someone more honest than kind had once commented. When Elmore walked into the kitchen, Daisy was awake at once and lifted her head to look at him. With her tongue lolling out of her mouth in a sort of dog smile, she slapped her tail happily against the brick floor when he put down a bowl of water for her.

"You great lazy thing." Elmore scratched her head affectionately. "Gonna sleep all day, are you? You're not so old, yet." But, really, he could hardly fault her for her sluggishness. The heat made him want to sleep, and he didn't have to wear a fur coat. "Drink some, eh?" But when he made to push her dish of water a little closer to her, Elmore found that it had been usurped. "Harold? And where did you creep in from?"

Harold wasn't Elmore's dog, but a stray who tended to wander in or out of the house when the mood suited him. He'd come for the first time several years ago and apparently found the household to his liking. Ever since then, he'd made a habit of dropping by nearly every day, and Elmore didn't see any reason to chase him off. Harold was smaller than Daisy by half, and his sleek, almost skinny body was dwarfed by her. His coat was a hodgepodge of colors, all brown and yellow and black. Small eyes as bright and blue as a winter's morning sky constantly shifted around, even as he concentrated on lapping up the water. Elmore had always found Harold to be somehow rat-like.

Though he gave off not one sign of being friendly, Daisy went to Harold and lay down beside him, leaning against him. She might have crushed him had she not been mindful, but Harold allowed the show of affection. When he'd finished off the water, he gave Daisy's face a lick while she waited patiently for Elmore to refill the bowl.

"Uncle!"

Elmore stood up and scowled when his nephew, Jacob, rushed into the kitchen. "You holler in this house again and I'll take you over my knee."

Jacob, red-faced and panting for breath, had obviously been running. He paused, leaning over to rest his hands on his knees until he'd caught his breath and then, with a smile on his face that said he didn't take the threat to heart, he said, "I found work for you!"

"Oh?" Elmore raised an eyebrow. "And what do you plan to use to pay me? I know full well you've nothing in your pockets but lint. What do you want with a coffin, anyhow? Not feeling well? Or did you throw stones at someone you shouldn't have?"

"No! It's not for me and it's not a coffin. I met a—"

"And what are you doing out of school? I only sent you off a short while ago. Did you even have time to step in the schoolroom? If you're spending your days lollygagging about town ..."

"I wasn't. I mean, I was going to school, but I met these people and we got to talking. They're new in town, haven't even unpacked their belongings—you should see all the crates he's got—and he needs something built and was asking if I knew where he could find a carpenter."

"Well, what's he want built?"

"He didn't say, but he said he has directions and he just doesn't have the," Jacob paused a moment and frowned. "He said he hasn't got the touch. What's that mean?"

"I suppose he doesn't work with wood, o' course. Funny way to say it, though."

"And I know you'll say you're too busy, but I was thinking that if you are, maybe you could take on the new job and ... and I was thinking ..." Jacob trailed off a moment, looking at his feet almost shyly before he took a breath and started again. "I was thinking that if you haven't got the time to do all the work on your own that maybe ... maybe I could do the coffins for you. They're just big boxes, really, nothing fancy at all, and I know I could do it!" Jacob met Elmore's eyes squarely, but he lowered his gaze almost at once and went to where Daisy and Harold lay, squatting down to pet them. In a far more subdued voice, he said, "I'd get my schoolwork done, too. Honest."

"Would you, now? Just like the time you swore you could bring home half a tree on your own?"

"It was worth a try and this is different; I know I can do this. How am I ever going to get better if you don't let me at least try once in a while? And if I do foul it up somehow, I'm sure you'll tell me and show me how to fix it."

"You're sure of a lot of things today. I'll think on it, but I don't want you getting this too much into your head. You're not going to be a carpenter." He easily ignored Jacob's sulky pout. "Now, what's the name of this new customer?"

"Fa Tseng. Funny sort of name, isn't it? He doesn't dress a bit like folks around here; I think he might be from China."

"Wouldn't surprise me. God knows we've got plenty of folks from all over."

Jacob stood and faced Elmore with his hands clasped behind his head. "I didn't stop to talk to him, really. I stopped to talk to Fa Mei. Isn't that an interesting name? It sounds fierce, but really she isn't a bit. I was on my way to Saint Peter's and she was there, right outside the door of her house, sitting on a crate. She was watching the ships. I just wanted to talk. She dressed funny, but I liked it—she had tiny black shoes and she wore long skirts with flowers sewn on them. She looked awful sad when I saw her, so it seemed mannerly to chat and try to cheer her up. She didn't talk to me, though. She wouldn't even tell me her name. I was going to leave when Mister Fa came out —he's her grandfather, and he told me that she's dreadfully shy about meeting new people, so he introduced me to her. Anyway, he asked if I knew where he could find a carpenter, and I don't think it's just the boxes he wants. He's so new that his house is sure to need work, and weren't you just saying the other day that you wanted something to do other than just coffins?" He took hold of Elmore's arm and pulled him. "We have to go. Now. I told Mister Fa how good your work is, but if you wait, he might just get tired of waiting and hire someone else. Let's go!"

Much as Elmore hated to leave his work unfinished, Jacob was quite right when he'd said that Elmore had been griping that the work was dull. It would be nice to do something different, even if it were only a couple of boxes and maybe a table. True that it wouldn't be so interesting as patching a leak on a sinking ship or fashioning a peg leg for a suddenly crippled shipmate, but it would be a change, and he had no immediate work after the coffin was finished. Not that Elmore was worried about work not turning up—there was never a lack of the dead—but he'd never seen any good reason to turn down paying work.

He shook Jacob's hand off his arm and took off his apron, which he left on the unfinished coffin lid. He dusted off his clothes and said, "We'll take a walk over there, then, but you give me some time. I'll not leave the house in my shirtsleeves and looking like some tramp."

He splashed water on his face and arms to get off the worst of the sweat before heading upstairs, where he put on his best coat and dug out his newest shoes from under the bed. There were only a few scuffs on the leather, and the buckles were nicely polished. Before he left his room, Elmore took a moment to check his reflection in the glass of the window to be sure he was presentable. A quick run of his hands through his hair to push it away from his face, and he was satisfied. That done, he belted on his cutlass, tucked two loaded pistols into the band he wore across his chest, and tucked a dagger into a sheath at his side.

Dressed, armed, and reasonably clean, Elmore went back down to the workshop of his house, where Jacob paced around the unfinished coffin. He watched the boy, unnoticed, and reflected that impatience was characteristic of Jacob. For as long as he'd known Jacob, the boy seemed to overflow with energy. It was as if he didn't know what to do with himself. At times, it seemed to Elmore that Jacob was nothing more than a half-mad rabbit bouncing around inside a boy-shaped costume.

As they walked to the home of the new patron, Jacob chattered, as children tend to, about his schooling and friends, and, most of all, the new people. He'd thought Mei was very pretty, even if she didn't dress like the other girls in Port Royal. Their first meeting hadn't begun well. "She ran into her house when I tried to talk to her, even after her grandfather introduced us. And I think that was sort of rude, don't you? It wasn't as if I was doing anything, and she just ran away."

"You likely scared her."

"But I smiled at her, and I was friendly as anything."

Elmore just shrugged and let Jacob carry on, bemoaning how his efforts of neighborliness hadn't gotten a warm reception. It was good to see the boy smile. Five years ago, he wouldn't have been able to coax a smile out of him for an armful of sweets. The lad had changed in those few years. The sullen, angry child Elmore had met at St. Peter's Church was mostly gone, and had left behind a boy that was eager to please and a joy to know. The boy had been a trial in those first few weeks, but Elmore was proud of him. It was, he believed, one of the best decisions he'd ever made when he'd agreed to take the boy in.

They left their home on Barrier Street and went to St. Elmo's Street, which ran along the ocean, and turned to the right. They passed many people during their walk; three Spaniards laughing uproariously and ladies in carriages pulled by white horses. There were a couple of doxies with low-cut blouses, one of whom held her skirts shockingly high enough to show off her pale, skinny calves. She'd coyly asked if Elmore wanted to spend time together, but he'd rolled his eyes and told her, "Not interested."

Jacob had hardly noticed the woman. He was too busy rambling, having moved on from his new friend who'd run from him to the fact that his teacher, Reverend Roberts, might be providing Elmore some work, too. It seemed that his desk had broken. It wasn't termites, Jacob had gleefully told him. No, this broken desk had come about all thanks to one of Jacob's newer schoolmates who, unused to the strict discipline enforced by Reverend Roberts, had risked mouthing off. He'd been so spoiled by an overindulgent upbringing that, when he'd been brought before the class to receive a well-deserved caning, he'd had a temper tantrum and kicked Reverend Roberts' desk, breaking off a weak leg.

"You'd have thought he was three instead of thirteen, the way he carried on." Jacob was clearly delighted by the scene his classmate had made. "Reverend Roberts turned red as a cherry when his desk broke and collapsed right on the floor. I thought he'd strangle Marcus. Grabbed him by the ear and dragged him right out of the room. I wonder what Reverend Roberts ended up doing to him. When he came back to the room, he was alone and didn't say anything about Marcus. He just went on lecturing like nothing had happened."

"That don't bother me none. He's not my boy. You are, and I'd best not be hearing of you doing anything so disrespectful to the good reverend, or you'll be looking forward to a sound thrashing at home as well as the one he gives you. I don't pay good money for you to make an ass of yourself."

"I can outrun you," Jacob crowed with a grin. "Besides, I don't get into trouble. I'm a good boy and I'm Reverend Roberts' favorite." And he threw an almost angelic look to Elmore. Completely false, but it was a good show that had gotten him out of trouble more than once. Far more likely than not was that Jacob just didn't bring home tales of his misdeeds, or that he simply didn't get caught.

It wasn't until they reached the fish market that Elmore became aware that they were being followed. He could feel eyes on the back of his head. He turned and took note of the faces in the crowd behind them. A few minutes later, he looked back and saw two of the same faces.

"Lad," Elmore said, putting a hand on Jacob's shoulder. "What street are we headed to?"

"Butchers."

"Then you run ahead and tell that Mister Fa that I'm coming. I wouldn't want him giving away me job just 'cause I can't walk fast enough." He gave Jacob a pat on the back. "Off with you. Run, now." He watched while Jacob took off at a sprint, dashing down the street, until he was well out of sight. As soon as he could no longer see the boy, Elmore turned and faced the two men who'd been following them.

The dirty, shaggy men were grinning. They stood a few feet apart but didn't stop walking until they'd come to stand only a yard or so in front of Elmore. One of them smiled. His teeth were crooked and rotting. The other watched Elmore with piggy eyes while he absently scratched his armpit. They had tense, hungry looks to them: all eager eyes and twitchy fingers that clutched at the hilts of still-sheathed swords.

"That's a fair lame walk you've got, friend. Let us give you a hand."

The reassuring weight of his cutlass made Elmore feel a bit more at ease, but how much better it would have been had they been unarmed! "No friend of mine would dare suggest it."

Elmore tightened his hand around the head of his walking stick. "Get away with you. You're wasting your time—my purse is empty."

The two men moved closer, never taking their eyes from Elmore. "A fair gentleman like yerself?" The second man looked Elmore up and down. "Such fine clothes? Why, those shoes be something worth a deal, and what with the soles falling off mine, I'd prize them higher than gold."

"Aye," the first man shifted closer still. His hand slipped under his coat. "You let us judge what you've got, friend. We're not looking to hurt no one."

The street was far from deserted, but there was a wide, empty area between the three of them and everyone else. Some people ignored the unfolding scene while others watched as if they were seeing carnival jugglers. Nobody did or said anything to help. It was to be expected. Elmore opened his mouth to speak when he caught sight of a movement on his left and it made him start turning. A third man was there swinging a fist that Elmore was only just fast enough to dodge. He turned his bad leg in a way that made pain shoot down to his ankle and right up his back, but was able to stay on his feet. He swung his walking stick like a club, but missed the other man. He started to draw his cutlass, but he was struck hard from behind and knocked down to the ground. He heard his walking stick clatter to the ground. They swarmed over him, keeping him pinned down with their hands and forearms and knees, while they dug through his clothes.

He groaned and let out a sound somewhat close to a growl, straining and struggling to shift them. He barely heard the yell of a frighteningly familiar voice before one of the bodies on him was rammed off. He turned his head just enough to see that his Jacob, kicking and swearing blue lightning as fluently as any common man before the mast, had joined the brawl with gusto.

The man still holding onto Elmore was distracted enough that Elmore was able to wiggle an arm free. He threw his elbow back and caught the man in the ribs. His other hand had finally found his dagger, but he couldn't twist his arm around far enough to do much more than slash blindly. One of those blind strikes found a target, there was a yelp and another weight was taken from Elmore's back. With that, he was able to roll himself over, but just as he got himself to his knees, he was tumbling with the third attacker. One sharp jab with his fist to the chin and he had the man flat on his back. Elmore surged to his feet the minute he was released and, in an instant, he found Jacob on the ground with the man he'd attacked half-kneeling over him with a fist raised to strike.

Elmore saw red. He grabbed the man's fist, and when the man whirled around, Elmore slashed at him with his knife. He snarled when the man pulled away, but he'd swung the blade so hard that he couldn't stop moving and ended up spinning halfway around, giving the enemy the opportunity to kick Elmore's leg out from under him and put him back on the ground.

One of the thieves was on him, kneeling on his chest and pummeling blow after blow to his head and stomach.

"Off! Off!" Jacob screeched and threw himself onto the thief's back. He took a handful of hair and pulled back, while he punched at the side of the man's head with all his might.

The man staggered under Jacob's first blow, but recovered quickly. He reached over his shoulder and grabbed Jacob's arm to pull him off, but couldn't without pulling out his own hair as Jacob doggedly held on. They struggled like that until Elmore's head cleared enough. He took the man by the shirt and tossed both him and Jacob aside. He raised himself up on his elbow and looked up.

The third man loomed over him with his sword drawn. "Just die," the man rasped with a voice that was harsh. "We only wants yer coin."

A shout went up among the bystanders. "Soldiers!"

The three men ran, the injured one more slowly than the others, and in a breath they were gone. Even the people who'd only been watching the fight ran, scattering until only a young soldier with a rifle over his shoulder was left with Jacob and Elmore in the street.

With his leg, back, and stomach throbbing, Elmore got to his feet. Before he'd even straightened his legs, Jacob was at his side, having slipped under one of Elmore's arms to help support him. Elmore shoved the lad away, then took hold of his arm and pulled him close. "Am I going feeble, or did I tell ya to get yerself to Butchers Street? Don't ya think I've got a shining good reason for what I tells ya?"

Jacob didn't flinch. "Yes, but you just said you wanted Mister Fa to know you were coming. I told him, and he said you didn't have to hurry; he didn't want you to hurt yourself. He sent me running back to you." Jacob turned half away from Elmore, rubbing his right arm near the shoulder. "And what did you want me to do? Run away when I saw them go at you? I'm not a coward!"

Elmore gave the boy a shake hard enough that he was sure he'd rattled the boy's teeth. "You dratted, senseless brat! You might have been killed!" But he had to admit the lad looked well enough. Nothing but a split lip and dusty clothes to show he'd been in a fight with full-grown men. Elmore's throat tightened. It could have all turned out far worse. If his pistol had been fired, the boy might have caught a stray shot. His mind ran wild, taking him on a nightmare of a path of a sword slash or push that would crack Jacob's skull on the street. "You just do as you're told!"

Jacob glowered. "If I'd stayed away, you'd have gotten a worse thumping than you already got. Your face is swelling."

There was a hearty laugh that made both Elmore and Jacob turn towards the soldier. "Your boy has a noble heart, sir. He's a regular young knight." He smiled genially at Jacob. "But even a knight must bear in mind that he does no good to anyone if he gets himself killed." The soldier was quite young—perhaps ten years younger than Elmore's thirty-five years—and had a most unusual appearance. His dark, almost coffee-colored skin, was a marked contrast to his fair eyes which stood out against his skin as brightly as candlelight in the night. His hair was a mass of golden curls. His uniform was bright and clean, neat as a pin. He smiled widely and easily, showing off bright white teeth. He was so pristine that he looked quite out of place on the street.

Elmore stepped between Jacob and the young soldier. "I did nothing to start any trouble and was only defending myself. You want the troublemakers, then you go after them!" He jabbed a finger in the direction that the thieves had gone.

"They separated and went their own ways. Rather than wear myself out by chasing people I would be unlikely to catch, I thought it best to stay and see that you and the boy hadn't been hurt too badly." He held a hand out to Elmore. "Forgive my poor manners. Lieutenant Jeremiah Bowe, at your service. I'm pleased to meet you."

Elmore regarded the hand suspiciously. He sheathed his knife, making a show of pushing his coat aside so Bowe could see he was well-armed. "What'd you stick your oar in for?"

Bowe kept smiling and didn't withdraw his hand. "It was the right thing to do."

Elmore had never heard such nonsense before. Still, he took the offered hand. "Elmore Finch—coffin maker. This here's me nephew, Jacob Scratch."

"If you would indulge me, sir, I would be pleased to accompany you to your destination. It would be a great shame if those thieves returned with hard feelings."

The offer pricked at Elmore's pride and he turned away from the soldier. "I've lived here a good many years and I fancy I can look after myself. That's not the first fight I've been in, and I suppose it won't be the last. We don't need an escort, so you can be about yer business."

"It's fortunate that my business is patrolling the city streets, then." Lieutenant Bowe wasn't to be dissuaded. "I think we'll both be amused to find that my patrol route follows your path exactly for quite a long while."

Bowe was too cheerful and bright for Elmore's taste. There was nothing malicious or sly about the young man, but Elmore was so unused to such a person that he was made uneasy and wanted the man to be away, despite his earlier, timely help. How to refuse, though? The man, no matter what his disposition, was a soldier, a man of the governor and certainly not one to offend. No matter what his rank, he was uniformed, and a single poor word from him could make life difficult for Elmore and Jacob. And what harm would there be in allowing him to accompany them? Elmore had to concede that it would be safer, even if he didn't particularly want to be seen in the company of a soldier.

"You're going to insist, aren't you?"

"I am."

Elmore grumbled and scowled. "Then we best stop wasting daylight and start moving. I'm a working man and I've too much to do to spend time gabbing away out here like some lord at his leisure." He started walking when Jacob retrieved his walking stick. His leg had taken more strain than was good for it in the skirmish and pained him terribly.

They walked quietly, though Elmore did keep an eye on Bowe the whole way there. Bowe would linger a moment to exchange a pleasant word with some passerby. Each time he stopped, Elmore would try to hurry his step enough to leave the soldier behind, but he just couldn't move fast enough to elude Bowe, and within moments, Bowe would reappear at his side with that infernally cheery smile and an amused glint in his eyes that told Elmore, as sure as anything, that Bowe had known perfectly well what Elmore had tried to do, but he didn't much care whether or not he was unwanted.

"Is it hard to be a soldier?" Jacob suddenly asked, as he looked around Elmore at Bowe. "How do you get to be one?"

"You would have to enlist, and after that you would be trained. It is hard, but there are advantages."

"Like a fine uniform?"

Clearly, Jacob had taken a liking to the bright red coat and those splendidly polished brass buttons. Elmore scowled at the boy, but Jacob took no notice and kept right on with his open gawking. Such rudeness was so downright shameful that Elmore snapped at Jacob to mind himself. Though Jacob contritely turned his eyes back to where they were walking, Elmore knew he would have to keep his eye on the sudden admiration the boy showed for Bowe's uniform. Curiosity was all well and good, but he wouldn't have the boy putting too much thought into the life of a soldier. The boy certainly wasn't ever going to become a soldier—not if his da had anything to say on the matter, and Elmore knew very well that Jacob's da had a great deal to say on the matter.

"Actually, the uniform isn't so splendid as it might seem." Bowe answered Jacob as if he hadn't heard the scolding. "Oh, it looks grand enough, but imagine all the polishing I have to do—buttons and boots, you know."

Jacob nodded sagely. "True. But you must get a lot of respect."

Bowe laughed. "You would think so, wouldn't you? Sadly, just wearing red doesn't grant instant respect. That's where the hard work comes in, and it *is* hard work."

Their conversation kept to such light things, and Elmore grew somewhat easier as they walked. Bowe didn't seem to be anything other than a genial man bent on taking a stroll with new companions. He was easy and didn't give any real cause for Elmore to be apprehensive. No matter how he tried to convince himself, Elmore was relieved when they reached Butchers Street and the house Jacob pointed out as being the one where Mister Fa lived, as he knew that would be the end of the soldier's company.

CHAPTER 3: FLASHES

The house Jacob led them to was really no different than the thousands of other buildings of Port Royal—two stories tall and built of brick squashed on either side by another building that was almost identical. Each building had some little thing about it to differentiate it from its neighbors. They were minor differences, such as lace curtains in one window—undoubtedly the pride of the mistress of the house—or heavy shutters to guard against the frequent storms. The doors might be painted different colors, or maybe more garbage than usual was littered around outside the house, but, for the most part, the houses were all alike. That minor difference for Mister Fa's house was a small collection of wooden crates and bags piled up outside the front door.

Elmore leaned more heavily than normally on his walking stick. The pain in his knee was like liquid fire, and it boiled not only at the knee, but up and down his leg so viciously that he wished to do nothing more than sit and rest. Resting wouldn't put food on the table, and a little pain was survivable. He kept walking. Jacob's concerned look didn't surprise Elmore, as the boy was apt to be worrisome, but the lieutenant kept casting what he likely thought were discreet glances at Elmore, which felt like an insult. Elmore scowled and quickened his pace, as if he might distance himself from the pity he guessed was brewing in the lieutenant's mind.

As they drew near to Mister Fa's house, a little girl stepped out. She was a tiny thing. Her skin was pink with a faint sunburn, and her long hair was tied into two pigtails that hung down her back.

"Hello, miss!" Jacob shouted. He sprang away from Elmore and hurried towards the girl. "Good morning!"

The girl looked up at them with dark eyes. She regarded them with a strangely somber expression that looked too old for a child's face. She went very still when she saw Jacob, and she got such a look in her eyes that made Elmore think of a rabbit startled by a fox.

If Jacob noticed her unease, he ignored it entirely and went right to the girl without even a hint of hesitation. "I'm back, and I brought my uncle as I said I would. Are you going to talk to me, yet? You really should, I'll be a great friend. I know all the very best places in the city, and if you come to school I'll stick up for you if anyone pesters you. I told Uncle Elmore all about you and your grandfather, so we've come to meet you. Oh! And here's another friend." He stepped a little to the side to make a proper introduction. "Please meet Lieutenant Bowe. He was a great help—saved Uncle's life!—and he seems nice enough, but I don't really know him well and—oh, come on! Wait a bit!"

But the girl didn't wait. As Jacob had been talking, she'd looked carefully at all of them with wide eyes, then quickly stepped back inside her home and closed the door behind her.

"Well! What did she do that for?" Jacob wrinkled his nose at the door before he looked at Elmore. "I was only being friendly."

Elmore patted Jacob on the shoulder and chuckled. "Like as not, my chatty brat, you went and frightened the poor little bird. Did you rush up and start jabbering at her like a magpie when you know she's shy and in a new city? On top of all that, you go and bring two more strangers to her door, one of them a soldier. Are you sure she even speaks English?"

Jacob huffed and crossed his arms. The stance was eerily familiar, as Elmore couldn't count the number of times he'd seen such an expression on the face of Jacob's father. Another look at the door, then Jacob looked back up at Elmore and said, rather sulkily, "But I was smiling. She should've been able to tell I was being nice, even if she couldn't understand me."

The door opened, again, and an elderly man with a long,

white moustache stepped into the doorway. Jacob had been right—the man was clearly from China or some other part of the Far East. He was a small man, but held himself with an air of utmost confidence even though he had to look up at Elmore. It was always a peculiar feeling when Elmore found a grown man that he had to look down at. The old man looked at them all with clear, sharp eyes that seemed much younger than his face suggested. Elmore was fairly certain they were being judged and wondered how they measured up. The old man smiled softly when his eyes fell on Jacob.

"Welcome back, young man. I am honored to have you, once again, at my door." He spoke with a heavy accent, but was clearly understandable and spoke with no hesitation or apparent discomfort. He next looked between Elmore and Lieutenant Bowe and gave them each a bow. "Welcome to my home. I am Fa Tseng. I believe you've already met my darling granddaughter, Mei." He moved a little to the side to show the little girl who nearly hid behind him.

Jacob, the earlier insult plainly forgotten, waved cheerily.

"Elmore Finch, at your service, sir." Elmore offered his hand, but withdrew it when Fa Tseng ignored it and gave another dignified bow. "Ah. Yes." Elmore gave an awkward bow in return. None of the Chinese men he'd ever known had objected to handshakes, but, he reasoned, it seemed likely that this man had come straight from the east and it was likely he didn't know any different manners, yet. "My boy tells me you're in need of a carpenter. Some boxes, he said. Maybe more. I'm a fair hand at it and have had a good many years of practice under my belt."

"Indeed. Will you enter and kindly accept my hospitality? I will apologize to you now for the lack of welcoming warmth I have to offer." He held the door open and allowed them to walk in. There were several more crates inside the house, but little else. The house was small, like most, and the crates made it seem all the smaller. There was no furniture at all, not even a table or chairs, and Elmore couldn't fight the little surge of joy at the sight of such opportunity and nearly felt a chill run down his spine. Mister Fa interrupted Elmore's calculating thoughts with, "Please, make yourselves as comfortable as possible while I get you something to drink."

Jacob dropped to the floor with a laugh, obviously amused by the novelty of sitting on the floor. Elmore wasn't nearly so taken with the idea. He glared at the floor and thought about the pain that getting down on the floor would create, with his knee already aching wildly from the fight. Still, he couldn't be rude to a prospective customer by refusing hospitality. Resigned to the pain, Elmore put his weight on his cane and started to carefully ease himself awkwardly to the floor.

A little hand gingerly tapped Elmore's arm and he paused, looking down at Mei.

The girl backed away a bit when he looked at her, but seemed to find her courage and stood up straight. She pointed at the floor, then at Elmore's cane and, then, waved her hands at him.

Elmore had no idea what she was trying to tell him.

Mei went to a crate that was long and low and started pushing it towards Elmore. Whatever was in it was clearly heavy, for she heaved with all her strength and could only slide it a few inches across the floor. She paused a moment, then started pushing, again, bracing her feet on the floor and gritting her teeth as she did.

Lieutenant Bowe moved to push the crate with her and didn't blink when the girl darted away as fast as she could when he apparently got too close for her comfort. "Such a little lady," he laughed. "Looks like she doesn't want you to strain your leg."

Elmore sat on the crate when it had come close enough and, smiling gently, he touched his forehead with a finger and gave the girl a nod. "My thanks, little bird."

Mei gave him a little smile, then went to the cold fireplace and began to stack wood and kindling in it.

"It is so good to meet neighbors," Mister Fa said when he returned. "And now we have guests only hours after our arrival.

I am sure this is a good portent of our future here. Sir," he looked at the lieutenant, then gestured to the long crate Elmore was sitting on. "Please, be seated."

With all the charm of a man accustomed to getting his way with a smile, Lieutenant Bowe stiffly bowed his head. "I wouldn't think of sitting if it means my elder is left standing, sir. Please, make yourself comfortable."

With an approving nod, Mister Fa sat on the crate with Elmore and set a small tray with a few cups and a little teapot between them. "The boy told me much of your skill, Mister Finch. He was very pleased to tell me how well you could furnish my new home. Though I have no chair to offer for your comfort, I may at least offer you tea as soon as we have some hot water." He made a gesture to Mei and, just as Elmore turned to look at her, she struck a flint and steel together and sparked the fire. There was the faint smell of smoke and a dim glow before Mei leaned in close and blew gently on it. Then a tongue of flame shot upward only moments before the whole fire danced to life and cast a bright glow into the room.

Elmore blinked.

***

Fire.

Heat.

Choking ... *can't breathe.*

Screaming. She was screaming, and it filled Elmore's world, echoed inside his mind. She screamed.

The fire was immense, it soared up into the sky. All around it, in a terrible ring, people had gathered and watched. Some jeered, some stared, but none took their eyes from where she burned in the fire. The sound died around him and all was silent. He saw people's mouths moving, saw the furious fire moving and twisting as it reached higher, but he heard nothing. She was crying. He saw the fire's light reflecting off the tears on her face.

Elmore blinked.

Pain! It near swallowed him. There was fire. A raid gone wrong, and the ship was on fire. Pain and fear melted together into one nightmare after the spar had fallen and pinned Elmore to the deck as it crushed his knee. Pain and fire and smoke clinging to his throat ... he couldn't breathe ... he couldn't breathe ...

Elmore blinked.Back in the home of Mister Fa and his little granddaughter. The fire was nothing to fear, just a cheery warmth to heat a kettle of water. He breathed in deeply and let it out slowly. He put one hand on his still-aching knee and discreetly squeezed, deliberately causing more pain that forced his mind to the here and now rather than old memories he had no desire to get lost in. He inhaled, again, held it for a moment, then breathed out. He tightened his hand on his knee and the dull ache that had shot up and down his leg. He repeated that several times as he listened to the conversation, distant and faintly muffled, carry on without him. He had no idea what was being talked about.

The tea was poured and handed around and Elmore took it without hesitation. Heat in his hand. The teacup had blue flowers painted on it. A weight against his leg made him look over and he saw that it was Jacob, still chattering merrily with Mister Fa, who had leaned against him. He didn't look at Elmore, didn't say a word. After a few more moments, when he could hear the words being spoke around him and felt as if he were no longer teetering between "now" and "then," he reached down and gave Jacob a pat on the back.

"... and Reverend Roberts will teach girls, too, so Mei can come to school with me." Jacob was telling Mister Fa, though he kept stealing glances at Mei where she had sat next to her grandfather to drink her tea. "It's lots of fun, but there aren't any other girls. We used to have Prudence Appleton, but she's not there now. And Reverend Roberts seems mean to look at him, but he's a very fine teacher."

The lieutenant started to laugh. "And you'll get no more glowing endorsement. He may not want to send her to school, young man, especially not with a bunch of boys."

"I will give it due consideration," Mister Fa told Jacob with far more respect than he had any reason to, consider than Elmore had expected Mister Fa to send the children out of the room while they spoke. Mister Fa set his cup on the table. "Mister Finch, I would very much like to thank you for coming so promptly, and though it would please me greatly to sit and pass a leisurely morning in your company, I would not be so selfish as to take up any more of your valuable time. To business. I would like to commission some boxes approximately so big." He showed the size he wanted with his hands. "Three, for now. Perhaps more at a later time."

"Easy enough, I reckon. Might I be asking what you're needing to store in such a shape? Not going to be able to put much in a box so small. I can do you something bigger; might be more practical." Though with the crates he already had, that didn't seem more practical, either.

Mister Fa didn't change expression, though it seemed to Elmore that he held himself a little more proudly, as impossible as that seemed. "Aside from my profession, I am an artist. A painter. These boxes you will make are necessary to send my paintings home to friends. This island is beautiful, and few in my homeland have ever seen anything of its like. They will be most pleased to see my work."

Elmore nodded, though he'd never really understood artists. He'd met one, once. Flighty as a jaybird. The fellow kept going on about light and shadow, and then painted a right mess that didn't look like much of anything. Still, so long as Mister Fa paid, it really wasn't any of Elmore's affair how he chose to spend his time. "You said you'd a profession?"

"I am a physician."

"Really? Well, that's a right fine thing, and I think we can always use more doctors hereabouts." But really, he didn't see many of Port Royal's residents taking their business from Doctor Branson to a foreigner. "You'd be from China, unless I miss my guess."

"True. It has been a long journey, and I fear the culture will take much getting used to. My poor Mei has already begun trying to learn the language and finds it a great challenge. No help for it."

Lieutenant Bowe leaned forward a little and said, "Forgive me, sir, but I am surprised at how well you speak English. Have you been traveling so long that you were able to learn it since leaving China?"

That almost made the old man smile. "You flatter my intelligence, officer. No. As a child, a missionary taught me to speak both English and Spanish at my father's request. Considering how many traders and merchants come to China, he thought it prudent that I know as many languages as possible."

"Why did you leave?" Jacob asked, taking another sip of his tea. "If it's such a long trip and all your friends are there, why come here?"

Mei very suddenly burst out, "My brother! My big brother is here. Or near. He is here and we will find him!" Her eyes shone and a smile brightened her face when she spoke. She was so excited that she nearly bounced where she sat until her grandfather chuckled, and she appeared to take hold of herself and take another sip of tea. "He is here and we must find him."

With an affectionate smile at his granddaughter, Mister Fa said, "Yes. Mei's brother is somewhere in this part of the world, and we have plans to join him. He is quite a bit older than her and left home to seek his fortune some time ago, but had always found time to write to us. He sees much opportunity on this island and has written, asking us to join him here. How could I refuse such an offer? My family is not wealthy, so this is a welcome chance for the future."

He glanced quickly at Mei, and Elmore knew that he was thinking of her future, not his own. Elmore understood. He'd give up his whole world to benefit Jacob's future.

Elmore looked into his tea and hoped they would find the boy. Port Royal wasn't an easy place to find anyone, and it must have taken them months to travel all the way from China, in which time there surely couldn't have been any message from him, so who knew if he was even still on the island? It was easy enough for a person to run into trouble, and he might have found it necessary to leave, even if he knew his family was coming for him.

"Would you like some help to locate him?" Lieutenant Bowe leaned forward a little. "I'd be more than pleased to ask around, if you can give me his name and description. Perhaps someone at the barracks had seen him."

Elmore frowned at Lieutenant Bowe. "You're not long here, either. What makes you think you can find him?"

He shrugged with a grin. "It won't do any harm to try, and I have some free time now and again. It's no hardship to be friendly, after all."

Elmore drank his tea in one gulp. Such kindness was rare, and he wasn't entirely sure he trusted it. For his own good, Bowe had best not go around making such offers to all and sundry, or he'd find himself in a world of hurt. Mister Fa seemed a harmless enough gentleman, but there were plenty of others in the world who would take advantage of a good-natured man.

The kindness of Lieutenant Bowe was well appreciated by Mister Fa and he poured another cup of tea for the lieutenant. "My grandson's name is Bingbang. Fa Bingbang, and he is really very ordinary-looking. I'm afraid there is no unusual feature I may give you to identify him."

Bingbang. Elmore went still for a moment before he finished his tea in a single swig.

"Oh!" Jacob couldn't let a discussion go on without him. "I'll help, too. I've lived here just about forever, and I know everywhere and lots of people. I can ask around and help you look. If he's here, we can find him. Of course I haven't always lived here, but I've been here for so long that I'm sure we can find him, and Port Royal isn't all that big so it shouldn't take any time at all. So you don't have to worry about that at all and—"

Elmore gave Jacob a nudge with his foot and Jacob, always a quick boy, stopped talking.

Mister Fa had smiled the whole time Jacob let his mouth

run freely. He looked at Elmore. "The boy is kindhearted. A joy to any parent."

"Yes. He is." Elmore felt his pride for Jacob swell inside him. "He's also not as polite as he ought be with folks he don't know, and too easy at letting himself take on tasks he's got no business volunteering for when he's got school to be thinking of."

He saw the protest in Jacob's eyes and knew the boy well enough that he could guess that it was on the tip of his tongue to say he could help Mister Fa after school and even before and that he could help so much, but Jacob kept his mouth shut.

"If I could be so bold," Lieutenant Bowe spoke up. "It seems to me that you'll be needing a good deal of things other than boxes." He looked around the room but said no more.

There was nothing in the room. It was a bare, brick room with nothing to show but the walls, floor, ceiling, and the crates Mr. Fa had brought with him. The place was empty and had the same cold atmosphere that all abandoned buildings had. It wasn't a home, not yet, and possibly not for a good long while. If they found his grandson, it was likely that Mister Fa would be able to make the place comfortable, but Elmore wondered if the man would stay on the island if they didn't find his grandson. He wondered if they could leave. From the state of their clothes, it didn't look at if they had more than a few pennies to their name, and Mister Fa was old enough that he might not be able to work. Mei was too young to work unless he was able to get her into service at one of the few good houses on the island. To travel so far and have nothing at the end of the journey, how terrifying was that idea? But he wasn't Mister Fa, and Mister Fa took no apparent notice of Elmore's unease.

He laughed. A low, easy chuckle. "Yes, we have much need of everything, but it would be too much to ask a busy craftsman to drop all he had to furnish my new home. We have need of beds and chairs and a table and many other things, but I see no reason why I cannot find such things secondhand to purchase. There will surely be someone willing to sell what they do not need."

A polite way to say he couldn't afford the cost of new

furnishings, and Elmore appreciated the frugality.

Mister Fa continued. "There is much to be done, but I must say that furnishings are not the most important of my concerns. It is food. All else we can suffer with. We have blankets, even if we must sleep on the floor for a time, and a sturdy roof to keep out the weather. We are very fortunate."

The house wasn't bad. Not really. It was bare and more than a little dusty, with filthy widows that hardly let in any light at all, but Elmore had seen far worse. "You're lucky you found this place, if you came here without arrangements."

Elmore tried very hard not to think that the grandson must have been a real snake to bring an old man and a little girl so far, to a strange land where they surely had no other friends waiting for them, and not even make arrangements for them. To be generous, their ship may have arrived earlier or later than anticipated, as the whims of the sea and winds respected no one's schedule, but that was no excuse to leave them alone once they'd arrived. Perhaps the grandson was just a thoughtless boy, or perhaps he was an inconsiderate worm who'd sent for his family, but lost interest and moved on to some other venture. No matter the reason, thoughtlessness, disinterest, or an unexpected end, Elmore kept his peace. It wasn't his business. "It may be bare at the moment, but, you're right—it's sound. You'll have to do little but make it comfortable. You go to market and you're sure to find someone to sell you some chairs and whatever else you'll be needing." He did not mention that they would likely be to his shop in less than a week to get beds, as those would be harder to come by than chairs or a table.

"I will surely make use of your suggestion," Mister Fa nodded his head. "My grandson will find us shortly, I am certain, but I must see that Mei has a good life. I would not have her be uncomfortable. To that end, may I ask for directions about this city?"

It was, of course, Jacob who sat up on his knees and eagerly —even proudly—announced, "I can help! I know everywhere in Port Royal. I wasn't born here, you know, but I have lived here for years and years. I used to live up north, in the colonies, with my mother. We lived by the sea in a beautiful house, but ... but I came to Port Royal to live with Uncle Elmore, and I've been here long enough that I know just about every nook and cranny in the whole city, and most of the people, too. What do you need?"

Elmore sighed. Jacob really needed to learn when to hold his tongue.

When many adults might have been annoyed with Jacob's overactive mouth, Mister Fa outright laughed with bright sparks in his eyes. "It sounds as if you are the correct person to ask, then. I merely need directions to a market where food might be purchased. As I've said, we have only just arrived and have little to our name, but I do have some small savings to tide us over until my grandson finds us. In fact, it's been mere hours since we left the ship, and even less time since I bought this house. Mei has not eaten well since we left home, and while there is much to be done, I wish most of all for her to be well-settled here, and I think she will sleep deeply with a full stomach tonight."

"I beg your pardon for asking," Lieutenant Bowe leaned forward and rested his elbows on his knees. "But have you considered taking a room at an inn? There are many about, and you would have food when you pleased."

"I had considered it, but it has been hard for Mei to be without a home these many long weeks at sea. It will be good for her to have a permanent place to call her own. Unfortunately, this bit of comfort means that we don't have the convenience of readily available food."

Jacob quickly put forward, "I can take you to the market. It's not too awfully far, and on the way I can show you everything else. There's the tailor's shop and the butcher's and the tobacconist and the cobbler. We've got a fine church, Saint Peter's, and—"

Elmore cleared his throat meaningfully.

Jacob grimaced. "Or not. I should probably go to school."

"And you'll give my apologies to Reverend Roberts, and tell him I kept you on family business," Elmore told him, sternly. He waved a hand at Mei. "And take the girl with you. Let her see what school's about before Mister Fa decides whether to send her or not."

There was silence in the room, but Elmore pretended not to notice.

Slowly, Jacob nodded. "Umm ... yes, of course." And he smiled brightly, though Elmore would bet his pipe that the boy was still confused. He held a hand out to Mei. "Come along. I'll introduce you along to everyone, and Reverend Roberts is sure to like you."

Naturally, Mei didn't move an inch until her grandfather, with a suspicious stare at Elmore, gave his permission.

"I'll take care of her," Jacob promised before the two left. "I'm a gentleman."

Elmore set his cup on the crate beside him and tried to think of the least horrible way to say what he thought should be said.

Mister Fa cleared his throat. "I expect you have a reason for wanting my granddaughter away?"

"Yes. You come walk with me a bit. Yes?"

The three of them, with Elmore in the lead and Lieutenant Bowe following silently behind, went to a small church on the outskirts of the town. It was small but well maintained, and to the side, there was a modest-sized graveyard. There, Elmore took Mister Fa to a small, nondescript grave marker. He took off his hat. "Here. He's here. I made his coffin some weeks ago."

Mister Fa was silent.

"I'd not have remembered, but his name struck me. I haven't heard the like before."

"Do you know what happened?" Mister Fa didn't look away from the grave of his grandson.

"Your pardon, sir, but no. Every now and then I'll get a commission from a church to do a coffin for someone who's got no family to see to them. I thought maybe you'd be wanting to tell Mei yourself, rather than me bringing her here."

"Yes. Yes, thank you for that consideration. It is

appreciated."

They stood there without speaking for a time, and it seemed only respectful, given the shock Mister Fa must have suffered, and surely *suffered* was the most accurate word. Mister Fa was pale, and looked many years older than when Elmore had first seen him. His shoulders were slumped, and his hand trembled at his side.

"Should I have not brought you here?" Elmore asked, after some time. "I wasn't intending to hurt you. Didn't seem right to let you hope when I knew the truth."

"No. Of course." Mister Fa drew in a breath and turned to Elmore. "You have done me a kindness in bringing me here. I would have spent the rest of my life looking for him. Better to know the truth than to wonder. And do you know... what caused him to die? He was healthy."

"I don't know the whole of it. From what I saw, looked like a fight."

What Elmore had seen had been the result of a savage killing a knife wound to the gut that would have killed, but wounds on his hands and arms. He'd been young, like too many that Elmore worked for. Older than Jacob, certainly, but a far cry from a mature man. No reason at all to go into such details, not when Mister Fa was struggling to hold himself together.

"He was very peaceful. He didn't fight."

"Maybe not, but someone wanted to fight him." Elmore put a hand on Mister Fa's shoulder. "Maybe it was something so small as he'd bumped into a drunk who was itching for a fight. Maybe he'd got work with some bad characters."

"What did he do for work?" Bowe asked.

"He was an artist. He drew. Exploring the world was passion." He ran a hand over his eyes. "I ... I must have food for Mei."

The change of subject was not unexpected, and Elmore was pleased to give Mister Fa the escape. So he obligingly said, "I'd be pleased to show you to the market. It's on my way, at any rate. Before then, we'll go by the school and fetch your Mei."

Mei was found just where Elmore knew she would be—in Reverend Robert's school, sitting next to Jacob at one of the tables Reverend Roberts had set up for his half-dozen students. She was wide-eyed at the lecture Reverend Roberts gave, but sat very still, as if afraid to draw attention to herself. The moment Elmore opened the door of the classroom, every eye went to him, and Mei, upon seeing her grandfather, leapt to her feet and ran to him.

"Mister Finch," Reverend Robert looked down his long nose at Elmore. "Jacob explained that you were speaking to someone about business and had him bring the girl here in regard to that business. He didn't elaborate, but I presume there is more of an explanation."

Elmore glanced behind him to ensure that Mei wasn't paying him any attention before he told Reverend Roberts what had happened in a hushed voice. "Didn't want the girl to learn about it like that. Your pardon for disturbing your day."

"No pardon necessary. I will call on them later, to see if they need help."

And with that, Jacob was sent back to his lesson, while Elmore continued on to the Market with Mister Fa and Mei behind him and Lieutenant Bowe trailing silently at the rear. As always, the marketplace was furiously busy in the late morning. The air was filled with the smell of fish, a scent that Elmore, for all of his years at sea and then settled in Port Royal, had never been able to get used to. The smell didn't seem to bother anyone else, though, so he kept his opinion to himself in favor of keeping an eye on the city's newcomers.

Mei was feverishly curious about everything and couldn't seem to stop staring at each little object, animal, and person she saw. No matter how curious she was, though, she didn't once let go of her grandfather's hand or attempt to stray from his side, and that was good because Mister Fa was didn't seem ready to let her go out of his sight any time soon.

Elmore had never known either of his grandfathers or his grandmothers.

***

Young Elmore once complained to his father, "But William, my friend at school, has a grandfather and two grandmothers. Where are mine?"

Connor Finch had been a softspoken man, modest and mild as a spring afternoon. His hands were large and calloused from a life of hard work, but his eyes were bright and danced with merriment. He was never one to send Elmore away because he was too busy or too tired. There was always time for his boy.

On that day, late in the afternoon when they'd had time to sit together as a family, Elmore's mother sat crocheting with her basket of yarn, and his father poked at the fire in the fireplace with a long stick of kindling before tossing it into the flames and watching it catch light. The fire crackled and popped cheerfully, giving light to the room, as the afternoon would soon fade into night as well as warmth that was dearly needed so late in the year. The small house was the only home Elmore had ever known and, though it had been a good deal smaller and emptier than the house Farmer Hanson's family lived in, Elmore had never wished for anything different.

That afternoon, six-year-old Elmore had crawled into his father's lap and leaned against his chest. He looked tired, even to little Elmore. There were dark circles around his eyes, and his smile couldn't reach its normal brilliance, although it was as warm as ever when he hugged Elmore to him. "Your grandparents are back home. Still living in the same house your granddad was born in."

"And my parents," Bronwyn, Elmore's mother, said without looking up from her work, "are in Coldstream, where they have a small farm and a herd of sheep." She glanced up at Elmore. "Ah, they would have adored you. Your grandfather would have taught you to play the pipes. He plays so beautifully."

Home was Scotland, not Virginia. Home, to mother and father, was across the raging sea and where they'd grown up. It wasn't the house where Elmore had been born, not the forest where he played, or the rivers and ponds where he'd learned to swim and fish. Home was distant and far and a place they never expected to be able to show Elmore. They'd talked about it many times.

"Are they going to come live with us?"

"No. The journey's too far and too hard."

"Then we'll go live with them?"

Elmore's father's smile disappeared altogether. "We've got three more years to work off this indenture, son. Maybe ... after I get my own work started and we get a house of our own, we can think about it."

It never happened. There were many nights idled away with stories from faraway Scotland and family and old songs. But he had never seen Scotland, and before he'd reached his tenth year, all of his grandparents had passed away.

***

Just beside Elmore, little Mei chattered something at her grandfather, who answered her softly.

"How old is little Mei?" Lieutenant Bowe asked at one point. "Seven?"

"She is ten years old. My granddaughter has always been small." There was no missing the fondness in his eyes when he looked at Mei as she gawked at a woman walking with a young girl at her side. Both wore the customary gowns, and the woman had her hair piled neatly up on the top of her head. A moment later, a man joined them. He put his arm around the woman and leaned down to kiss the little girl on the top of her head. Mei watched them for a moment, then turned her suddenly cheerless face away and pressed herself to her grandfather's side. She sniffled miserably.

"Well, now, what's this then?" Elmore asked.

Mister Fa patted Mei's back. He opened his mouth, but Mei spoke first.

"Mama and Baba," she whispered. "They are killed."

Another knock to the little family. *But*, Elmore thought, *how fortunate for little Mei that she has an obviously doting grandfather to protect and shelter her. Any orphaned child in* the world who had even one defender could count themselves luckier than most.

With whispered words in his own language, Mister Fa stroked Mei's black hair before he looked up at Elmore. "Forgive us. It has been a trying few months for her." He would say no more on the matter and, shortly, they arrived at the market. Elmore spent some time showing Mister Fa around to the different merchants until they had bought a basket to carry things in and enough food to fill it. Unsurprisingly, Mister Fa had no interest in lingering, and very soon they parted ways at the door of his home.

When the door closed behind them, Elmore knew that Mister Fa had to tell Mei about her brother. What a blow to them both.

"They won't have an easy time of it—without the grandson, I mean." Lieutenant Bowe stepped up to stand next to Elmore and stared at Mister Fa's door. "He'll have to try to find work."

"At his age?" Elmore huffed and started walking back to his home. "Who's going to hire an old man when this city's so full of young men and boys, eager for work?"

He wasn't a bit surprised when the young lieutenant started after Elmore without invitation. What a sight they must have made! Common Elmore with his sawdust-covered coat and the polished officer walking side by side. Bowe kept pace easily with his long strides and, more than likely, even slowed his step to let Elmore keep up with him.

"If the girl was older, then he might have hope of her marrying and bringing in her husband to take care of them." Bowe shrugged a little. "I suppose there is hope that she might find work in service with one of the finer families in the city. He wouldn't have to support her, and she could send him her wages."

"A chance of it, I suppose." Elmore didn't like to think about what might happen to a young girl going into service if she found a position in a house with no one to protect her, and there was no point in commenting about it. "Nothing to be done about it. They'll figure it out." And it wasn't as if he could do much for them, anyway. He had his own to take care of, and that meant getting back to work.

As Elmore walked, he cast a discreet, sour look at Bowe, smiling and nodding to all they passed. Seemed it was too much to hope that the lieutenant was just going to give up on his bizarre quest to befriend Elmore and, indeed, he didn't show any signs of turning away as they walked together. Elmore sourly asked him, "Ain't I gonna be rid of you?"

"Eventually, I expect. I do have to go back to the barracks at some point." Bowe ignored any and all of Elmore's attempts to get rid of him. He nodded politely to each woman they passed, whether she was a lady or not, and gave a coin to a beggar boy who was missing two teeth. All in all, he was a pleasant and agreeable companion and, as they walked and Elmore considered the situation, he decided that having Bowe about wouldn't be a bad notion. He was a soldier, and even though he was little more than a pup, a soldier as an ally could only ever be useful. The only troublesome worry that nagged at Elmore was about Bowe's aim in the friendly overture. Elmore had no influence to speak of and no wealth that anyone knew about. There wasn't anything for Bowe to gain out of befriending him. Why not use his time to cozy up to someone who could actually do something for him? It was a mystery, but as all the gain in such a relationship was solely in Elmore's favor, he saw no reason to worry too hard over it.

By the time they got back to Elmore's home, he was on the verge of inviting Bowe in for a flagon of something to gentle the heat of the summer sun, but stopped as soon as he opened his door and saw the two unexpected, but not unwelcome, visitors in his workshop.

One man, lean and fair, stood with his back against a wall and his arms crossed, while the other man, tanned very dark from years living under the sun, had brought in a chair from the kitchen and sprawled comfortably on it as if it had been his own and, to be perfectly honest, it may as well have been.

"Friends?" Bowe asked. He stepped up to stand beside Elmore and, though that was all he did, the sudden tension that fairly seeped from him was enough to make Elmore cast a quick, curious look at him. He still smiled, hadn't even twitched a hand towards his weapon, but he was on guard and Elmore, who knew his visitors well, almost laughed at the idea of a soldier defending him.

"Aye." Elmore stepped in and, when Bowe stepped in after him, said, "Old shipmates of mine. Gabriel Scratch," he gestured at the tanned man, still in his chair, before indicating the lean man, "and Raynard Passy."

Elmore was unsurprised when Gabe gave only a cool nod to Bowe as greeting, while Raynard smiled and held out a hand to Bowe as warmly as though they were long lost friends.

Bowe accepted Raynard's offered hand, but his smile, even to Elmore, who'd known him barely an hour, seemed meaningless. It was like the smile of a porpoise—just there, with no indication as to actual feelings or thoughts. "Greetings. It's always interesting to meet new people, and this certainly has been a day for that. I do hope you will forgive me not staying, but I am on duty and will have more than enough explaining to do when my superior wants to know what I have spent my morning attending to. Good day to you all." He gave them all a nod before turning briskly and walking out.

CHAPTER 4: FAMILY

The very moment that the door had closed behind Bowe, Gabriel Scratch burst out into hearty laughter. His broad, whiskered face was full of amusement; the coolness it had worn in Bowe's company was gone as if it had never been. "What's this?" He grinned wickedly. "You keeping company with the king's men? Will I see you next at Sunday brunch with the governor's wife?" Over the years that Elmore had known him, Gabe's heavy Irish brogue hadn't diminished one bit. He still had that easy smile that everyone around him found so appealing, and he still had a presence that was somewhere between commanding and affable. He would never be the captain of any ship, Elmore knew. Gabe didn't care enough for the power that being captain would give him. He'd far rather enjoy a good round of dice with his crewmates than worry about keeping his position.

"Not hardly likely." Elmore happily took Gabe's hand and didn't resist when he was pulled close for a quick embrace. "When did you two get to port?"

"Near sunrise." Raynard gave Elmore a quick embrace and, as was the custom of his people, a brief kiss on each check. He was a fine-looking fellow and had been as long as Elmore had known him. He was tall, with a friendly face, and wore a splendid coat of rich purple. "You know Scratch, here. He couldn't keep away from his boy long. He's been talking about nothing else for hours. I was headed in this direction myself, so I thought I'd accompany him."

"Will you stay and take a meal?" Elmore asked.

Raynard held up a hand. "Forgive me, but I am unable to stay, as much as I would like to. I have business today." His French accent had faded a good deal over the years, but it was still strong enough to be recognizable. "I just wanted to see you before I left, in case we had no chance to meet later. It seems like a good long while since we've spoken." Raynard smiled amiably. He'd always had an easy sort of disposition, which was surprising considering how much he had to be bitter about.

Elmore certainly wouldn't have blamed him. He'd left the ship shortly after Raynard had been voted down as captain, but, as he saw it, there had been little reason for Raynard to be deposed. He'd been a fair and just captain, and, until a single raid had turned ill, a well-liked and respected man. It was an unlucky raid that ended Raynard's command. Several mates had died: one shot in the face by a Spaniard's pistol, one gutted like a fish who screamed till he'd died. Another poor soul had been driven to Davy Jones, plunging to his death when one of the Spaniards brandished a pistol, startling him badly enough into taking a single, fatal step backwards. That boy hadn't been much beyond his seventeenth year, and his mother would never know what had become of him.

For all that, the failed raid wasn't Raynard's fault. It had just gone wrong, as things often do. Regardless, after their escape from the fruitless attack and after the wounded had been tended, the angry crew called for a vote. Only moments later, Raynard had become just another hand, while their quartermaster, Nathaniel Harrington, was made captain of Raynard's ship. Even after all that, Raynard was quick to smile.

"It's been well near a full year since we last met," Elmore protested. "Can't your business wait? Long enough for a drink? I've even got some coffee."

"I'm afraid not. It's rather urgent."

Gabe frowned at Raynard and dug at the wax in his ear with a finger. "You didn't say nothing about no business. You was happy as anything to get here."

"I am happy to be here, and I didn't say anything because I didn't know of this business before we came ashore. I saw an old acquaintance in town. I didn't know his ship was in port, but seeing as I do now, I can't put off this errand." He gave them a cheery wink. "Owes me a good pocket of money, and I don't see myself letting him set sail with my coin in his pocket, again."

After Raynard had taken his leave and Elmore and Gabe went into the kitchen, Gabe took Elmore by one shoulder and swung him around so they faced one another. With a wide grin, he pulled Elmore into his arms and hugged him tightly. Then he pushed him away and said, "Give us a kiss!"

"Get off me!" Elmore whacked Gabe on the leg with his cane.

Gabe yelped and hopped away and went to sit at the small, square table. "Yer cold to an old mate!"

"I'll clobber an old mate if he don't mind himself." He shook his cane at Gabe.

Neither of them took the other very seriously—it was an old game, to them. It was a game that was both familiar and comfortable, like a well-rehearsed play in which they both knew their lines by heart. They smiled at one another before Elmore asked, "Gonna be in port long?"

"Cap'n Harrington didn't say. We only set anchor today. Sun weren't hardly risen when we came to harbor." He wrinkled his nose and sighed forlornly at the cup of water Elmore set on the table for him, but he didn't complain or ask for anything stronger. "Where's my boy at?"

"School," Elmore answered.

Gabe took a long drink, then wiped his mouth with his sleeve. "You still on about that? I had in mind that he learn a useful trade from you."

"He is. He's got a good eye and a steady hand. The lad's helped me time and again, but you take a look at what I got for all my life of work." Elmore spread his arms wide. "A workshop and three rooms no bigger than walnuts. It's mine, thanks be to saving and pension for this damned leg, but I'll not likely ever have more. It's hard on a man to know you'll just make by as long as you can work. I'll work as long as I'm able, but my health will give out sooner or later and that'll be it. I'm done for. I want more for the boy."

Gabe thumped the table with his fist, spilling his water. "You fool. Why'd you think I brings you me share of the spoil? It ain't your—" He stopped abruptly and looked away. "You get most all of what I get. It's for a nicer house and a proper workshop."

"What's wrong with my house?"

"Nothing. Not a blasted thing, but you could have a bigger place."

"What? And do more cleaning? I'd rather have a tooth pulled."

"A horse, then. And a cart to carry yer wood in."

"Where would I keep a horse? And how would I feed it? Hard enough keeping Daisy fed."

"Better food and clothes, then."

Elmore scowled. "If you weren't my friend, I'd guess you were insulting me. I keep a perfectly good table and I hardly dress the boy in rags! I do well enough by the boy with my own work. Everything you give me is being saved—every penny."

"What for?"

"For later. The boy's learning his letters and numbers at the school. Speaks Latin, you know. He can read a fair treat. Those are his." Elmore gestured to the three books on a shelf near the door. "A Bible, some poetry book, and one he practices his own writing in. He's a right smart lad, and I'll not have that wasted. When he's got all he can get from here, I'm using your savings to send him to England—to Cambridge."

Gabe's eyes widened with disbelief. "What? The university?"

"No, Cambridge the tobacconist. Of course the university! He'll be a doctor, maybe, but I'd put my money on him being a lawyer; he's mighty good at talking."

Gabe shook his head and wrapped both hands around his cup. "A carpenter can have a good, respectable life. And I don't know what you're talking about—your health? You'll live as long as any man, and when you get too tired to work, then Jacob takes care of you—just like every other family in the world. No reason to send him so far off."

"No reason but for his own sake," Elmore told him. "You've got to stop thinking of yourself and think of what a good life you could buy him. He'll be a respected gentleman and—"

"And nothing! Thunder!" Gabe stood up and slammed down his cup on the table hard enough to dent both the cup and the table. "I'm not thinking of me. He'd be happy here. You know I wants the boy to have an honest trade, and here you are making such decisions about me boy without even asking. He ain't yours and I don't wants him in England! I wants him here. I put him here for a reason."

Elmore knew. To be able to freely see his son without the fear of hanging for piracy was the main reason to have Jacob raised in Port Royal. Most of the world wasn't nearly so tolerant about pirates or privateers as Port Royal.

"What you want isn't important. Yours? You ever once held him after a nightmare? You mended his torn trousers? Have you cooked his meals for near on five years?" Elmore snorted. "You're a ruddy fool if you think I've no say in his life. He's my boy as sure as if he had my blood in his veins, and I'll have my say in planning his future. Matter of fact, if yer fixin' to die on the waves, then what do you care where Jacob is or what he does with his life? You wanna have your say, then get yourself an honest living, and it won't matter where the boy is; you'll be able to have him with you. And anyway, there isn't one reason why he can't come back here to live after he's done his schooling, if he likes."

Gabe's fury, as it always did, vanished as quickly as it had erupted. He glared a bit and paced around the kitchen before finally plopping back down on his chair. "Well? We gonna see him? I brought him a gift."

"I told you—he's at his schooling. No sense in bothering him. He'll be home soon enough."

In the meanwhile, there was booty to be hidden.

The bag Gabe handed over wasn't as full as it had been in the past, but it was a respectable handful of silver, profits from the sale of sugar, he'd told Elmore. They took it upstairs to Jacob's room, where Elmore pried a wallboard loose and set to the side. For the first time in a great long while, Gabe saw the six shelves that had been built between the studs and the boxes on those shelves that held the booty from five years' worth of life at sea. It was more than Elmore would ever earn, even if he hammered together coffins for another fifty years. Elmore was a bit pleased to hear Gabe's breath catch at the sight of those plain, unadorned boxes.

"You really haven't spent a bit of it." Gabe looked up and down the shelves, all the wooden boxes of coins, jewels, and jewelry. He reached out a hand and ran his fingers over the small boxes. "It's all here."

"Five years of hard work—yours and mine, my friend—and it's going to set Jacob up for the rest of his life. So long as he's smart and careful, he'll never have to want for anything."

Gabe didn't look happy, but he also didn't argue, so Elmore took it as a victory.

***

Several hours passed in peace as Elmore worked and Gabe spoke about what had happened since they'd last seen one another—George had left, taken a wife up in Virginia, and young Liam was dead from a fever—and alternated between wandering the room and sitting in a chair he'd pulled out from the kitchen.

Elmore carefully choose some of the nicer pieces of his scrap wood left over from coffins and began to piece together boxes for Mister Fa.

"We set anchor at Tortuga some weeks ago, and what a wild place that is."

Elmore said nothing and, when he saw that one of the pieces of wood was a bit too big to fit well against the others, he took out his saw to cut it down to size.

"There was a game of dice and I wanted in so bad, but I'd nothing to wager, so I sat back to watch. They both cheated, and it were so bad, they both caught each other at it at the same time. The fight was a real glory and ended up with both of them rolling right off the docks and into the water!" He laughed as if it were most hilarious thing he'd ever seen.

Elmore rolled his shoulders a bit as the tension of the day's normal stress slipped away.

After midday had come and gone and Elmore could see out the open door that the sun had begun to creep closer to the horizon, Jacob swaggered through the door with his usual cheery, "I'm back!"

But Elmore happened to be looking at Jacob's face the instant he saw his father. He watched as Jacob's face froze, that wide smile turning into an uncomfortable mask, and the light in his eyes turned into ice. Like a statue, he stood in the doorway, his slate under one arm and the other on the doorjamb as he stared at his father.

Gabe awkwardly stood. He tried to smile, but it came out strangely weak for a man who was so often far too pleased with himself. "Good to see you, lad."

As the silence from Jacob dragged on for a few very long moments, Elmore shifted his eyes back and forth between them and warred with himself about what to say or, indeed, if he should say anything at all. Mayhaps if he'd known Gabe were coming home, he might have had time to plan how to ease the difficult reunion, or at least he might have prepared Jacob enough that the boy could show some decent manners. As it was, he chose to let it play out and deal with the ashes when the fire died.

With an utterly blank face, Jacob turned and went upstairs. A moment later they heard the door of his bedroom close a little too loudly.

Gabe let out a sigh and ran a hand over the top of his head. "This gets harder every time."

"You didn't really think he'd jump into your arms, did you? You didn't even tell him you were leaving, last time."

"I didn't have a choice. We was all called to set sail at once. You understand."

"Aye, and so does he. He just doesn't like it." And because there was no other path to take, he gave Gabe the only advice he had: "You go talk to him. Now or later, it will have to be done, and it won't get any easier for the waiting with him stewing in his sulk and you stewing in your guilt."

"I don't feel guilty. A man's got to make a living." Yet, Gabe stared morosely at the stairs.

Elmore sighed and ran a hand over his hair. "As you say. No matter what you feel, I tell you, making the boy wait will make a volcano out of a candle's flame. I maybe raised him up, but he's got his father's temper through and through."

With a heavy sign, Gabe squared his shoulders. "I'd rather he'd have inherited my nose. Time to lance the boil." He started up the stairway, though he couldn't have moved much slower if he'd tried.

Elmore watched him go and, while he was fairly certain that he knew how the meeting would fare, as he fancied he knew both Jacob and Gabe very well, he was surprised by how short it was. He hadn't even managed to pick up his hammer before he heard raised voices above his head and then the slam of a door. Gabe barreled down the stairs, growling curses, and headed for the front door.

"Where are you going?" Elmore asked.

"I need a drink!"

Elmore opened his mouth, but before he could warn Gabe against drinking, Jacob, standing halfway down the stairs, shouted, "Don't come back neither!" He was red-faced and scowling. One hand was braced against the wall on his right and the other held a metal cylinder in a furiously clenched fist. "I don't need your stolen presents!"

Gabe left without another word.

Jacob was tense, almost vibrating with anger as he glared at the closed door.

Elmore barked, "Hey!"

It seemed to break Jacob out of his state. He took a breath and started downstairs, stopping at the half-finished coffin. "I don't want his presents."

"I heard. He's your da."

"I don't need him. He's never here."

"Don't be ungrateful. He's paying for your schooling—your future. He's only not here 'cause he's doing his work to give you a decent life, and you know it to be so."

Jacob, looking a healthier color than he had moments ago, sat at the table where Gabe had been. "I don't see why you set such store in all that. I can be a carpenter. I'm good at it and I don't need to be a rich gentleman. So long as I've got a home, I'll be happy."

Elmore grinned and said, "Your da said about the same. He doesn't want you going off to England. You'd be too far away."

Jacob set his arms on the table, then put his chin on his arms. He set the metal cylinder, a small spyglass, on the table in front of him. "It doesn't even work. Stupid, broken garbage."

Elmore picked up the spyglass and decided that it wasn't quality work. The metal was dented, and it wouldn't unfold as it should. He put it to his eye and turned to the window, but saw only darkness. "Maybe we can get it fixed."

"It's not worth it." When Elmore put the broken spyglass back on the table in front of Jacob, Jacob pushed it away. "He acted like I should be happy to see him. All he does is drop off money. We don't need it. If I tell you I absolutely won't go off to England so we don't need his money, would you tell him to stay away?"

"No. I won't throw away your future just 'cause you want to be foolish, and I won't chase off one of the only people I can honestly call a friend because you're angry at him. Grow up and be thankful. How many boys do you see sweating on the docks, wishing they could go to school? They'll still be there in ten, twenty, forty years. They'll never leave, likely. The old men you see mending fishnets? They'd been doing that for years, and they'll do it 'til their hands are too twisted and knotted to go on, and then what do they have? Nothing. If they're lucky, they'll have family to support them. If not, they'll die begging for food.

I won't have that for you. You have a good chance to do more than ... just more."

"I like working with wood."

"Aye, and I likes Italian wine. I likes a velvet waistcoat and a fat, roasted turkey. No man can have everything he wants. Damn it, boy! Be grateful for what he provides. A good many other children don't even have a father willing to lay claim to them. Yours brags on you, he's that proud."

Jacob said nothing. He stood and took the poetry book from the shelf before he quietly went upstairs.

***

For the rest of the day, both Elmore and Jacob waited for Gabe to return. Jacob said nothing about it. He cleaned the house and fed the dogs, quietly ate dinner with Elmore, but there was no possibility that even the most indifferent person could have missed how Jacob kept an eye on the door, clearly expecting it to open at any moment. It wasn't until well after dark, after Jacob had gone to bed and Elmore was ready to see his own bed, that the front door opened and Gabe staggered in, reeking of rum and looking as beat up as a belligerent alley cat. His left eye was swelling, and a cut on his forehead bled weakly. His clothes were a sorry sight, what with one sleeve of his coat torn and his trousers wet from the knees down. Elmore wasn't all that surprised to see him staggering drunk and red-nosed, but he scowled blackly at the wench who giggled at Gabe's side. She wasn't the best-looking woman he'd ever seen and was well-past the bloom of youth, but her eyes were clear and she seemed moderately clean.

"You been paid?"

The woman didn't look nearly so drunk as Gabe. She shook her head.

"Then get out."

Gabe swung his arm in front of him and thundered as well as a man could with a heavy, drunken slur, "'S not yer affair! If I want company," he pulled the woman closer and shook his fist at Elmore. The sudden movement almost toppled him off his feet.

"Then, by God! I'll have company!"

It wasn't a surprise to see Gabe so drunk, it was expected, really, but that acceptance did nothing at all to soothe the anger Elmore felt that Gabe would bring a street doxy into his home. He spoke as evenly as possible when he said, "All fine and good. Then you take your company somewhere else."

"What?" Gabe's face twisted. "Yer a papa, now, so you go all moral? Taking the boy to church, are you? You ain't no white lily!"

"She ain't staying in my house! You come or go, I don't much care, but she's not staying!" Who was fool enough to bring home a rented woman? "You go to her house or rent a room at a tavern. Find someplace else."

Gabe fumed. He went tense all over and breathed hard though his nose with his lips pressed tightly together. He also seemed to forget that the woman was still with them.

Elmore looked at the woman. "Get out of here."

She bristled. "No skin off my nose, but this one owes me for my time. He agreed."

"And what price did he agree to?"

She looked between the two of them, then answered.

Elmore gestured at Gabe. "Pay. Now."

"I ain't paying for what I ain't had."

It was always the same. Get angry. Get drunk. Get stupid.

Elmore shoved Gabe, not hard, but along with his drunkenness, he fell. While he sat on his backside and looked confused as to how he'd come to sit on the floor, Elmore reached into the inside pocket of Gabe's coat and pulled out a few coins. He carefully counted out the right amount, and the woman left in a good humor. And why wouldn't she? She'd been paid without working. How much better could her night get?

"Bastard," Gabe growled after the door had closed behind the woman. "Not yer business."

"My house. Don't you ever try to bring a doxy in here, 'specially not when you're too drunk to keep her from robbing me blind. Do it again and I'll toss you out on your ear."

Gabe surged to his feet and charged, but Elmore easily stepped to the side. Gabe kept going, right at the sawhorses where Elmore had left the nearly finished coffin lid. Gabe fell right on the lid and snapped it in half.

Elmore closed his eyes and, when he was calm enough, pulled Gabe to his feet. "Steady. Are you done? You lummox. You ruined hours of work. You gotta stop the drinking."

Gabe feebly tried to move away from Elmore but had knocked the wind out of himself and, in the end, allowed himself to be helped.

After setting down a few blankets on the kitchen floor for Gabe to bed down on, Elmore looked down at him. "You made such a point of telling me you went without the wine and women to provide for the boy, then you go and do this?"

Gabe's eyes filled with tears and his lips trembled. He pulled one of the blankets up to his chest and huddled around it. "'E hates me. Me own boy hates me. Said he wished he'd never set eyes on me. Would rather be an orphan." The tears began to flow, and Gabe curled himself into a ball as he began to sob miserably.

Elmore couldn't have been more tired if he'd just run around the whole island. He bent over as much as he comfortably could and patted Gabe on the shoulder. "He don't hate ya. He's angry, is all, and just a child—"

Gabe was already asleep, snoring noisily.

Elmore looked over his shoulder at the broken coffin lid and overturned sawhorses. "Too much trouble, matey. You're just too much trouble." He was out of wood.

Everything else was needed for the coffins he hadn't even started, yet. Some of it could be salvaged, of course, but the large pieces meant to be the coffin lid were ruined. He could, he reasoned, use the remains for the boxes for Mister Fa. Those wouldn't take much. Other than that, he'd have no use for the wood unless he got an order for a child's coffin. That meant money wasted, as he'd need to make the long trip to the wood cutter's home in the morning.

When Elmore turned away from his workshop, he saw

Jacob standing on the stairs and staring at his father with an utterly blank expression. As Elmore watched, Jacob's face darkened and his lips twisted in disgust. "He's drunk, isn't he? I heard him carrying on."

"He gets like this sometimes."

Any anger or bitterness in Jacob was swept away as he looked down at his father. His eyes were sad, and his shoulders slumped. "Yes, sir. I know." Jacob turned and went back upstairs.

Elmore began to follow him. His eye caught the spyglass and made him pause. Such a gift. Whole or broken, it wasn't going to win over Jacob. He set aside the broken spyglass in the kitchen between the flour canister and a basket of potatoes before he blew out the lantern and made his way to his bed for the night.

CHAPTER 5: BOARDED

*E**lmore was nine years old and walked at his father's side on a warm, foggy dawn. The fog was heavy, like a February snowfall. His father looked tired. He always looked tired lately. His eyes were heavy, with dark bags under them. His shoulders sagged and he walked slowly, almost dragging his feet. The fields were blanketed with dew the morning that Elmore walked down the lane at his father's side, fairly bursting with pride as he looked up at his father. It was the first day he'd been allowed to help in the workshop, and Mother had set them off with the taste of eggs and potatoes still in their mouths.*

The path underfoot was wet and muddy and squished noisily at every step they took. Ahead, nearer to the barn than the house of the landlord, Elmore could see the vague glow of the fire in the smithy though the veil of fog. Elmore turned to look at his father, but his father wasn't there. He'd fallen and laid on his face on the path a few steps behind Elmore.

He remembered this. A memory dream. The realization that he was dreaming hit Elmore hard.

Then Elmore was in the graveyard, holding his mother's clammy hand as she stared—transfixed—at a hole in the ground that he knew would be his father's resting place. The air was sweet and filled with the scent of lilacs. Great bundles of the small purple blossoms hung heavily on the tall bushes that lined the graveyard. The minister was speaking, but Elmore couldn't hear any of it other than a mumble. His ears seemed to be buzzing, and he looked away from the coffin to the faces surrounding the grave site. All somber faces, all familiar—the man who'd worked with father in the carpenter's shop, the milkmaid with dry, cracked hands, and the old woman who sat for hours on the back porch of the landlord's house and did his mending. The landlord hadn't come, but no one had expected him to take time out of his day for a funeral.

Everyone dressed in their finest clothing for the funeral, and Elmore was no different. He had nothing black to wear, but his trousers were brown and his waistcoat was gray. It was the best he could do and, after all, that was all that could be asked. His shoes pinched his toes, but his clothes were soft and smelled of soap, as his mother had been meticulous in giving them a good cleaning. His hair had been combed into a very respectable pigtail at the back of his neck and tied with a small, black ribbon. If it had been any other time, any other circumstance, then he would have felt so proud to look so fine.

Someone nudged Elmore in the back, perhaps his mother, and made him walk towards the coffin, as was expected. It felt like it took hours to walk the few feet. Then he was looking down at his father's still, pallid face and knew something was wrong.

Something changed in that moment, and while Elmore didn't know exactly what had changed, he did know the instant that what he was experiencing changed from a memory into a nightmare.

Father's eyes sprang open, empty and staring, and his mouth moved to let out a whisper: "Danger."

Elmore woke abruptly.

For a time, all he could do was breathe, and even that was an effort. His lungs burned, and he felt unnaturally cold. The blanket covering him had been kicked off, and the linens on the bed were soaked with clammy sweat. He couldn't move for the longest time; he felt altogether frozen. The blood in his veins may as well have been ice water. Everything seemed darker, shadowed in the memory of his father's dead eyes and that awful, hollow voice. Finally, Elmore took a great gulp of air, and his head began to clear.

That memory had never faded. He'd once been told that pain was dulled by time, but that memory was as fresh as ever. He could see the worn patches on the mourning dress his mother had worn, and he could smell the apple blossoms from the orchard next to the graveyard. He hadn't cried over that memory in years, though. Because with it, he remembered the quiet dignity his mother had shown when they stood at the grave side, despite the shaking of her hands, and how proud he was of her strength. He could also, when memories began to grow grim, remembered his father's smile, the love and gentle affection that his father had always showered on his family. Those memories overpowered the grief and held it at bay.

There were other dreams, dreams that had nothing to do with his father in a coffin, and at night they haunted him. So ghastly was the terror that the haunting inspired his cold sweats in the night, and, once was woken by a frightened Jacob shaking him and telling him that he'd been screaming. He dreamed of a far-off fire burning in the mist.

Danger.

The word flew around in his mind like a trapped bat.

With his feet bare, Elmore left his room. The house was utterly silent, as it should be. Uneasy, still, he went to Jacob's door and peeked in. Moonlight from the single, tiny window shone down on Jacob to show his peaceful face. Elmore wished to always see Jacob like that, like a child. At twelve years of age, he wouldn't be a child for much longer, and if Elmore hadn't had such grand plans for him, the boy would have left school ages ago to work with Elmore in the carpentry shop, or perhaps start an apprenticeship. But Elmore had a plan, a vision for Jacob's future, and that plan involved schooling.

He sat gently on the side of Jacob's narrow bed and just looked at him for a time. He was safe and, if Elmore had anything to say about it, he'd stay safe. He smiled down at Jacob before he stood and patted his head, lightly, and then went downstairs. In the kitchen, he found Gabe on the floor right where Elmore had left him, still sleeping off the drink that had put him there in the first place. He was safe, too.

Everyone was safe. So the dream meant … nothing? No. That couldn't be right. Such a powerful dream couldn't be "nothing." It had to hold some meaning. They were messages from some other place. He wasn't sure if it was messages from

God or the dead or something else altogether, but they were messages. All he had to do was puzzle it through.

***

Before dawn, Jacob and Elmore sat together in the kitchen eating bread and cheese, as was their habit. For the sake of Jacob's pride, Elmore pretended not to see the furtive glances Jacob kept sneaking at his still-sleeping father. As for that man, Elmore was half-tempted to strangle him where he lay for the trouble he'd caused. There, Gabe lay on his back in the middle of the kitchen floor, looking innocent as a newborn lamb, snoring away like he'd no worries at all. Much as he liked Gabe, there were many times when Elmore really wanted to give the man a good beating. A solid kick in the head, Elmore often thought, might do the nitwit some benefit, and maybe he'd wake up with some good sense.

"You done your studying?" Elmore asked Jacob.

"Some," Jacob didn't look at him. "It was hard to concentrate."

Elmore couldn't find it in himself to reproach the boy too harshly. Yesterday had been a very distracting day. "Well, pray for luck, then. Reverend Roberts won't give you any points on that exam for excuses."

"He'll let me try, again, though," Jacob said, assuredly. "I should go."

"It's early, yet."

"The church isn't locked, and I can study in the classroom."

"You can study here."

Jacob glanced, once more, at his snoring father. "I think I'd rather study at the church."

Once Jacob had gone, there was no reason for Elmore to put off his own work. He stood and gave a shrill whistle. "Daisy!"

There was a thud and a tremendous clamor of heavy feet running down the stairs. Daisy, the muscular black and brown dog Elmore had bought as a fluff-ball puppy two years earlier thundered into the kitchen. She sat at Elmore's feet and looked up at him in adoration, with her long tongue flopping out the side of her mouth. She was, Elmore had to admit, dumb as a brick, but she was useful and good company.

"Let's go, girl. Get your gear on." The harness had been commissioned especially for Daisy, much to the amusement of the local leather worker. Elmore slipped it over her head and fastened the straps at her shoulders and chest. In the workshop, he pulled his small wagon—a low bed on wheels, really—and attached it to the harness. All the while, Daisy's tail wagged with almost pathetic joy. She so loved working.

He loaded one small child-sized coffin onto the wagon. For anything bigger he'd have had to rent a proper wagon, but Daisy's little cart was perfectly suited for small jobs.

Elmore hadn't known the child, but the mourning father had come to him a week ago and asked that it be built. He hadn't asked the circumstances, but an accident or sickness wouldn't have been uncommon ways for a child to meet their end.

The delivery errand took only a short time, but he and Daisy were in no rush to return home, and the unhurried walk was a good time to think as they walked down the length of the harbor. He admired the ships that had come from all over the world—all the sloops, schooners, frigates, and a sluggish-looking barquentine. The forest of tall masts brought back such memories—not all happy—and he took time to admire the flags hanging from the tall masts; Spanish, Dutch, British, Portuguese, and even one French flag flapped in the strong breeze. He even stopped for a bit to talk with old crewmates on the *Indigo Running,* his mind drifting back to the days when the ship had been home.

Nothing much had changed but the faces. He found himself wondering what had happened to old shipmates, but couldn't bring himself to ask. There wasn't much point. They were dead, or retired to some berth in a harbor town where he'd never set his sights on them again. Perhaps the law had caught up with them, and they'd met their end with a rope and a callous, cheering audience. More dreadful to Elmore's mind was the idea that perhaps some of them had been caught unawares by the press-gang and were, even now, serving aboard some navy vessel. The new faces—some younger and less touched by life, and some hard and angry—watched Elmore with caution or barely controlled violence or mere curiosity, but no one approached him other than the one or two who remembered him.

Elmore left, quickly. The ones who remembered him were not friends or even people he'd liked. The amount of fond nostalgia he felt when *Indigo Running* came into port diminished each time another familiar face was replaced, and every time he felt that small pang of disappointment that things were changing, he though too deeply of his former life and the freedom he had been forced to give up. And there was no time to be reminiscing, anyhow. There was work to be done.

As he slowly made his way down the docks, Elmore unwillingly found his mind settling back on the trouble at home. He'd hoped to be distracted by going to the *Indigo Running*, but that had worked about as well as a rabbit trying to ignore a hungry wolf, and he found himself brooding over Jacob and Gabe and wondering if he was doing either of them a kindness by letting Gabe stay at the house.

He didn't like Jacob's anger—though it was understandable—and he wanted to have the two make peace, but he no idea how to go about promoting such a thing. Jacob was so stubborn when he set his mind at a thing, and he'd gone and set his mind on not forgiving his father. Gabe had always stayed at the house when his ship came in, there was no question about his welcome … there never had been any question of it before that day.

Since the day he'd come into Elmore's home, Jacob had always been obedient and well-mannered. In the beginning, Elmore suspected that the boy might have been frightened that he'd be turned out on the streets if he were in the least bit cheeky. He wasn't a blood relation of Elmore's, after all, and the two of them had never met before the day he'd gone to fetch the boy.

It was only natural, he'd reasoned, that the boy would be scared and would have done anything he could to please so as to secure a place of safety. Not only had Elmore been new to him, but Jacob had been taken away from the town he'd grown up in and brought to a place practically on the other side of the world. As time had worn on and they'd grown accustomed to one another, Jacob's fear had all but vanished, but his obedience had never faltered. He'd had a few incidents of rebellion, as all children have, but by and large, he was a pleasant, agreeable lad. Such a display of near wild anger worried Elmore. He'd never seen Jacob so furious as he'd been when he'd woken up the morning after the last time Gabe had shipped out so unexpectedly.

It hadn't been kind to leave as he had, but, despite all his faults and queer habits, Gabe was a good man and a loving father who worked hard to provide for his boy. That hard work was rough and dangerous, but Gabe had no other skills except those of a sailor, and no schooling to be an officer. So he sweated and bled, and would likely keep doing it as long as he could. Luckily for Gabe, piracy seemed to suit him. "Can't give the boy nothing without a living, can I? And what could I give him on a sailor's wages? Navy don't pay half so well as the life of a gentleman of fortune." He did the best he could, even if he didn't walk the most moral path a man could take. He honestly didn't deserve the bile Jacob had spat at him.

If Elmore had the right words, if he knew what to say that would make Jacob take notice, then he would tell the boy what unbearable pain it was to have family taken away. That Jacob would thoughtlessly throw away his father … the boy just didn't understand. Elmore would never again see his father or mother, and he wouldn't wish that on Jacob.

By the time Elmore returned to his door, it was nearly midday. Daisy was as energetic as if they hadn't just gone parading all over the city, and her long tongue lolled out of her mouth as she happily bound to the front door. Once there, however, she stopped and sniffed frantically at the threshold. When he put the key in the door's lock, she barked and then whined, looking up at him with worried eyes.

Elmore froze and looked down at her. Daisy never barked. Elmore looked back at the door just as another dog barked, but from inside the house. He smiled and felt the tension ease away from his shoulders. "There you are," he gave Daisy a pat. "It's only your gentleman what's in there. Everything's as it should be." Elmore put his key to the door, but it swung open at his touch. He stared at the open door, then stuck the key back in his pocket. Harold certainly hadn't unlocked the door.

Elmore took time to quickly detach Daisy from the wagon and pulled his pistol from his belt, while he held tightly to her harness to prevent her from running in as she normally would. That done, he pushed the door open wider and peered into his home.

Harold, Daisy's sly-looking gentleman, sat inside, in the middle of a ransacked room and watched the kitchen door.

Elmore just stared, stunned at the wreckage of the room and absently said to Harold, "How did you get in here? Weren't here when I left." He gave Harold a pat on the head.

Harold turned his face to look up at Elmore, showing off the blood on his muzzle, before he went to Daisy and gave her a sniff. Then, he started towards the kitchen, his head held low, but without hesitation.

Elmore allowed Daisy to follow Harold, as she usually did, while he looked around his workshop. Destroyed. Everything was ruined. Turned over or broken, it looked like a madman had gone through the place. His tools—his precious tools!—were strewn on the floor like fall leaves. Elmore felt sick. He looked at the door and found that the lock had been broken. Someone had forced their way in. The wood around the latch was splintered, and the metal latch itself bent so badly that he would have to take it to the blacksmith to be repaired.

Elmore felt something inside of him begin to burn. "Gabe? Where are you at?"

In the kitchen, the clay flour canister had been emptied onto the floor, and the canister lay in the white mess, broken into three pieces. A chair lay on its side. The small door of the stove was open and ash had been dug out of it, onto the floor, mixing with the white flour. The little wooden box hidden in a cabinet near the sink had been emptied of the money Elmore kept there.

Breathing hard and almost overcome, Elmore stared at the empty box a moment before he realized his hand was shaking. Angrier at his lack of control than the missing money, he picked up the box and threw it as hard as he could, and managed to accomplish nothing more than making it clatter against a wall and fall back onto the floor.

The treasure. Elmore's head spun when the thought stuck him. He barreled out of the kitchen and up the stairs as quickly as his leg would allow, nearly falling halfway up. However, when he got to Jacob's room, he found that the treasure was entirely undisturbed. The wall hadn't been touched as near as he could tell. Not even the quilt on the bed had been rumpled. Puzzled, Elmore went to the next room, his own bedroom, and found that, too, untroubled. Whoever had done such a job on the workshop and kitchen had clearly gotten what they'd wanted and hadn't bothered going up to the bedrooms. Still. .. he rushed back down to the workshop for his hammer and pry bar. Once the wallboard in Jacob's room had been taken off and he could get to the little hidden boxes of treasure, he let out of a great sigh of relief. It was all there. Not a bit of the treasure had been touched, and seeing all those full boxes sitting on their shelves was like the taste of cool water on an August afternoon—an unspeakable relief. He sealed up the wall, again, then went back downstairs.

There was blood on the kitchen floor, just near the table.

"Weren't a rat or a cat you got your teeth into, were it?" Elmore asked Harold. If it had been an animal, it would have lost far too much blood for it to have lived, and he'd have found it dead unless Harold had eaten it. Not that Elmore was soft enough in the head to believe that an animal had ransacked his home. A person, though … "Did you get in a tumble with Gabe?

You've met him afore." But Gabe wouldn't have broken up the whole house unless he was drunk, again, and he wouldn't have been. Not after the row he'd had with Elmore.

The drinking was only a bad habit, as far as Elmore could tell. Every time Gabe stepped ashore he went and got himself roaring drunk, just once, then kept away from it altogether. That drinking binge was always embarrassing, as Gabe completely lost control of himself when he drank, but he never took to the drink more than once each time ashore. Never. Then again, Elmore had never seen Gabe so upset by Jacob, before. If Jacob's childish fury had gotten under Gabe's skin more than Elmore had guessed, then perhaps Gabe might have given into temptation. God knew that men had been known to lose themselves in drink for less reason.

"He wouldn't have broken the door," Elmore told himself. "He has a key." But if Gabe had lost it or if that doxy had picked his pocket and taken it ... he'd certainly been insensible enough the previous night to be so stupid. Elmore thumped his fist against the wall. "Damn it, Gabe!"

The house was silent as death, but for the soft clicking of toenails on the floor as Harold and Daisy trailed behind Elmore. He'd been invaded. His home had been boarded, rifled through like a drunkard's pockets. The rising bile of his gut and a sudden, throbbing headache made Elmore wanted to scream, stomp, and make enough noise to wake the dead. The treasure was safe, but his home suddenly wasn't. He'd worked hard—damned hard!—to make a good home and to have it thrown in his face that it could be so easily ruined was devastating. If Jacob had been at home ...

Daisy leaned against his leg and Elmore put his hand on her head. "Is alright. It's only things." And he set to work putting his home back to rights.

***

A rainstorm set in before long, and when Jacob returned from his classes in the early afternoon, he walked into the house soaked head to foot. As was expected of him, he arrived in a cheery mood; the shadow hanging over him from the row with his father had lifted, somewhat. He walked into the house with a bright smile and his hair hanging in his eyes like that of a wet dog. That smile faded into a look of shock. He silently looked around the room, and the disappointment in his eyes was almost painful to Elmore, though he knew it wasn't directed towards him. But Jacob didn't waste time with questions or accusations or anger. His shoulders slumped, showing the same resigned defeat that Elmore felt, before he set aside his books and started in the kitchen with the cleaning while Elmore straightened up in the workshop. Jacob worked without a word for more than an hour until Elmore went to check on him and found him standing in the middle of the kitchen, glowering at his feet.

"What've you got an ugly on for?"

"It's gone."

"What is?"

"My spyglass. Da's present. Did you throw it away?"

"I put in on the counter. There. You're sure it didn't get thrown somewhere? God knows everything else did. Likely as not, it's somewhere in here."

"I cleaned everything. It's not here." Jacob's eyes were shiny and he pressed his lips together. "What a stupid thing to steal!" He stormed out of the kitchen and up to his room.

Alone in the kitchen, Elmore stared at the countertop where he'd last seen the broken spyglass.

CHAPTER 6: A SAILOR AND AN OFFICER

It was still raining when Elmore left his home early the next morning and made his way to the blacksmith. In addition to commissioning a new lock for his door, he traded three pouches of tobacco for the loan of the blacksmith's ugly horse and a wagon. The beast was serviceable, if not much to admire, and saved Elmore quite a bit of aggravation as he started out on his extra trip to see the woodsman. As wood was hard to come by in any city, the woodsman made his home and business well outside the city, where trees were tall and plentiful. Unfortunately, that meant that either Elmore had a long, hard day of walking on a sore leg, or that he would lose some tobacco.

Elmore chose to lose some tobacco.

Elmore looked up at the gray sky while he rode and cursed loudly at the weather. There was no one about to hear or care but the ugly horse. What a lazy creature he was. No matter how Elmore kicked his heels or slapped the reins, the horse would go no faster than a meander as they left the cobblestone streets of Port Royal and moved onto the dirt path that led into the lush forest around it.

It was only when he finally came in sight of O'Donnell's home, nearly a half mile from Port Royal, did the rain begin to slack off into a gentle drizzle. By the time he pulled the horse to a stop outside O'Donnell's home, the drizzle had faded into nothing more than a fine mist.

O'Donnell's home was small and, naturally, built of wood rather than brick. The grass and weeds and brush around the house were well overgrown. It was all a familiar sight, as Elmore had paid many visits to O'Donnell over time due to his trade.

The shouting coming from behind the house, however, was not expected.

"Now look, I'm not trying to hide anything; I came to YOU! Why are you—"

"You'll mind your tone, sir, or you're liable to find yourself spending time behind bars to teach you some respect!"

"No. No, I'm sorry, surely I am, but I didn't hurt anyone. And if I did, what kind of fool would I be to bring you here?"

Elmore slid off the horse as carefully as he could. With the horse's reins in hand, he went to the corner of O'Donnell's house and peered around the edge. Behind the house, in a state of obvious agitation, were O'Donnell and two red-coated soldiers, along with a small wagon and a horse that looked too fine to be pulling a cart. O'Donnell's own flat-bedded cart and mule were off to the side, with the mule calmly ignoring the scene in favor of grazing. And it was quite a scene, what with the one officer who stood stiff and tight as a bowstring while he shouted, a nearly hysterical O'Donnell, and the other officer, Bowe, calm and placid in the middle of it all, like the eye of a storm.

Bowe saw Elmore first, in fact. He gave a smile and a nod, before he turned back to say something to the other soldier, a mustached captain who looked decidedly unimpressed with O'Donnell's hysterics. He didn't listen to any more of it before dismissing O'Donnell with a wave of his hand and turning, instead, to speak to Bowe.

O'Donnell was clearly astonished at being so dismissed and looked around, as if he didn't know what to do with himself, before his eyes fell on Elmore. "Finch!" He combed his shaking fingers through his curly, black hair as he rushed over to Elmore. "Well. Well, I can't get you much. Not today. There's some in the shed, but it's only fit for burning, really, and I wouldn't trust myself to try cutting down a blade of grass, what with the state I'm in. I know this sort of thing happens in the city, but this isn't the city and it shouldn't happen here, not right in my own backyard! Why, I thought my heart might have leapt out of my mouth when I saw him just ... laying there."

Elmore tiredly rubbed his face with one hand. "Hold then. What are you on about? Who did you see?"

O'Donnell's eyes grew wider as he leaned a little closer and whispered, "A body. A man. Someone's been killed here! I was going out to start the day and I found him just lying on the ground." O'Donnell pointed down the path that led from the main road behind his home and into the forest. As far as Elmore knew, O'Donnell was the only one who ever used it. "I went for the law, of course, and Captain Brown there came, but oh! They're sure to think I did it!"

"Rubbish. Why'd they think that?"

"I don't know. But they've been asking so many questions, and why would they want to know where I'd been and what I'd been doing? And if I knew the man, and was I really sure I'd never seen him before if they didn't already think I'd done it? I don't cause trouble, never had a bit of trouble with the law, so why would they think I had anything to do with it? And why would anyone come out here to get killed in the first place? Everyone going from the city to the plantations uses the main road or goes by sea. No one just wanders about these woods. I never see anyone out here unless it's for business."

Elmore brushed that aside. "Folks can hide if they've a mind to, and you don't take pains to keep yourself secret or even quiet. I've been out there with you, remember? Anyone lurking about out there would be well and gone or hiding themselves when they hear you singing or the trees falling. How'd he die?" He looked over at Bowe and the captain, who had gone to stand together near the horse and wagon and spoke together with hushed voices. From where he stood, Elmore could see two booted feet, as if the dead man were simply laying on the ground, but that was all he could see of the body.

"I haven't a clue. Really. I found him and panicked, shamed as I am to say so. Poor Ham hasn't had to run in years." He looked sadly at his mule. "I don't think he liked it much, but we rushed to the city. That young lieutenant was very helpful, but I don't think his captain's awfully enthusiastic. I suppose the man might have died naturally. His heart, maybe. Or if he was a tramp, he might have just come out here to live alone and gotten sick."

"No." Bowe wasn't smiling when he stepped over to them. "It was murder. I'm willing to lay wages on it." The grave expression he wore made him look older. "He wasn't a tramp, either."

Elmore asked, "You'll get bawled out for standing about chatting, won't you?"

"I doubt it." Bowe smiled lightly. "Captain Brown doesn't much care for this duty."

Captain Brown's stormy expression said as much as he ignored the other three men and stared out at the forest with anger fairly rolling off him. He stayed there only a moment before he started into the forest.

"He's going to have another look at where the body was found," Bowe said.

O'Donnell burst out that he had no desire to have another close look at the body, but Elmore followed Bowe back behind the wagon where they'd laid out the body on the ground. The man, Elmore saw when they moved closer, had been near about thirty years of age. It was hard to tell, as a person looked so different in death than they did in life, but Elmore could swear that there was something familiar about him. He couldn't say what, exactly, and he was reasonably certain that he'd never met the man, but something about the shape of the man's face gave Elmore pause.

A stiff, unfriendly presence stepped up behind Elmore. He turned and found himself looking up at Captain Brown. Captain Brown had been in command of Port Royal's garrison for nearly ten years, since the British had taken the Point from the Spanish, and Elmore had seen him around the town plenty of times. He was hard-nosed and set in his ways, an excellent soldier if not greatly liked. Fortunately, for many of Port Royal's less-than-honest citizens, he was also easily bribed.

Captain Brown raised his chin a little and glared down at

Elmore before he nodded sharply at the dead man. "You know this man?"

"No. How'd he die?"

"A knock on the back of his head broke his skull. What are you doing out here?"

Elmore raised an eyebrow and tried very hard not to sound sarcastic. As satisfying as it might have been, mouthing off to a soldier could never do anyone any good. "O'Donnell's a wood cutter. I'm here for wood, sir."

"Very well. You hear anything, get word to the garrison." He looked sourly at the body, as if it had offended him merely by having had the gall to die in such an inconvenient location. "Get that body covered decently, lieutenant, and get it down to the undertaker."

"Yes, sir," Bowe replied with a sharp salute. He waited until Captain Brown went back to where O'Donnell stood nervously by his mule, no doubt to finish his questioning, before he took a white sheet from the bed of the horse cart and started to cover the body.

It wasn't often that Elmore saw such genuine reverence anymore when caring for a body. He'd seen burials at sea done with all the ceremony that God-fearing seamen required, and as a child he'd gone to churchyard burials presided over by the holy fathers, but when it came to the unnamed in Port Royal, they never seemed to garner any respect. He'd seen men buried without caskets and without a single word from any holy man. To see young Bowe so carefully laying out the shroud over the murdered man who, for all they knew, could have been nothing but a drunken tramp, struck something in Elmore. He felt a sudden, inexplicable need to do something for Bowe, considering as how the dead man was forever unable to repay the kindness given to him. Normally, he wouldn't bother to involve himself, but it didn't seem as if there would be any harm. So he cleared his throat to get Bowe's attention and said, "If it helps you any, the man wasn't just a sailor, he was an officer."

Bowe turned his head a little to the side and narrowed one

eye as he looked up at Elmore. He bore a striking resemblance to a confused puppy. "What makes you think so? He's dressed like every other sailing man who walks the streets of Port Royal."

"Oh, yes, he does seem like any other salt, doesn't he? Skin's brown as leather. 'N his clothes—loose trousers and shirt. A kerchief around his head. You see dozens of men just like him every day. But you just take a closer look. Those clothes are new. Not a single mended tear, or even a worn spot."

"Then he just bought them."

"Possibly. Why don't you pull out his knife for me?"

With a puzzled look, Bowe squatted down next to the dead man and pulled a long knife from the sheath at his hip. It was quite long, almost eight inches from tip to hilt. Bowe shook his head at it. "It's just a knife. I have one like it myself."

Elmore reached down and tapped the sharp point carefully with his finger. "It's still got its tip. You ever been a sailor? No? Well, there's a number of captain's out there what make it an order that the knives of all the deck hands are to have their tips knocked off. Helps to discourage mutinies and killing fights. Only officers are trusted enough to have proper blades."

"And unless I miss my guess, the officers having proper blades would be another means to discourage mutinies?"

"It is a method that works."

"If he is an officer, why would he dress like a common deck hand? Where's his uniform?"

"Couldn't say why he's dressed as he is, but my best guess would be that he doesn't want to be known to be an officer."

"Yes, or he has a captain who isn't too worried about mutiny. Or he bought this knife when he came ashore, perhaps at the same time he bought his new clothes."

Elmore couldn't rightly gainsay the speculation. There were captains—fools that they were—who allowed their crews to keep intact knives and there surely was no shortage of blacksmiths eager to sell whatever they could. But Elmore had no doubts at all that this man had been an officer on a ship. "He's an officer, mark me." Elmore balanced himself on his good leg and used his walking stick to push away the man's coat. At his side was a pistol in a holster. He smiled at Bowe. "Men before the mast don't carry firearms. Some captains may be lax enough to let their crew have untipped knives, but I've yet to hear of even one who would let the men go around armed with a flintlock. You know how many men would just love to have one clear shot at a captain that was too fond of the cat-o-nine tails? You'd have a hundred ships on the seas without captains. This man was an officer."

"Like the knife and the clothes, he might have bought the pistol ashore."

"What for?" Elmore stood up straight when he saw, from the corner of his eye, Captain Brown look over at them. "Buy new clothes, new arms … why? Out at sea, a man only cares if he's decent and warm. There's no point in new clothes if there's no one to show them off to, and if he'd been a naval man, he'd surely have been in uniform. The weapons would have been taken away or destroyed as soon as they were discovered, and discovered they would have been. Aboard ship, there's nowhere to hide anything. No privacy for even a minute."

Bowe considered it seriously, lightly tugging on his ear before he suggested, "He may not have intended to go back to his ship. He could have been making his way up to the plantations to get work there. He might have wanted new clothes to impress prospective employers, and the knife … well. Perhaps that was in case his shipmates caught up with him. I've heard that deserters are not looked upon with any great mercy."

With a snort, Elmore said, "If he were part of any navy and his shipmates had caught up with him, they'd likely have joined him at the plantation. I spit at the navy, the low scum! But for a private ship, then you may be right. If a contract had been signed, he'd be expected to honor that. If he were deserting and trying to stay hidden, then he'd have gotten himself dressed like a farmer. Or a blacksmith. Or any ordinary man in town. He'd not have dressed himself as a sailor."

"Perhaps he wasn't deserting. He might have been retired

and simply preferred this manner of dress."

"At his age? Can't be more than thirty at the most, and I never heard of any crewman who could afford to retire 'til they weren't able to work. He looks hale and healthy as anyone, so I don't see as he'd have been allowed to leave 'cause of his health. Well ..." Elmore checked himself. "He *was* healthy, anyhow. And if he was retired, then it was by God's own grace smiling down on him and making him a wealthy man."

Bowe fell silent for a time. He put his elbows on his knees and cupped his chin with one hand. "A pirate, perhaps. He could have afforded to buy new clothes and weapons with his share of the looted treasure. He would need good weapons and wouldn't have to hide them from any aboard his ship, because everyone aboard would have been heavily armed."

"Perhaps, but I don't see it as likely. A pirate would have bought secondhand to save what he could for drink and women." Elmore laughed. "Not many would waste money on something like new clothes."

"Not many, but some?" Bowe raised an eyebrow.

Reluctantly, Elmore nodded. "I've known a few dandies in my time what put a bit too much value on what they wore. Some would have sooner given up drink altogether than go about in patched clothes, but those are few and far between."

"So it's possible, but more likely this," Bowe gestured broadly with one hand at the man, "man was probably an officer dressed to blend in with the crowds in the city. And he wasn't robbed. Any thief worth his salt would have taken the weapons."

"Sure as I'm standing here, they would have. They'd have also taken his coat and those fine, new boots. Don't look like they'd been worn for longer than it took him to walk from Port Royal to here."

"He didn't," Bowe didn't even look up, he was so intent on studying the victim. "There isn't a bit of mud on his boots, and it's been raining. He was brought here and dumped like a sack of rubbish. You know, I truly hate mysteries. This city is full of sailors, never mind the rest of the island. This man could have come from a harbor on the other side of the island, for all I can tell. His name will be a real trick to uncover, let alone the reason for him to have been murdered and who did it." Bowe frowned, but not at Elmore. It seemed more like he was puzzling over the information. He put one hand on the side of the dead man's face and tilted his head to the side. "And another sign of a seaman." The man's hair had been tied into a short braid and was coated in something thick and black, making it stiff. "He's tarred his braid."

"Sure enough he did, but come away." He slapped Bowe's arm. "Your captain's looking none too pleased. See me away afore you get yourself into mischief."

The warning came too late.

"Lieutenant!" Captain Brown barked at Bowe. "Get this civilian away. This is a proper investigation, not a fair."

Bowe saluted his captain and, again, waited until his attention turned back to O'Donnell before he softly said to Elmore, "Sorry. Orders are orders." Bowe looked down at the dead man, rather sadly, then pulled the white shroud over the man's face. He stood then, and silently escorted Elmore to the road with a hand on Elmore's elbow, presumably as a show for Captain Brown, as Elmore wasn't making the faintest effort to linger.

"None of your doing. No point in apologizing. Your captain's in a right state, isn't he?" Elmore said once they'd moved a good distance away.

"It's not been a good day for the captain. Gossip—to which I never give any credence—says that he rashly said something rather unflattering to his superior. The result of that unfortunate statement is," he spread his arms wide, "this assignment." They walked silently together passed Captain Brown and O'Donnell until they reached the main road. Once they were well out of earshot, Bowe said, "It's not really important to him, you know. He doesn't care at all whether or not this gets solved. If Major Dunville hadn't been upset with the captain, I would have been sent to collect the body, gotten a statement from Mister O'Donnell and delivered the body to St. Martin's for a pauper's burial. There would be no investigation. No one important has been reported missing, so whoever this man is, he doesn't matter. People are killed every day, and the number of them who are never even named, let alone given justice, is shameful." He looked back at the unnamed man, the fine sailor. "He should at least have a name."

Elmore shook his head. "As you say, people die every day and no one cares. It's not just your superiors. You can't catch every man with a score to settle or thief who found himself a mark who decided to fight for his purse."

"I'm not a dove in a gilt cage." Bowe smiled, though half-heartedly. "I know justice is often neglected, still ... the right thing should be done. It must be done."

It had been a very long while since Elmore had seen the world as such a black-and-white place, but he couldn't help liking Bowe for his naive sense of right and wrong. For all they knew, the dead man had been a murderer whose last target had fought too well, but was frightened that the law would judge him too harshly for defending himself and, so, had tried to dispose of his attacker's body. "The will of God be done, so the good book says, I think. Maybe this is justice, passed down by a court higher than that of Governor Modyford's."

Bowe didn't look at all impressed and merely shrugged. "Maybe. Regardless, at the very least, I have some information to go on. Our victim was most likely an officer on a ship who was in disguise as a common seaman for some unknown reason. The crew of his ship must be expecting him back and, as it's very probable that he's from the nearest harbor—ours—all I'll have to do is hunt through the docked ships and hope someone will recognize his description. If not, I'll have to expand the search to the rest of the island. I'll have the murderer, yet."

"Don't you plan on telling your captain?"

"I'll have to if the other harbors need to be searched. If nothing else, I'll have to ask for leave to travel there. Captain Brown will, naturally, argue that whatever ship this man belonged to will have sailed by the time we get there to ask any questions."

"So would I," Elmore replied, honestly.

Bowe shrugged. "Be that as it may, if I have to or if Captain Brown shows any interest, yes—I'll tell him what's going on. Right now, though, he doesn't care in the slightest. He'll do his job, but that's as far as he'll go."

"Should you be going any further? If the man had friends enough to care, they'll get revenge for him."

"How would they know who to get revenge on?"

Elmore laughed. "Just 'cause you don't know who did the deed doesn't mean no one knows. His friends are likely to know who might have held a grudge. You figure out who he is, and you'll be halfway to finding the killer. As we know he wasn't robbed, then we know this was personal. He wasn't killed out here but brought from somewhere else, so we know whoever did this wants to keep it secret."

"Very personal." Bowe looked, again, to where they'd left the body. "His eyes were closed, you know. Mister O'Donnell said that he found the man lying on his back, with his hands folded on his chest. His eyes and mouth closed. He said that it looked very much as if the man had just lain down to sleep."

"Leastways, you know you've got a kindhearted murderer out there." It was almost enough to make Elmore laugh. "Bludgeons a man over the head, but hides him so poorly that he must have meant for the man to be found. He even leaves him in a respectable state. Quite makes a body wonder if he went and brought a holy man along to give last rites, too. Maybe he felt a stab of guilt after the sin and he makes sure to lay out his victim all nice and neat. Maybe he's hoping the ghost won't haunt him. Well, as I said, you find his mates. One of them will likely know who did this to him. And who's to say it weren't one of them? It's close quarters on any ship, close enough for men to start grating on one another. I'd not be a bit surprised if that man is never named and his killer walks free 'til his dying day. It happens often enough."

Bowe's eyebrows drew together in disapproval. "That's the trouble with this city. Apathy. How can you think that way? What about Jacob? Do you want to see him murdered because no one cared enough to stop the killer the first two or three times they'd killed? Maybe this wasn't a personal killing. Maybe the killer is twisted in the head. Maybe he killed for killing's sake. He could strike at any random target. Isn't it better to stop him now before he stumbles across your Jacob?"

A flash of something cold ran down Elmore's spine, like a terrible hand of ice, at the idea of Jacob crossing paths with such a person. He swallowed hard. "A fine speech, and it has some sense, I'll admit to that, but there's no force on God's green Earth what can keep a body perfectly safe always. 'Course, I'd lend a hand stopping this killer if we'd any way to find him; I'd no sooner have Jacob hurt than I'd cut off my own arm. That being said, you worrying about every evil out there won't do nothing but give you a headache. You say 'apathy,' but what else is a man to do? Nobody, not even your good self, can bring to justice every man with blood on his hands in his city. It's not apathy, but common sense. Why, you likely passed a half-dozen killers on your way here and never even knew it."

Bowe's shoulders fell and his head face lowered. "You're not the first to tell me so, but if no one even tries ..."

With a light slap on the arm, Elmore told him, "Don't let me ruin your plans, lad. Sounds to me as if you know what you want and how to get it—that's more than most men have. I'm just telling you how things stand. Maybe you've the right of it, after all's said and done; just don't be too let down if things don't work out as you're planning." He would admit to himself to being pleased when Bowe's disheartened expression lightened. There was no good reason to discourage a good man from trying to do good—there were few enough of them as there was, and he couldn't deny that he rather hoped Bowe would succeed. Such idealism could be dangerous if Bowe let it overcome his good sense, but it seemed that such fire for a goal should be result in a profit. "Well, who am I to criticize? Maybe finding this killer will get you rewarded in the hereafter."

"Sooner than that, I should hope." Bowe slowed his pace as they turned the corner and went out of sight of the watchful Captain Brown. "I have it all planned out, you see. This is just a very helpful circumstance, not to make light of the situation, you understand." They reached the horse and wagon that Elmore had borrowed and Bowe petted the horse's neck, though he watched Elmore for a long, quite moment. It was like being studied, and it wasn't an entirely comfortable feeling.

Judged.

Elmore was distinctly aware that he was being judged, and by a man who was hardly more than a boy, at that! Certainly, Bowe had no cause to judge Elmore, he knew nothing about him, and there was no reason at all for Elmore to feel such an ugly, twisting uncomfortable feeling in his gut, because he knew himself, as well as his crimes, better than anyone. There wasn't a single thing Bowe could say that Elmore didn't know and accept about himself, and yet Elmore wondered how someone like Bowe—utterly devoted to the rule of law—saw him. Not well, if he knew all.

With a sudden brightness to him, Bowe said, "I trust you. I haven't told anyone this, as I think it may cause trouble if some of my fellows know my plans, but I can trust you."

Elmore scowled. "Why?"

"I'm a good judge of character. Anyhow," he glanced around, yet again, before he leaned close and lowered his voice to answer. The light in his eyes was bright and sharp, showing that whatever it was that Bowe envisioned in that moment was as clear as daylight to him. Elmore guessed that Bowe could see it as well as he saw Elmore standing in front of him. "Finding this killer will be a stepping stone to power that I need to make a difference."

"And you think catching this one killer will get you some kind of power? Don't be addled. He'll get hung, and you'll go back to patrolling the filthy streets."

Bowe shook his head, and the corner of his mouth

twitched upward into a tiny smile. "Governor Modyford has made it clear to all his troops that he wants to bring more order to Port Royal. It isn't good for a governor to be in charge of the wickedest city on Earth. Makes him look incompetent to the king. Governor Modyford is eager to show His Majesty that he is able to subdue and civilize the city. All soldiers have been given orders that criminal activity is to be severely punished."

Elmore laughed. "And you think there's a hope of every soldier in this city suddenly going out of their way to catch criminals? Half of them *are* criminals."

"Oh, there isn't a hope of it. Not even the slightest chance and, rather sadly, that disinterest will do nothing but benefit me and help me to achieve my objective. A great many of my fellows are pleased to ignore crime. They're often bribed to suddenly be looking the other way. I will be one of the very few who brings a murderer before the governor, and he will remember me."

"Remember you? For one killer? Boy, you're dreaming. The hanging of one killer isn't going to clean up this town and you, alone, can't turn Port Royal into a respectable city."

"I can and I will."

"This city's been lawless for near as long as there's been a city. Sea gentlemen come and go by the kind invitation of the governor. They are the only navy we have, and without them, Port Royal would be defenseless, unless the king decides he can increase the size of his navy and spare us a few ships, and that won't happen." Elmore chuckled. "Why should he go to any expense when he can have his territory guarded without any lightening of his purse? Port Royal will stay as it's always been."

"You're wrong. I will change it. People will change when they realize that their lives will be safer and easier with law. Port Royal deserves justice as much as any city in this world, and I will see that it gets that justice."

There was such conviction in his voice, such unflinching certainty in his face, that Elmore was tempted to believe him. "You're only a soldier."

"Not for long. When the governor sees how useful I am to

him, I will rise in the ranks. And one day, I will be governor."

"Lofty ambition."

"A man is nothing without a goal."

Elmore gave Bowe an appraising look and slowly nodded. "Aye. I think you may just have the gumption to reach that goal, and I wish you the best of luck. I truly do."

CHAPTER 7: JUSTICE

Without the wood to replace what had been irreparably damaged, Elmore set about doing what he could once he returned the ugly horse to the blacksmith and got himself home. One plank might be salvaged for a smaller coffin, he reckoned. The wood that couldn't be used for a coffin could maybe be used for something else, so he stored all of it away and tried to think of something small, something that might sell. Maybe he could use some of it for the boxes Mister Fa wanted, though considering the Fa family's situation, Elmore wasn't altogether certain Mister Fa would have the money to spare for even something as simple as wooden boxes.

Still, Elmore thought, holding one of the smaller planks, broken into sharp points on both ends. *Got no other use for it. Wouldn't do any harm to make it a gift for the gentleman. Better than just burning it, anyhow. Maybe a toy for the girl ...*

For the better part of the afternoon, he fixed what could be fixed and contemplated whether or not he should sacrifice the kitchen table and use it to make a new coffin lid rather than have to tell a paying customer that he couldn't deliver. They couldn't let any income escape. He set down the wood in his hands and walked to the kitchen, where he put the palms of both hands on the table. It was strong and just big enough that it would do. He stood up straight and rubbed a hand over his face. His money jar was empty. But the treasure saved for Jacob's schooling was still there, entirely untouched, and it would tide them over until he could get some income. It would be enough for food and ...

Elmore felt sick. It would be like robbing the boy.

He swallowed hard and stared hard at the table. He could make a new table.

The front door opened and Elmore turned, ready with a practiced smile for whatever customer had walked in, but that smile faded instantly when he saw his visitor.

Gabe. Stone-cold sober and looking as wretched as a rainy November morning, he stepped in Elmore's house and every step closer he got to Elmore, Elmore's temper rose. With his hands in his coat pockets and his face humbly lowered, Gabe stood in the kitchen doorway and made such a pathetic sight that it might have been enough to get him some sympathy if Elmore hadn't gone through a similar scene every time Gabe visited. Or if Elmore hadn't spent a respectable amount of time making a fruitless trip far out of town and lost some good tobacco in the process. Out of the corner of his eye, Elmore watched as Gabe stood awkwardly near the door. Every time they'd gone through this, Elmore always forgave Gabe. They were the closest of friends, and Elmore had never seen any reason to let Gabe's bout with drink stand between them. This time was different. Elmore felt such a terrible fury at the sight of the man that he couldn't trust himself to speak.

Gabe wasn't one to let a silence drag on unchallenged. He cleared his throat and took a tentative step into the room. "See here, now. I ... ah. Yesterday. You know I meant nothing by it."

Elmore shot Gabe a harsh look and brushed by him to go back into the workshop, where he picked up a plane and resumed work on the one surviving plank, making long curls of wood as he shaved it smooth. He knew right well that Gabe hadn't caused havoc deliberately, but the fact was that he had done it, and Elmore had little hope that it would never happen again.

"It were more than the habit," Gabe went on, as though he didn't notice Elmore's dark temper. "It were Jacob. He said I were no good if I weren't around. Now I ask you: how can I makes me living and provide for him without taking a berth aboard a ship? You know I got no other trade, but he won't understand. That boy got me so boiling mad, I just had to get some peace and take me thoughts from him. You know what he says to me? Says he wished I weren't his da!"

"And right now I wish to God you weren't his pa, either." Elmore slammed the plane down on the wood and looked up at Gabe. "By thunder, what you did here!" Elmore spluttered, shaking. "If I'd a pistol in my hands now, I'd orphan Jacob properly! You and your rages, letting the drink make a mess of everything. First my work, then my home!" He surged to Gabe so quickly that Gabe didn't even try to move when Elmore seized him by the shirt and pushed him against the kitchen door hard enough to bring a grunt from Gabe. "It stops now! All of it!"

Gabe took hold of Elmore's hands, but didn't try to push him away. He grinned. "Finch, I like a brawl better than most anyone else, but what roused this tempest?"

Fire burst out in front of Elmore's eyes and then his fist hurt, and Gabe was on the floor, rubbing his jaw with an astonished look on his face. Elmore growled, "You think this is a joke? Making light of what you did?"

"No. I—"

"The only reason I haven't tossed you out that door is that we've been friends a good many years. Right now, standing here, I want to gut you. This is no time for your games, man." The words were growled out, more like an animal than a man. "Did you take it?"

"Take what?"

"The spyglass you gave your boy. Did you take it, or can't you remember? I don't rightly care one way or the other, but you get it back to him. Jacob was in a right state when he found it had gone. And my money box! All I had for taxes and you went and ... and what? Drank it away? Did you lose it on dice? How am I to go about feeding the boy with no money? How do I keep a roof over his head?"

The grin slid off Gabe's face. "What are you on about? What money? The spyglass?"

"I came home, after leaving you on the floor in your stupor, and when I gets back you're gone, and my home's been ransacked! My work destroyed, everything broken, the money gone, and Jacob's toy gone! He cried, you know. He cried for it.

He thought more of it than he let on, and now what have you done with it? Thrown it away or just lost it when you got drunk, again? And you had better have been drunk, 'cause if you'd done this knowing what you were about, then I would kill you."

Gabe shook his head and got to his feet. "I did nothing. I swear it. I woke and all was well. I let that ugly cur of yours in and gave him water, but then I left. I even locked the door. I swear, I weren't drunk! You know I only do that once—ONCE!—when I come ashore. Can't drink aboard ship, I don't handle it. I drink ashore once, then keep away from it. I'm no fool; I know I'm weak when it comes to spirits. I went to see Dora—the girl you took a dislike to—then back to *Indigo Running*. I figures you wouldn't want to be seeing me for a spell. We've been mates near ten years—you know I wouldn't steal from you, not even drunk. I'd no sooner rob you than I would my own mother."

"I know you took a swing at me, and I know you fell and broke one of my boards."

"That were an accident!"

"Look here, enough! Just tell me: did you take the spyglass? If you want Jacob to think well of you, then losing that spyglass was altogether the wrong way to go about it."

Gabe drew himself up straight and put his hands on Elmore's shoulders, looking right into his eyes. "No. All was well and good when I left here this morning, just after the church bells rang eight bells. I had a devil of an aching head, and I went to visit Dora. Ain't been back here 'til now. My word on it! Believe me."

If Elmore had learned one thing about Gabe through their many years' association, it was that Gabe couldn't tell a convincing lie to save his life, so he stepped away from Gabe to collect himself. "Then you have my apologies. I'm well worn out." He gestured to the room. "There's much to be done. I wasted the morning going to the woodcutters for more wood and, when I couldn't get it from him, I came back to do what I could here. I need to make boxes for a new customer, and I still need to see Reverend Roberts about a new leg for his desk … it's a bit of stress, is all. I don't like being so far behind. I can't see how I can get started on the desk leg 'afore tomorrow. Even if I had the time, I don't have the wood. I'll have to take another run to the woodcutters tomorrow or send Jacob for some. He won't mind the holiday, I guess. O'Donnell's a good enough man not to cheat the boy and send him home with a bit of rubbish fit for nothing but kindling."

Gabe nodded and looked Elmore up and down. "Anyone get hurt in the break in? Did the boy get hurt?"

"No. He weren't here. Thank God. He's upstairs studying. Whoever broke in didn't take much, but what a ruddy mess they left me! Curse them! I can see why they took the money, but why the spyglass? Why destroy the place?"

"Maybe they thought it were a working one. You said Jacob were upset?"

"Damned near had a tantrum when he couldn't find it."

There was no mistaking the pleased look that flashed across Gabe's face. "Think he'd have another tantrum if I goes to talk to him? You say he's upstairs?"

When Elmore silently nodded, Gabe headed upstairs with a cheery, "Maybe he needs a little rest from the studying. Wouldn't want him to ruin his eyes with too much reading."

Elmore waited a moment, then went up as quietly as he could. Near the top of the stairs, he heard them speaking and stopped to listen.

"I know you got reason to be angry, but it's all I know how to do. I got no other way to provide for you."

"Uncle does well enough. You should be here. You could help him in the shop."

"I'm no carpenter. The sea is all I know; the tides and waves and ragin' storms—it's my life. Don't think I could live away from her, no matter how I wished it. She's got me well chained to her. And, anyhow, it wouldn't be right for me to impose on Elmore."

"You're family. Uncle wouldn't mind."

"I'd mind. A man's got to make his own way in the world,

not leech off another. Your ma would want me to do right by you."

"Uncle never talks about ma."

"He didn't know her. Do you remember her?"

"I remember she wore a blue dress and her hair was braided. I remember her voice. She used to sing to me."

"Ah, but she were real fond of singing. Had a right pretty voice, even when singing those raunchy tunes at the tavern. She were a good woman. Don't you let anyone fill your head with fire and vinegar for street women. They's just as good, most of them, as any lady in silk finery and pearls around her neck. It's only fortune what sets them apart."

"Reverend Roberts says we're all the same—all God's children."

"And right he is. Your ma was the loveliest girl I'd ever set sights on, for all her patched skirts and sweat-stained blouses." Even through the door, Elmore could heard the warmth in Gabe's voice and wished, not for the first time, that he could have had the pleasure of meeting such a woman who could inspire that sort of emotion in a man like Gabriel Scratch. "Her eyes … they sparkled like the stars on the waves. When I heard the fever took her, I was about lost. I didn't have a clue what to do about you. You were such a little thing, and I had no honest way of raising you up."

"Padre Gomez was kind."

"That Catholic priest? Well. Be as that may, I didn't know him, and I do know Elmore. He's a real friend. I knew he was a good man, and he lived here. I wanted to be able to see you, and there ain't too many places where I'm able to weigh anchor for any stretch of time." Gabe paused. "I don't leave you here 'cause I don't care for you. I do it for your sake. Elmore's a sight smarter and steadier than me. You're better off with him. I'm sorry you don't like that I last left without saying nothing, but when cap'n calls, I gots to go running. No choice unless I want to go against ship's articles, and that's no good at all. I signed my name to it, same as all the crew, and a man's got to stand by his word. Look, you, I'll get you another something to replace that spyglass. It were garbage, anyhow. I'll get you something better. A pistol of your own and I'll teach you to shoot, too."

Elmore jumped when a sharp knock at the front door grabbed his attention away from Gabe and Jacob. He went to the front door as quickly as he could before the noise disturbed what was happening upstairs. He was more than a little surprised to find Bowe and two lower-ranking soldiers at his door.

Bowe was serious and sedate—not a trace of his earlier good humor—when he stepped in without invitation and brazenly looked around as he took off his hat. "Forgive this visit, but we're looking for your friend. He was here the other day when we met."

The other soldiers stayed in the doorway, blocking the exit, and neither of them had even a trace of Bowe's polite manner.

"Which one? I'd two guests, then."

"His name is Gabriel Scratch."

Elmore felt a sickening weight settle in his gut. "What do you think he's done?"

"He's been brought to my attention in regards to a crime. I need to speak with him. Now, if you please."

Elmore took the broom from where it rested near the kitchen door and started sweeping up the shavings and sawdust that littered his floor as he pondered the wisdom of lying. "What is this all about? What crime is he supposed to have done?"

"Murder. I did tell you that I would find the killer, although I really didn't expect my hunt to lead me to your door."

"You've been led off course, I can tell you that truly. Gabe's no murderer."

"He was named." Bowe sounded disturbingly certain. "A person who'd somehow heard of the murder gave testimony that Gabriel Scratch had good reason to want the victim, First Officer Leopold Passy, dead."

He looked back at his men. "Look everywhere, but mind that you treat this home as if it were your own. I don't want so much as a chair overturned."

Elmore watched, helpless and furious, as one of the soldiers went to the kitchen and the other started up the stairs. He went to follow the soldier going up the stairs without any idea of what he would do or say if he actually caught the man, but Bowe caught his arm.

"Please, don't ..."

A great crash from above and yelling made Elmore's stomach flip. Jacob gave a frantic cry and that was it for Elmore. He wrenched his arm away from Bowe, but before he'd even reached the foot of the stairs, the soldier who'd gone into the kitchen rushed by and pushed him out of the way.

Thrown off balance, Elmore's bad knee twisted hard enough to make him cry out and fall against the wall. He had just righted himself as Gabe, with one arm around Jacob's shoulders and his sword held tightly in his free hand, rushed down the stairs. They stopped halfway down upon seeing Bowe and the second soldier.

Both soldiers, one at the top of the stairs and one at the bottom, had their rifles up and aimed.

Gabe, wild-eyed and sweating, held Jacob tighter to his side.

The two soldiers were yelling and Gabe yelled right back. His face turned red with the effort. Elmore didn't hear any more of their noise than he would have heard a mosquito buzzing. He could focus on nothing but Jacob's pale, frightened face.

"That is enough!" Bowe thundered, bringing everyone, even Gabe, to silence. His smile had gone when he stepped to the foot of the stairs and cast cold looks not at Gabe, but at his own men. "Put your arms down unless you plan to kill a child not yet old enough to shave! Both of you! Be ashamed!"

Too slowly for the sake of Elmore's heart, the rifles turned towards the floor.

Bowe seemed taller, then. Pride and power appeared to have instantly made him grow. "A fine show you put on, the pair of you! Mister Finch, Mister Scratch. I apologize for this severe lack of civility. I had thought my men could control their zeal. To you, too, Master Scratch." He smiled at Jacob. "I hope you weren't too frightened."

Jacob raised his chin a little and shook his head. "No, sir."

"Good. That's good." Bowe looked at Gabe and kept smiling, speaking with a soft, even tone. "Mister Gabriel Scratch? We met yesterday."

Gabe nodded, sharply. "I remember." His hand, still on Jacob's shoulder, tightened around the boy's shirt. His wild eyes didn't ease. "That one," he jerked his head to indicate the soldier behind him at the top of the stairs. "He said I'm wanted for murder. I don't know who's spewing such lies, but I'm not a murderer! I've been here, at The Blue Dog Inn, or aboard *Indigo Running* all the while we've been docked."

The soldier at the top of the stairs sneered. "*Indigo Running* is a pirate ship, sir. Liars, murderers, and thieves—all of them."

"I'm no murderer!" Gabe spat. "And *Indigo Running* is a privateer. Cap'n has a letter of marque, signed, as is right and legal, by Governor Modyford."

Bowe held up both hands in a placating gesture. "I'm not here to question your profession. There is suspicion against you, Mister Scratch. A man has said that you had motive and opportunity to kill a man we've found. Our orders are to take you to the prison for questioning. We aren't escorting you to execution dock. We're not going to kill you in cold blood. If you don't believe me, then fine, but you will be taken to the prison. The boy should go to Mister Finch. Now."

Jacob looked up at Gabe. "Da?"

He didn't want to let Jacob go, that much was obvious. Gabe licked his lips and shifted his eyes around to all the soldiers.

"If you're considering fighting or running," Bowe said, "please remember that if we aren't all quite civil to one another, this situation could turn unpleasant. I see no reason for anyone to get hurt, but it would be best to get the boy out of harm's way. I'm sure you wouldn't want him hurt or killed because of a misunderstanding."

"I won't hang for a crime I haven't done," Gabe hissed.

"If you aren't guilty, then I won't see harm done to you. I will fight for your justice." The sincerity in his voice was arresting. "But right now we have orders and we must escort you to prison with or without a fight. Please, let the boy go."

There was no way out. Much as it ate at him, Elmore knew he was no match for the soldiers, even if he had been armed. And what good would it have done to fight? Even if he killed one of the soldiers or managed to make enough of a distraction to give Gabe a chance to run, he'd get himself killed, and where would that leave Jacob?

Gabe took his arm off Jacob's shoulders and gave the boy a gentle push. "Go to your uncle, lad." Then he glared at Bowe. "Don't you lay a hand on him, or I *will* be guilty of murder."

Jacob rushed between Bowe and the other soldier and went straight to Elmore, but then turned and kept his eyes fixed on Gabe and the soldiers.

"Thank you," Bowe gave Gabe a little bow. "Now, the sword. Put it down and we'll go."

Gabe may have had a rough temperament, but he wasn't stupid. With a curse, Gabe did as he was told, laying his cutlass on the steps then walking down to Bowe. When he was nearly at the bottom step, the soldier at Bowe's side grabbed Gabe's arm and yanked him down the last few steps until he stood on the floor.

Bowe scowled at his subordinate. "No need to get overenthusiastic. Mister Scratch is coming willingly and will be treated with due respect. Search him for weapons. We want no mistakes. No more misunderstandings." He looked over at Elmore without even a hint of pleasure or pride in what he was doing. "Justice must be served."

Justice?

Justice was a lie; nothing but a sweet fable.

Elmore kept an arm around Jacob as Gabe was led away. Neither spoke. Was it justice to lead an innocent man away? Gabe had no lawman to speak for him, and certainly didn't know the law well enough to defend himself with words. In the end, it wasn't about justice, anyhow. It was all an excuse to bring someone before the governor, parade him up and down as some ruthless killer, so the governor could feel that he was doing his duty to king and crown.

They watched at the doorway until Bowe's soldiers, with Gabe sandwiched between them, rounded a corner. Gabe looked over his shoulder at Elmore and Jacob just before he was led out of sight, and Elmore suddenly found himself years in the past, watching his mother be led away. He shook himself and tried to squash down the burning anger in his chest that had ignited at Bowe's empty word—justice.

All through his life, Elmore had seen time and time again that justice was a meaningless word. It was enforced when suited. The rich could buy themselves free of guilt, and no one really cared whether or not the poor were wronged. He'd seen too many times when justice was ignored or perverted to serve a purpose. If Bowe hadn't cared to further himself, if the governor hadn't needed to prove himself to the king, would anyone have bothered to look for the murderer? No. Bowe had admitted as much.

So why Gabe?

Why should he suffer, when there were so many others in Port Royal—so many others the whole world over—who led far worse lives?

Jacob was shaking as fiercely as if he'd been caught in a blizzard and he clutched so tightly to Elmore's sleeves that it felt as if he had some great prey bird latched onto his arms with its talons. It seemed to pain the boy to take his gaze away from where his father had been, and he whispered, "What are we going to do?"

"Do?" Elmore gave Jacob a quick squeeze around the shoulders. "You're going inside to practice your schoolwork, and then you're going to start some dinner up for us. We've got pork enough for stew."

"No!" Jacob's eyes went alarmingly wild. "What about da? What are we going to do for him?"

"Nothing we can do."

Jacob flew into a temper. He pulled against Elmore, trying to get loose, but Elmore's arms were strong and he held tight. And all the while, Jacob roared and used words that Elmore knew he'd learned from hanging about the harbor.

"Belay, boy!" Elmore hugged Jacob close enough that Jacob couldn't so much as budge his arms. "I said, belay! What demon's come to you?"

"Let me go! I'll get him out! I'll get him! I won't let them take him!"

Though he was lame, Elmore was not to be overpowered by a half-mad child. He took hold of Jacob's skinny arm and hauled him back into the house. He slammed the door behind him and rounded on Jacob. "You check yourself!"

Jacob rushed him, as if he thought he might be able to push by Elmore.

With one hand, he grabbed Jacob by the collar of his shirt. He spun Jacob around and tucked him under one arm, while he used the other arm to land him a hard smack to the backside. It took two more smacks before Jacob began to calm. Elmore held Jacob like that only long enough to be certain that the fight had gone out of him, then he pulled Jacob upright and, doing his best to ignore the tears on the boy's face, said, "I hear such words from you again, and I'll thrash you 'til you can't sit for a month! You aren't going to talk or even think about putting yourself in the sight of any soldier!"

"We can't just let them have him."

Of course they couldn't. He was family. Every part of Elmore screamed at him to do exactly as Jacob wished to; he would storm The Hold and free Gabe. But that was madness and would end in nothing but failure. He took Jacob's chin in hand and forced the boy to look, to meet his eyes. "You will leave this alone. Understand? I'll go talk to your pa and see what he's got to say."

"But he didn't kill anyone. You know he didn't." Jacob paused and licked his lips. The anger and panic that had filled his eyes drained away, leaving nothing in their place but fear. "He didn't, did he?"

CHAPTER 8: THE HOLD

The prison on Hamshaw Street was most commonly known as The Hold. It was an understandable title, as any sailor who'd ever set foot below deck of a ship could testify, for the stone building was dark and damp as any ship's hold.

Several hours after Gabe had been taken away, Elmore made his way to The Hold. The soldier on guard led Elmore from the door to the guard's room, and then through that, to a long hall lined with doors. At the end of the hall, a tiny window, barred and too small for even a child to squeeze through, gave some light, but couldn't chase away the shadows or the shining, inhuman eyes of rats staring out of the dark corners as they lurked and waited for any chance of food. The soldier who'd led Elmore into The Hold carried a torch that added light, but also smoke, and the heavy smell of burning wood that couldn't quite blot out the smell of mildew and filth that filled the prison's air. The smell of the place was nearly unbearable; urine and vomit and sweat and blood all mingled together to make the air heavy and foul.

There was very little noise, but the soft moans and cries of someone sobbing in their dark cell sounded miserably loud in the stone hall. One man peered out the tiny window cut into the wooden door of his cell with shining eyes that seemed eerily like the rat's small eyes lurking at the edges of the hall. The man muttered insensibly to himself as his eyes rapidly shifted this way and that, as if he were desperately searching for something.

At the far end of the hall, the guard opened the door to Gabe's cell and Elmore stepped in. Surprisingly, Gabe didn't look as poorly as Elmore had feared he might, even after only a few hours locked away. Elmore had seen prisoners in worse shape after less time if the soldiers guarding them were in poor spirits. Gabe sat on a rough wooden bench in a cell no more than four paces wide and long. A bucket under the bench was undoubtedly the source of the pungent smell.

The soldier hung his torch in an iron holder just outside the cell, enough to give some dim light. "I'll tell you when your time's up," the soldier said before closing the door behind him.

In the silence and stench and near darkness, Gabe and Elmore stared at each other until Gabe let his face drop into his hands. "This ain't any fun. They don't do anything. I just ... sit here."

"That's better than I'd hoped for." Elmore moved to sit next to Gabe on the bench. "You're a sight better off than I'd expected. You're gonna need a shave if you're here any longer, though."

Gabe laughed, a bit hollowly. "I'd grow a full beard if it would mean getting me out of here. They say I killed some Frenchman."

"Did you?"

"Damn you, no." He sounded tired. "I told them the truth back at the house. I've been nowhere but your house, the ship, and that inn. That's it and I swear my soul to it!"

Elmore leaned back, resting his back against the cold wall. "I don't like all this."

"You trust me or not?"

"Aye. Soldiers ready to open fire in my home with Jacob in the way? He was upset enough by the robbery, and then having you hauled away when you'd just started making peace."

"Eavesdropping ain't polite."

"My house, I do as I please in it. Jacob, he wanted to break you out of here. I've a feeling I'll have a fight to keep that boy out of trouble in a year or so."

"There's to be a trial in five days. I'm gonna hang."

A terrible silence settled over them. "Did they say what their proof was that it was you?"

"Some dog said it were me. It were a sailor from a French ship we took; the one the spyglass came from. Someone says

I fought a man during the attack, and that Frenchman were found dead out in the forest. I don't remember there being much fighting at all. His name was First Officer Leopold Passy, they said. I don't make introductions during a boarding. They even had that French captain come here to say I were one of the attackers."

"Doesn't seem like sound reasoning. Just 'cause you boarded the ship and fought the dead man doesn't mean you killed him."

"Oh, I'm sure they got lots of reasons. They said some girl saw Passy getting killed and it was right outside the Blue Dog, just in the back. The barkeep said I'd left in a roaring state about the same time. My face … I'm marked up from fighting, but I don't remember it. I remember Dora, and then you went and knocked me down—"

"No. I didn't lay a finger on you. You charged me and I moved out of the way. You just fell."

They stared at each other for a moment and Elmore saw the desolate look flood into Gabe's eyes as the implications of his faulty memory hit him.

"Don't say it," Elmore growled. "Don't even hint that you don't remember that night!"

"I didn't think I'd drunk so much."

Elmore grabbed Gabe's shoulder and shook him. "You keep your mouth shut! Understand? Answer me!"

"Right! Right! I'm not a fool. I'll say nothing."

Elmore stood. "When you went about that French ship, did anyone use your name?"

"What does that matter?"

"Just tell me. Did you or anyone else say your name?"

"No. I'm well certain."

At that moment, the guard reappeared and informed them that the visit was over.

Elmore nodded sharply and told Gabe, "I'll try to come back."

"Bring Jacob by before the end, won't you?"

Elmore nodded and left Gabe with his morbid thoughts, as he could think of nothing comforting to alleviate them. All through the long halls of the prison, Elmore's thoughts lingered not only on Gabe, but on Jacob as well. He wouldn't take it well—seeing his father in chains and ready to die. Jacob hadn't cried when they'd led Gabe away or when Elmore, afraid to leave the boy alone so soon after the robbery, had left him at the church with the good Reverend Roberts. But the boy was twelve and wanted, like all twelve-year-old boys, to be more grown-up than he was. He wanted to know what was happening to his father, but what could Elmore tell him? How do you tell a child that his father would hang?

The dreadful thoughts had so preoccupied him that he didn't notice Bowe waiting by The Hold's outside door until he called out. When he saw who had shouted his name, Elmore tried to hurry away and walked past him without a word.

Bowe wouldn't be ignored and easily caught up with him, matching his pace even when Elmore limped as quickly as he could. "I'm sorry. I never wanted to cause you or your nephew trouble. Honestly."

"What did you think would happen when your thugs bust into my home and draw arms on a man? Especially when he's with his young son? Did you think he'd take it easy?"

"Of course not, but I couldn't ignore the evidence. He's our best suspect. He was seen in the area where the victim was killed. He was seen leaving a tavern stumbling drunk and angry. His face is proof enough that he fought with someone, though he didn't say who he fought with. A witness directly named your friend and said that Mister Scratch had faced the victim in an earlier fight."

"Gabe told me all of that, and he told me you had the French captain come in to accuse him. Of course he'll speak against Gabe—he lost his cargo to Gabe's ship, and if that's not enough to turn any man bitter, then I'm sure I don't know what is. That Frenchman's lying!"

"If that was true, then I would think that Captain LeBeau

would have spoken against the captain of the *Indigo Running* instead of her quartermaster. Besides which, he wasn't the accuser who led me to Mister Scratch in the first place." Bowe looked over his shoulder, then back at the road ahead. "There are a few points I'm not certain of, some things that don't seem quite right, but my superiors have proven very eager to please the governor, much moreso than I'd guessed. They want to show off to the governor that they were able to catch the killer of a military officer, even if that officer is of an enemy nation. Mister Scratch is the easiest target around. They aren't willing to give him up just because a few lines don't quite connect."

"So, if your dead man had been a nameless tramp?"

"Then I doubt anyone would have shown enough interest to send me to your home."

Elmore rolled his eyes. *Naturally*. "Gabe said the dead man was found yesterday. Was it the man at O'Donnell's?"

"Yes, but I really can't speak about details."

Elmore stopped walking and looked Bowe square in the face. "Then you're no good to me. Be off. I've got work to do."

***

The snitch had to have been someone from *Indigo Running*.

Elmore had sat in his workshop for a long time after he left Gabe, puzzling and stewing over the idea when he should have been trying to work. At the kitchen table, with his pipe letting out a soft drizzle of smoke and his elbows resting on the tabletop, he sat and kept trying to figure another way around the mystery, but there wasn't one he could think of. Whoever had accused Gabe had to have been a crewman from *Indigo Running*.

Even that didn't make much sense, though. There were rules against such things and, well … it simply wasn't how things were done aboard a ship of gentlemen of fortune. Any personal trouble was settled between the men, and serious enough grievances would be grounds for a trial, with the crew passing judgment. To involve the law was an unforgivable breach of conduct and, as most avoided lawmen as a matter of habit and survival, it was almost unthinkable that anyone would even consider such a dirty act.

Perhaps that was why it had been done.

Elmore tapped a finger on the tabletop at that thought. No one would ever suspect, so whoever had done it would never be in danger of being found out. They would need it to be kept secret, too, as anyone willing to sell out a mate was a danger to the whole crew and, as such, risked torture or death for such a betrayal. Whatever reason the man had for putting Gabe in such a spot, it must have been a whopper.

What he had to figure out was: who? And why?

Whether it turned out that Gabe was guilty of the killing or not, Elmore wouldn't see him hung. Even if that infuriating ass gave a public, honest confession followed by the victim's corpse coming to life to accuse his killer, Gabe wouldn't swing so long as Elmore had breath left in his body. He'd seen hangings before: the short fall and the sudden jerk as the noose tightened and, if the damned were lucky, they died with a jerk as their neck snapped. If they were unlucky, they would dance in midair, fighting futilely for life as they slowly turned blue, strangling before a curious, gawking crowd.

Then Elmore found himself in a nightmare of a memory.

Mother was screaming, her fair hair wild around her face as it came undone from her bonnet. She was dragged to the old oak, two men holding her arms. Again and again, she threw herself around like an animal, desperate to escape. Little Elmore, held back by men much bigger than himself, could only watch.

That day had been hardly more than a month after they'd buried Elmore's father. Everything had seemed quite normal until news had come that his mother had been taken away and was held in the town jail for murder. Elmore had run the whole way and arrived in time to see his mother standing before a judge. He hardly recognized her. Her face was drawn and pale, her blouse torn and hanging off one shoulder. Her skirts were dirty and, again, torn. It was her eyes, as she looked up at the judge, that frightened Elmore the most. There was something alien in her dark eyes, something that wasn't the mother he loved. It was something big and frightened and angry.

She had killed Farmer Hanson and freely admitted it.

"I'm a Christian woman, your honor, and I won't lie. I killed him. My hand was the one that took his life. But I did not murder! He tried to force himself on me. He'd already gotten one poor young girl with child and had her sent away without so much as a good word for her sake. He caught me alone as I cleaned his kitchen. There were no servants about to see or hear at that hour, and his good lady wife was quiet in her room." She stood straight and proud and met the judge's eyes without flinching. "My hand fell on a knife and I used it. I didn't mean to kill, but I'll not let myself be dishonored for his sinful nature. And I won't say I'm sorry he's dead."

Reasons didn't matter, the judge said. The law had to be obeyed. Justice must be served. The judge declared her guilty and, as a confessed murderess, Elmore's mother would hang.

Elmore remembered screaming at the men who'd led his mother away, fighting for all that he was worth, but he wasn't strong enough and they kept tight hold of him. She hadn't known he was there until he'd started to kick up a storm, that much was obviously from the desolate look on her face when she finally saw him.

There was a crowd outside the courthouse at the base of the oak tree. Onlookers swarmed close to the scaffolds to get a good look at the condemned. They shouted when Elmore's mother was led outside and when the hangman roughly put the noose around her throat.

How Elmore hated them! Each one of them! They had nothing better to do than watch, to make a spectacle of her death. If he'd only brought along his father's rifle, he'd have killed them all!

Look away, she had mouthed to him. *Look away.*

But he couldn't.

The hangman had tightened the noose, and the noise from the crowd faded to nothing. Elmore became aware of nothing but her standing high above the crowd on the top of an old crate. She was crying and scared. Her small mouth was opened as she panted for breath, and she shook hard enough that he could see it from even where he stood at the door of the courthouse. He suddenly couldn't move or speak or even think. All he could do was watch.

Her eyes closed.

A jerk.

Twitching, kicking, bulging eyes.

Face turning red, then blue, then purple.

Then … stillness.

What did justice mean when a woman couldn't defend herself?

What was justice when a good man like Gabe …

Be honest, he told himself. *Gabe ain't always so good-natured. He ain't rightly "good."*

Elmore had no illusions; he knew that Gabe was a killer many times over, and he knew that Gabe traveled a far less-than-pious path. Gabe was a bad drunk: angry, swearing, and violent. The scene right there, in the workshop, when Gabe had tried to attack him, hadn't been the first time he'd found trouble while in the grip of drink. He'd broken bones of people he barely knew and didn't hesitate to fight for the slightest reason, or for no reason at all. Despite that knowledge, Elmore wished that justice had overlooked Gabe as it did to so many others. Gabe was his friend—all faults included.

But even with all of his many faults, Elmore had never known Gabe to kill in cold blood.

No! Don't think about that! Don't doubt!

Gabe didn't need a friend arguing against him, not when any third-rate lawyer could do it so easily. Even if they accepted that Gabe wouldn't hunt down a man he'd bested in a fight weeks ago, they could argue that the victim might have held a grudge and hunted Gabe down. If Gabe happened to be drunk at the time, then the French officer might have been dishonorable enough to have challenged a drunken man, thinking he would be an easy target. It wouldn't be the first time that a drunk got the better of his attacker.

The key lay in the accuser. There was no proof of anything other than the fact that Gabe and the Frenchman had met in a sea battle.

There was nothing else for it. He extinguished his pipe and pulled on his coat. He had no doubt that Gabe had been drunk nearly since his argument with Jacob and, being drunk, he wouldn't have thought to move the body of someone he might have killed. And if he were the killer, then why should someone else move the body? No. It wasn't Gabe.

All Elmore had to do was find out who had spoken against Gabe. In a city of thousands - many privateers, pirates, and other assorted criminals - he would have to find one particular liar.

CHAPTER 9: CIRCLE OF GLASS

The day after everything had gone so wrong and Gabe ended up in The Hold, Elmore went looking for Raynard. Raynard wasn't aboard *Indigo Running* when Elmore went in search of him, but Captain Harrington directed him to a likely public house Raynard was known to frequent, The Gull and Tern, where many of the ship's crew chose to spend their earned shares of booty on strong ale, gambling, and sweet-faced barmaids who never seemed to remember to fully lace up their blouses.

The Gull and Tern was only a short walk from the harbor and was as respectable as any public house in Port Royal could hope to be. The common room was large enough for five round tables and a bar, behind which a fat woman with rosy cheeks doled out tankards from a large cask, and even in the noise of a pleasant evening, her hearty laughter could be heard all around the room. Despite the thick fog of pipe smoke, the room was bright thanks to two large windows that looked out onto the street.

Raynard sat alone near the back with two half-drank tankards, one in his hand and the other on the table in front of him. He started when he noticed Elmore walking towards him. He wiped his mouth with his sleeve and set his cup down when Elmore wordlessly sat down opposite of him at the table.

There was no subtle way to say it. He asked if Raynard knew of a man who shared his family name and went by the name of Leopold.

Raynard's face fell. He took a deep gulp, finishing off the drink of front of him before he set that noggin down and picked up the second one and just held it with both hands. "You heard about my cousin, then. I wasn't keeping secrets, exactly, or planning to sell out the crew to any soldiers, if that's what's on your mind. Leo and I, we just went different ways in life, that's all. He'd not have asked me to turn traitor, anyhow. He was a good sort of man. Lord, I'm going to have to write his mother …" He shook his head, then blinked and refocused on Elmore. "How did you meet him, anyway?" He looked down at his drink.

"Soldiers came to my home today and took Gabe away." He told Raynard what happened and what he knew.

Raynard shook his head when Elmore finished speaking. "No. I don't believe it. Gabe isn't one to kill for no reason. He did set his sword against Leo—that I saw with my own eyes—but when it was done, it was done with him. Gabe was never one to hold a grudge and certainly not over business. You know that as well as I. When the battle was over, he was happy as a lark. No reason for him to kill anyone."

"He'd been drinking the night it happened."

Raynard's shoulders slumped and he put the noggin back down on the table. "Oh."

"What eats at my mind is that your cousin might have hunted Gabe down or happened upon him when Gabe were out of his mind with the drink. Maybe your cousin was one to hold a grudge. You know how Gabe is after a few; his good nature turns straight to vinegar." Elmore picked up the half-empty cup that smelled strongly, not of rum or ale, but real wine, which Raynard preferred when his pockets were full enough. "He can't control himself when he's drunk. He'll fight a preacher over one wrong glance."

Raynard looked thoughtful. "Maybe so. I don't like it, but he does turn into a mean cuss after a few. It's like the sun rising and setting, isn't it? Regular as anything, he'll drink as soon as his feet hit dry ground. And Leo always tends to dwell on wrongs done to him. Least ways, he always did. I spoke with Leo the other day. Remember? I said I had someone to meet? Well, that was Leo. He didn't seem upset about anything, and he'd have said if he were. He saw I was on the crew that boarded his ship, though he was good enough to say nothing."

"What I want to know is who pointed the law at Gabe. They were told his name and where to find him. Whoever turned on him knew about the battle. We can't blame your cousin for reporting his own murder."

"One of Leo's mates would be my guess, then."

"They couldn't know Gabe was staying with me and they wouldn't have known his name. He said no one used it during the attack."

"Then … one of us?" Raynard scowled. "Ah! Never. Gabe's well-liked, and he'd have told me if he'd been having trouble with …" His voice trailed away, and he tapped his fingers and looked down at the tabletop. His eyebrows drew together. His hand clenched into fists before he relaxed them and set them on his lap. A strange light seemed to flash in his eyes when he abruptly looked up with cautiously narrowed eyes at the people around them. The room was crowded, but no one seemed to be paying them any heed.

Raynard stood. "Walk with me."

They went upstairs to where Raynard said he'd taken a room for the week or so that they'd be ashore. Once they were alone and the door closed, Raynard spoke softly, as if he were still afraid of being overheard. "I'm not accusing anyone of anything, mind, but Captain Harrington and Gabe had an argument before the last attack. Gabe wanted to stay closer to the Gulf Stream, where there were sure to be more merchants, but Captain Harrington had a hunch to hunt in less-crowded pickings. We'd gotten caught in a hurricane and chanced upon Leo's ship just after the hurricane ended. Captain Harrington didn't like that Gabe spoke against him in front of the whole crew. He might have gotten the idea to get Gabe out of his hair by setting the law on him."

"Seems like an odd reason to throw away an able hand. Gabe's never been shy about speaking his mind, and this can't be the first time he or someone else has spoken against one of Cap'n Harrington's ideas. 'Sides, he's quartermaster. He's supposed to speak up when he sees something he doesn't think is right, whether his cap'n likes it or not."

"I know it doesn't make much sense, but think about it. He knows Gabe always goes to see you when we're docked. He knows Gabe gets himself insensibly drunk first chance he gets. Soldiers came around to all the ships in the harbor, looking to identify Leo. Captain Harrington could have seen it as a handy chance to have one less voice against him. The fewer against him, the smoother his ship runs." He shrugged and winced, rubbing his forearm. "I'm likely thinking too much on this. Maybe I'm wrong, but I can't think of any of the other crewmate he's had trouble with."

***

Elmore left Raynard in no easier a mood than he'd met him. He didn't know the current captain of the *Indigo Running* well—he'd left before Captain Harrington had joined the crew, long before he'd stepped up as captain—but it just didn't seem right. Why would any captain go to so much effort to get rid of a hand when that hand was doing exactly what he was supposed to be doing—speaking his mind? It wasn't uncommon for differences of opinions between a captain and his quartermaster to crop up. Happened all the time, really.

Back at The Hold, the soldiers guarding the front door refused to let him in to see Gabe. They didn't give a reason, but then, they didn't have to. No argument could persuade them to let him in and, in the end, he was turned away with only the hope that in the morning he would find more sympathetic guards.

A short distance away, he turned back to look at The Hold and felt a stab of pain. He'd known Gabe for so long; it would be shameful to have it all end in such a way. To have such a bright flame of life snuffed out with a rope just made Elmore's innards churn.

They'd met in Boston, years ago. It was a memory Elmore couldn't seem to forget, no matter how hard he tried. The thought of it still made him blush like a slip of a girl.

At seventeen years old, Elmore had made his way to

Boston for the first time. Before that, he'd spent his time traveling and working for his supper at the farms he would come across. There was always work to be done, and plenty of food for a hard-working hand. Boston was his first encounter with a real city. The streets were paved with brick and such tall buildings! Ladies in fine gowns trimmed with white lace strolled down the roads while men rode their horses without much concern for the people on foot. Elmore was consumed with gawking at the sights of such a big city when he turned a corner and found himself facing something he'd heard about, but had never seen.

The Atlantic Ocean.

It was so vast—that endless expanse of water—that he was left speechless and stood in the street like a simpleton for a great long time until someone bumped into him from behind and nearly knocked him off his feet.

"Watch yourself, youngster." The man was no more than five or seven years older than Elmore and wore whiskers on his chin. His skin was quite dark, like the color of a man used to living under the sun, and his eyes sparkled at Elmore. "Stand there so befuddled and you'll be lucky your boots don't get stolen from right out under you."

Elmore made to apologize, but it was waved aside and the man put an arm over Elmore's shoulders. "You look to be new hereabouts. What's your business?" He started walking, and the arm he'd put around Elmore ensured that Elmore would walk with him.

"Just passing through." Elmore shrugged and, when that didn't get the arm off his shoulder, he made a sudden spin and twisted away from the stranger's arm.

"Don't be unfriendly, like." The man laughed, but there was nothing malicious in it. He just seemed a pleasant, friendly fellow. "Here," he gestured towards a building just to the left. "Let me buy you a drink."

Before that day, Elmore had drunk nothing but water, milk, and, on rare occasions, cider. To be offered real drink and companionship when he'd spent so many long, lonely weeks between towns was too tempting to refuse. Life had taught him well not to trust, but there was something engaging about the stranger, something that made Elmore slide away from his caution and accept the invitation.

The public house the stranger had led him to was small and dark and decidedly unclean. But the serving maid brought a frothy tankard of ale and smiled knowingly even when she caught Elmore's new friend looking down her loose blouse when she bent over to set the drink on the table.

"She'd be a handful, boy." The stranger winked at Elmore when the serving maid sauntered away, swinging her broad hips as she did. "Ones like that, the ones with spirit, are always the most fun." He took his drink and gulped it. With a contented sigh, he wiped his mouth with the back of his hand and nodded towards Elmore's drink. "Go on, then. It's not too bad."

He drew deeply from the tankard, and though the ale tasted odd and not exactly what he would call pleasant, he managed to swallow and felt quite grown-up. That one drink was followed by another until he realized that the room had grown hazy and clouded, and his head had begun to spin. But he was calm, despite the gently spinning world, and his new friend was laughing about something …

… Elmore had woken up with the sun on his face. He'd winced and brought both hands up to cover his eyes. His head hurt horribly, and the sun was no help for it. He stomach churned unhappily, and he lay as still as possible to keep it from rebelling against him. After a time, he took his hands away from his face and blinked. He'd taken a few deep breaths to settle himself before he finally looked around and went still again.

The room he was in was plain and bare but for the bed he was in, a chair near the closed door, and a small window. He had never seen the room before, and he had no idea whose bed he was in … or who was in the bed with him. A man, with dark hair and taller than Elmore, lay next to him in the bed, facing away from Elmore.

Carefully, Elmore sat up. He forced his mind back to the public house and the taste of ale and the smell of smoke and his new friend … yes. The man in bed with him was the friendly stranger who'd bought him ale. Elmore had leaned closer to look over the man's shoulder and see his face. Yes. The same man. Elmore worried at the thin blanket covering his lap for a minute. He was mostly dressed, though his shirt had disappeared. A quick peek under the blanket covering them showed that the stranger was entirely dressed.

That eased his worry a little, but the fact that he really couldn't remember how he'd ended up in such a place made him feel a bit sick. Anything might have happened. He might have walked out into the street and gotten trampled by a horse or walked off the docks and drowned in the ocean. He could practically hear his father furiously bellowing and his mother crying all the way from the afterlife. They had often warned him against drinking for fear that the loss of good sense would lead him to trouble, and he had always heeded their warnings, but, sitting in a bed that wasn't his, next to a man he still didn't know the name of, he couldn't deny how nice it had felt to sit with a friendly person. He hadn't even realized that he'd been so lonely that he would lose all good judgment the moment he was offered the smallest hint of kindness.

"Yer deep in thought." The stranger blinked up at Elmore and rubbed at his face as he woke. He yawned, then grinned blearily up at Elmore before he reached both arms over his head and gave a full-bodied stretch, like a cat. The stranger put one hand one hand behind his head, apparently completely at ease. "And up with the larks after such a rough night. I thought you'd be dead to the world 'til midday with how you were carrying on." He gave a single, deep laugh. "And after only two drinks! Your shirt's hanging out the window so it could dry out, if that's worrying you." The man crawled out of bed and went to the room's only window. "You were far gone when you spilled your drink all over yourself. When you tried to stand, you swooned so bad that you fell and didn't get up again." He opened the window and pulled Elmore's shirt in from where they'd been hanging and tossed it to him.

As quickly as he could, Elmore pulled it on.

The man laughed, again, and went to a washbasin to clean himself up. "I'm Gabriel, lad. Gabriel Scratch. I was planning to get drunk myself, but it didn't seem like a good idea when my guest needed lookin' after. Charity is what was needed, I told myself. Brought you up here to sleep it off. It was either that or you'd be waking on the street right about now, if you'd lived through the night. Don't you think nothin' of it. I didn't do nothin' nefarious while you slept."

Elmore frowned. "What do you mean?"

Gabe shook his head. "You know."

"No. What kind of 'nefarious' are you on about?"

He'd clearly said something shocking, though he didn't know what, as Gabe looked at him, sharply. For a few moments, he just stared at Elmore with narrowed eyes. "You're serious? Strike a light, you are serious!" Then he laughed, not the chuckle or little bark of a laugh he'd given out before, but long, loud belly laughter that filled the room. "Lord save the innocents! Don't you worry about it none."

He left for a short time and returned with a modest breakfast of bread and ham and set them on the narrow bed next to Elmore. "Eat your fill and drink; it'll help with the pains in your head."

And that was that. They'd been friends since that day.

It hadn't been entirely good-natured, at least not on Elmore's side of things. In fact, as he walked through the streets of Port Royal, where danger lingered in plain sight, he was better suited for life in that city because Gabe had taught him so much of the world. Even back then, as they'd eaten breakfast together, Elmore had thought that Gabe, who was older and so sure of himself, could be of use to him. It would be handy to be with someone who didn't threaten him, but could stand with him, so he wouldn't be entirely alone against the world.

In hindsight, Elmore had to admit that he'd also been

desperately lonely, and Gabe had been unnecessarily kind. So Elmore allowed himself to enjoy Gabe's company after that day, even after he had learned that Gabe was not the most moral of men. He wouldn't forsake Gabe even then. After all, Elmore had seen the worst of mankind—he'd seen his father worked to death and he'd seen his mother hung for defending herself—so why would he renounce the only man to show him any compassion simply because that man might not follow every law?

Several weeks after their first meeting, Gabe had brought Elmore to Boston Harbor and, together, they hunted for a ship to take them to sea. Gabe had been a seaman most of his life, as had his father and grandfather and great-grandfather. He couldn't rest properly on land, he'd told Elmore. There was so little life in the solid earth. It was on a small fishing ship that Elmore had started to feel truly alive, for the first time in a long while, and it was on that ship that he stayed with Gabe until their fortunes changed.

Elmore's thoughts were still drifting in the past when he reached his doorstep, and he was only brought fully back to the present when he found Mister Fa standing in his workshop.

Mister Fa turned towards him when he entered and gave Elmore a soft, momentary smile. "Forgive the intrusion. Your nephew allowed us in."

A glance into the kitchen showed Mei sitting next to Jacob on the floor with Daisy's head on her lap. The girl wasn't smiling, but considering the news Elmore had delivered about her brother, he supposed the girl was doing well in not sobbing.

"You're welcome here, of course. I reckon you've come for the boxes? Well, I'm most sorry to say they aren't ready. We've had a rough time as of late, and it's going to take a little time to get things together." Elmore limped to a corner where he let his coat fall onto a small table and leaned on it a moment to rest his sore knee. Even with his cane, he'd been doing too much walking of late for it to be entirely comfortable. "It's just a delay, I give my word. Your boxes will be done by the end of the week."

"No. Please." Mister Fa's calm expression didn't change even a bit, but Elmore thought he might have heard a crack in those words. "Given our current situation, there is no hurry to add expenses to our household when other necessities must certainly take priority. That is the reason for our visit. I am sorry to say that I will need to cancel the order, as I can't say when I would be able to pay you."

Elmore nodded, though he knew he would be making them, regardless of pay.

A soft whine from Daisy made both of them look at the kitchen, where Mei tenderly stroked Daisy's head. This made Daisy lean against Mei heavily enough that she was nearly knocked over, until Jacob pulled Daisy back a little.

Mister Fa said, "Jacob has informed me of your situation. Can I help you at all?"

What a thing for a man to ask when he was in such a position as Mister Fa! Elmore rubbed the back of his neck. "No. It's good of you, but we'll get through this. The lad shouldn't have bothered you with family business, though. I'm sorry for that." Elmore frowned at Jacob, who certainly knew better than to be gossiping about family, but the boy hadn't even seemed to realize that Elmore had returned, yet. He was too busy chattering at Mei.

"Don't be angry with him, I beg. He, too, was concerned that I would be upset by the postponement. I would have left, but Mei has taken well to your dog, and I believe she is getting to be more comfortable around your Jacob, also."

The sincerity in Mister Fa's voice surprised Elmore, but he nodded and motioned Mister Fa towards the kitchen. "Come and sit with me. I'll see what I can find for you to drink and I'll offer you a smoke, if you'll take it. Maybe a snack for your girl." Lord knew the girl could use what comfort she could get, and if all Elmore could offer was an apple, then he would do it. "If I can make so bold, how are you settling in? I know you can't have had much time to do anything. It can get cold in the night. I hope you've enough warm things." And that made him think of the cold fireplace he'd seen in the Fa's home. They would need wood.

Jacob didn't give Mister Fa any time to answer, for as soon as he saw Elmore, he pushed himself to his feet and demanded, "Is he all right? Did they hurt him? That soldier promised they wouldn't!"

Should have been expecting that, Elmore told himself. "Hold your tongue and be still. He's as well as might be hoped. I'll go back to see him in the morning."

"I want to go."

"Like Hell. Your pardon, sir." He gave an apologetic look to Mister Fa, who seemed so proper that Elmore feared he might be offended by something as common as cursing.

Stepping over Mei and Daisy, Jacob took hold of Elmore's sleeve. "Please! What if it's the last chance I get to see him?" His face was scrunched up with equal parts anger and fear. "They'll hang him!"

"You stop your yowling!" Elmore snapped. "You're not going to the prison, not while I've got any choice in it. And we're not going to argue in front of a guest." He gave a nod to Mister Fa. "Now sit down and be silent!"

Jacob looked mutinous, but he nodded, grudgingly. He sat back in his place by Mei, who said something quietly to him in that musical sounding language of hers.

Elmore motioned for Mister Fa to sit. "Did you find all you need at the market?"

Mister Fa answered that yes, he had, and he was grateful to Elmore for showing the way. "Mei, though, I fear is lonely. It is hard to be different, and harder still for the young. And the loss of her brother makes these times all the more troubling. There aren't many of our countrymen on this island."

"Anyone giving you trouble?"

"Not in particular. However, children can be cruel without even trying. Mei hasn't missed the staring or whispers or laughter." He looked at his granddaughter with a still expression that might have seemed cold had it not been for the compassion in his voice. "And we have been here only a very short time."

He laughed softly and shook his head. "Forgive me. I am an old, doting grandfather, and she is my greatest joy. I would give most anything for her happiness."

"No shame in that. Why, I—" Elmore broke off abruptly and felt himself go cold. "Mister Fa," he said in as normal a voice as he could. "You'll do us all a grand kindness if you'll sit very quietly a moment, eh? And tell your Mei to do the same. No talking, no moving."

Without questioning the request, Mister Fa seemed to freeze after a whispered command to Mei, which she instantly obeyed, letting her eyes close and her hands fall limply onto Daisy's back. The atmosphere was awful, a tension like that before a battle suddenly filled the room and made the air so heavy that it was choking.

Harold, the insidious, creeping thing that he was, stood in the doorway.

Elmore stood up and held a hand out. "Here, mutt. Come along." He must have forgotten to close the door. There was no trouble when it was just Elmore and Jacob in the house, and even Gabe was tolerated, but Harold didn't like strangers. Not one bit.

There was a moment's hesitation before Harold did enter, but he didn't go to Elmore. Instead, he strode to Mei with his head lowered and his rat-like tail so low that it nearly dragged on the floor.

Jacob looked at Elmore in a panic, but didn't dare to move.

With a sniff of Daisy, who looked up at him with her usual happy tail thumping, and a curious look at Mei, Harold lay down and put his head on his forelegs. The tension in the room vanished as quickly as it had appeared.

"Well, that's that, I suppose." Elmore sat back in his chair. "It's safe, now. You can tell her to open her eyes."

Mister Fa looked at Harold, then at his granddaughter. "Is that animal dangerous?"

"Very, but not to either of you, I guess. He's a territorial sort of beast, and he claimed this as his territory. Doesn't seem much bothered by us, but he gets a little touchy when strangers come around." The beast in question didn't look so fearsome as he rolled his head onto Mei's lap and nudged her still arm with his nose. "Your pardon for the fright. I don't like him just walking in with strangers here. Still, all works out. Your Mei has a right charm with animals, it seems."

Mister Fa gave another command and Mei opened her eyes. She gave a tiny, hesitant smile when she saw that she had two dogs vying for her attention and began stroking Harold's head as she had been Daisy's.

Jacob started talking, and all was well again.

"If he is dangerous, why keep him?"

Elmore chuckled as he reached down to rub at his knee. It didn't help much. "He's a treat when it comes to keeping the place safe. The crawling slime that wrecked my work and ran though my home like a trouble-making imp got himself caught well and good when Harold came upon him."

"He hardly seems dangerous."

Harold rolled a little onto his side and his tongue lolled out of his mouth as Mei scratched his ear, and Jacob seemed to think it the funniest thing he'd ever seen.

Elmore couldn't help the stab of shame at his vicious attack dog turned into a little girl's lap dog. "He's not normally so affectionate."

"Your leg?"

The abrupt shift in conversation startled Elmore enough that it took him a minute to realize he was still rubbing his sore knee. "Ah. It's an old ache that won't stop haunting me. Too much walking and not enough resting. There's only so much a cane can do."

"Perhaps we might make an agreement. I have, as yet, not gotten any local currency, and I am reasonably certain that you would not wish to deal with what I brought from my homeland. You will recall that I am a physician."

"A kind offer, but there's nothing to be done. It's been tended, and it's just something I have to live with."

Jacob had apparently been paying more notice to the

conversation than Elmore had guessed as he broke his attention away from Mei to say, "It was a spar falling that did it. Crushed his leg during a fire aboard ship."

Mister Fa's calm facade shook a moment as his eyes widened. "A fire at sea. You are fortunate, then, that your knee is all you have to suffer." The shock on his face faded easily away. "But even that much you do not need to suffer. Allow me to pay you for the boxes by easing your pain. I am certain that whoever tended to your leg did their best, but in my homeland, medicine is quite different. There are methods that you likely have never heard of."

It was tempting until Mister Fa mentioned needles. How sticking needles into him could stop pain, Elmore had no idea and he didn't fancy trying.

"As you wish," Mister Fa stood and said something to Mei that had her standing as soon as Jacob helped roll the dogs off her lap. "Should you change your mind, you are welcome in my home. Perhaps I should get a recommendation from a pleased customer to entice your patronage."

"You've had business, already? I'd have thought it would take a bit longer. No offense meant to you, but you are a bit different than the usual sort of doctor folks see about here."

"No offense taken. I believe the man was in a bit of a dire predicament, and I was nothing more than convenient. Perhaps if he spoke to you …"

"No. I won't trouble you to try and track down someone here. They might well have sailed, by now, and if they haven't there's enough holes in this city to hide an elephant. And even if you found this fellow and he did give a glowing report of your skills, I'm still not up on being turned into a pincushion."

"There are other …"

"No. Thank you, kindly, but no. I've learned to live with it."

Mister Fa didn't press further. They stayed for a few more minutes before they took their leave. As they walked away, Elmore stood in the doorway and watched them go, and Jacob came to stand near Elmore, looking after them.

"Looks like you made a new friend."

Jacob nodded, solemnly. "I think I like her. I'm going to help her learn more English. Can we give them the broken wood? For their fire?"

Elmore looked back into his workshop where all the splintered wood, useless for his work or even to make the boxes for Mister Fa, and nodded. "It's a kindly thought. We'll get it to them before long."

Jacob turned to go back into the house. "I'll take it over now. They'll need something to make a hot dinner."

As Jacob collected the wood, Elmore watched him, curiously. Jacob had always been a good lad, compassionate and friendly. This was no new behavior for him, and he likely would have done it for anyone suffering through tough times, but he couldn't help but think that Jacob was growing up, and he wondered if, after a few more years of growing, the lad and little Mei might become fond of each other.

Elmore rolled his eyes at his own serious, foolish thoughts. It would be years before either child was ready for such things.

However, he had no intention of distracting Jacob from his self-imposed charity as it seemed to be nicely distracting him from his father's troubles, and Jacob dearly needed that distraction if he was going to stay out of trouble until Elmore could get Gabe free.

He had to be free.

There was no question about that, because one day Jacob wouldn't be too young to think of girls, and he would bring a wife and child to Elmore's house. Such things were far in the future, but that future would be upon him sooner rather than later, and it would be a pity if Gabe weren't there to see it.

Jacob left with the little wagon full of scrap wood, along with two blankets they could spare, and Elmore watched him go with pride. Someday, the boy would make something of himself. He'd be a real force in the world, and Elmore was bound and determined that Gabe would live long enough to see Jacob soar.

***

Before dinner, Elmore and Jacob, along with Daisy to pull the little wagon, took the long hike out to O'Donnell's house for the wood Elmore so dearly needed. Elmore walked rather than borrowing another horse and regretted it almost at once, as the pain in his knee seemed to grow with every step. Still, it had to be done. He didn't have any more tobacco to trade, and he wasn't willing to pay with the savings he'd kept for Jacob. Simply not going wasn't an option because, as worried for Gabe as Elmore might be, he couldn't take the chance of losing the pay for the coffins if he stopped working to fret.

O'Donnell met them at the door of his cabin and apologized vigorously for not being able to help the day before, but he'd been just too upset to think about business. After Elmore assured him that it was no trouble at all, O'Donnell took Elmore to his shed, where he kept logs and rough planks of wood, so that Elmore could pick what he wanted.

For a few copper pieces, Elmore bought a plank of wood five feet long and six inches wide. Elmore shook O'Donnell's hand, then looked around for Jacob. He didn't worry when he didn't see the boy at once; Jacob had been known to wander off on his own when the mood struck him.

"I think he went out behind the house." O'Donnell pointed to the small path that led behind his house, out to the deep of the forest where he cut trees and his mule hauled them back to be cut up for selling.

They found Jacob squatting on the ground a short distance into the forest, just out of sight of O'Donnell's home and off the little path. It was a picturesque place, all green with the bright sun shining down and bursts of color from flowers here and there.

"Lord above," O'Donnell muttered. He had gone very pale. "This is where ... where that man was. The dead man."

"What are you up to?" Elmore asked Jacob from where he stood on O'Donnell's mule path. "Time for us to get going."

"Someone lost something. I saw it shine in the sunlight." Jacob stood and pushed his way out of the bushes to Elmore and held out what he'd found—a circle of glass edged with a metal band. It did shine in the fading sunlight.

Elmore took the circle of metal. The metal around the glass had threads, as if it were meant to be screwed onto something.

"It's from the spyglass."

Elmore looked at Jacob. "What makes you say so?"

"Because it is. I'm sure of it. It's dented, just there. See?"

Indeed, there was a tiny dent on one side.

"I'm sure the spyglass was dented when Da brought it home."

Elmore showed it to O'Donnell. "Did you drop it?"

"Not me. I've never see anything like it. The boy could be right, though. What else could it go to but a spyglass?"

CHAPTER 10: A FOOL AND A COCKEREL

After the exhausting walk home, the last person Elmore wanted to see was Lieutenant Bowe. Yet there he was, out of uniform for the first time since Elmore had met him. He sat on the stoop of Elmore's home with his long legs stretched out in front of him, ankles crossed and his eyes closed.

"You got some business here?" Elmore demanded.

"Only a humble request for a few moments of your time." Bowe pushed himself up easily and dusted off his trousers. He looked up at the bright afternoon sun. "I do realize you haven't got any reason to want to see me—"

"Too right," Jacob muttered.

"—but there is some business that I really do think we ought to discuss, if you have the time." He paused. "Even if you don't have the time, I think you will want to talk with me about this."

"Then talk."

"Not on the street, if you please."

It was said with a perfectly pleasant smile, but something in Bowe's tone caused Elmore to look at him a little more closely. "Right, then."

He unlocked the door and had only just closed it behind him when a startled yelp escaped Bowe. It was Harold, and he didn't look at all happy with the newest intruder. His lips were curled away from his teeth and his ears laid back. A low, menacing growl filled the room. He stared obsessively up at Bowe with his small black eyes glittering. His raised hackles were enough to show that his outward calm in no way diminished the irritation he felt at having his home invaded.

"Just be still a bit," Elmore warned, quietly. "He's just a bit —"

"He's fine." Bowe was perfectly calm. He didn't even sound tense. His shoulders were relaxed and his stance easy. It was as if he didn't even see Harold, and no one Harold had ever met had given him that kind of reaction. "It's been a stressful day, hasn't it? You're strung tight as a violin string, and now some stranger just breezes in like he owns the place? Of course you get upset." He was looking at Elmore, but clearly speaking to Harold. "I'm harmless, though. Didn't even bring so much as a knife with me. I'm not here to hurt anyone, you can rely on that, friend." He spoke slowly and softly, his deep voice almost a gentle hum in the quiet room.

As he spoke, to Elmore's astonishment, Harold stopped growling. His hackles lowered, his ears raised, and his lips uncurled. It was the first time Elmore had seen Harold come down from an attack posture so quickly, and due only to a stranger's voice, at that!

But Harold was quite at ease and even allowed Bowe to pat him.

Jacob rolled his eyes at the sight. "Traitor."

Elmore slapped Jacob's arm. "You get to the kitchen and get the dogs something to eat and a drink. They've been working hard."

"But—"

"Now. And I'll hear no more of this vicious streak of yours. Isn't mannerly."

Like a sulking five-year-old, Jacob called to Harold and they went together into the kitchen.

After the door closed behind them, Bowe said, "Your dog seems a good guardsman. How do you get customers if he's so territorial?"

"He's not normally in my workshop. When I'm open for business, he gets shut up in the kitchen or upstairs or he's out roaming the streets. But he is a mean old beast, if that's your gist. You're lucky you seem to have a touch with animals and that he didn't take more offense to you being in here. You ever come here, again, just make sure you let me walk in first or that I'm already in. We were just robbed and Harold took a mouthful of the blaggard; he's still a bit on edge."

"I'll be sure not to antagonize him. Thank you for letting me in, though. I'm sure this isn't the sort of conversation you would want to have in public. I wanted to ask if you know anything about a spyglass Mister Scratch might have had."

Elmore was acutely aware of the tiny circle of glass in his coat pocket. He set a plank up on a pair of saw horses. "Why? What's that got to do with anything?"

Bowe hesitated and put a hand to the back of his neck. "I am ... not happy about Mister Scratch's arrest."

Jacob yelled, "Then you should have left him alone!"

"Get us coffee, boy! And you mind that voice when you're talking to a guest, however uninvited."

Bowe had the grace to flush. "Yes. I do apologize for the unexpected visit, but you must understand how urgent it is that I speak with you."

Elmore spared a glance at the kitchen to see that Jacob was still occupied before he asked, very quietly, "Tell me what makes you unhappy."

"I will agree with Captain Brown when he says that all evidence points to Mister Scratch as being the guilty party, but something nags at my mind. A man must surely be coldblooded to murder a man, then go to spend time with his young son. There are men like that—I have met many—but your Mister Scratch does not seem, in any way, to be coldblooded. Rather fiery, in fact. Also, your Mister Scratch had a visitor this morning. That French captain dropped by. I happened to be on duty and I may have been standing unnecessarily close while they spoke. Captain LeBeau, I believe he said his name was, was very focused on Mister Scratch and didn't seem to notice me, so he may have said things he didn't want made public knowledge. He was very keen to know where the spyglass was. He said that Mister Scratch had stolen it from someone during the raid of his ship, the *Juliet*, and that he had sent Lieutenant Leopold Passy to find it. Considering that Mister Scratch was staying with you, I thought you might have seen it or heard something about it."

"They've got a letter of marque, Gabe told you. It's all legal."

"I didn't say it wasn't. I'm just struck by the idea of a ship's captain going hunting after a spyglass. Why would he? He could easily buy another, but he asks the man that he believes killed his officer for it? Captain LeBeau said he'd searched the dead man's rooms but couldn't find it, so he believed Mister Scratch had to still have it. When Captain LeBeau left, Mister Scratch called for me and practically begged me to have you visit him and to have you bring 'the boy's spyglass.' Given the circumstances, I really must encourage you to do as he asks."

"I haven't got a spyglass. Gabe knows that." It was true, if not entirely honest. "Can I see him, now?"

"I doubt it. It's nearly nightfall and visitors aren't allowed in after dark. It'll have to wait 'til morning, but I'll be on duty, so I can see that you get in. If you haven't got the spyglass, why was Mister Scratch so eager to speak with you?"

"Maybe he's worried that the French captain will trace him here, as you did. It were no secret that he spent most of his time ashore here."

Bowe clearly didn't believe him, but that was all right. Elmore didn't need trust. He needed information, and he'd be blind if he couldn't see how useful Bowe might be. "Be honest with me, soldier—where does Gabe stand in all this mess?"

"On shaky ground. To save him, we need to prove he didn't have a chance to kill Officer Passy. Even better, find the real killer."

"I've been trying to do that." Elmore looked at Bowe, quickly. "You really don't believe he did it, do you? I've got reason to hope for him. He's been closer than a brother to me for years. When Jacob's ma passed on, he didn't abandon the boy like many would. He's a good man." He wanted to trust Bowe, but didn't. Trust wasn't easy, and he'd only known Bowe for such a short time. Still, he had to admit, Bowe hadn't had to help him when the thugs had attacked him. Elmore knew well enough that other people would have just walked away. "Why did you help me the other day?"

Bowe frowned. "It was the right thing to do. I thought I explained that. And if I found a friend in the process, then all the better for me."

"I'm not your friend."

"That's fine. I'm very likable; I'll win you over, yet."

Although Elmore just couldn't bring himself to trust Bowe, he had to concede that Bowe didn't seem to wish any harm to them, and Elmore would need help to get into the Hold to visit Gabe. Besides, Bowe had already done some investigation that helped.

"I haven't got the spyglass, but I did. We was robbed yesterday, and it was taken. It was the only thing taken but for a handful of coins."

"Nothing else?"

"Not so much as a spoon. It was an awful lot of effort for so little. You should have seen the place. There wasn't hardly an inch left untouched."

Bowe scratched the tip of his nose with a finger. "It seems someone found the spyglass, but it wasn't Captain LeBeau. If he had it, he wouldn't have gone to see Mister Scratch today."

"Gabe said he got the spyglass from the French ship, but it was broken when he got it. Why search for a broken spyglass? It must have some value to be searched for, but I didn't see it." He took a mug of coffee from Jacob and stared into it while Bowe thanked the boy for his mug.

That only got a sneer from Jacob before he stomped back to lean against the door jamb of the kitchen.

Frustrated, Elmore exclaimed, "If only that fool hadn't gotten himself drunk!"

Jacob burst into tears and fled to the kitchen.

Elmore left Bowe and followed Jacob. The kitchen had a back door that led to a small, walled yard. Jacob was there, sitting all forlorn on the doorstep with his face in his hands and his shoulders shaking with sobs. Daisy half-lay in Jacob's lap, and Harold lay at his feet with his eyes rolled upwards, watching Jacob sympathetically.

"What's all this, then?" Elmore sat slowly next to Jacob on the stone step. He stretched his bad leg out in front of him with a groan. "You burn your hand on the coffee or something?"

"I'm sorry! I didn't mean it! I'm so sorry!"

Elmore put an arm over Jacob's shoulder and patted his arm. "Sorry for what?"

"Making Da angry. It's my fault he got angry and went out to drink." Jacob scrubbed his eyes and looked at Elmore with bloodshot, puffy eyes. "I yelled at him and I told him I didn't want his rubbish present, and if he couldn't be bothered to hang about, then I didn't want him, either. He only got drunk because of me, and now he's going to die!"

Elmore silently cursed Gabe. "Fool boy. You know your da gets himself drunk every time he comes ashore! If you'd greeted him with a smile and a hug, he'd still have gotten drunk and found himself in this mess. You had nothing to do with any of it. Now get yourself inside. Reverend Roberts said you've got an exam to study for, didn't he?"

Jacob nodded, rubbed his face, again, and stood up. "Does Da have any chance?"

"Pray for him. It's all you can do."

Harold and Daisy followed Jacob inside and, a moment later, Bowe came out and sat beside Elmore in Jacob's place.

"We need an understanding," Elmore told him. He fixed his eye on Bowe. "I want Gabe out of the Hold and trouble. What do you want?"

"Justice."

He'd said that before. "Can we work together?"

Bowe hesitated. "You're that sure he's innocent? Let me warn you now that if we come across evidence that proves his guilt, I'll tighten the noose around his neck myself."

"I don't doubt that. Are you sure you aren't so intent on

impressing the governor that you'll find evidence against Gabe, whether it's there or not?"

Bowe looked offended and met Elmore's eyes easily. "The governor wants law and order enforced on the island. He doesn't want anyone killed for the sake of appearances. My superiors want to put the matter to an end. They have a reasonable suspect, and that's good enough for them. It's not good enough for me."

His disgusted expression was enough to make Elmore snort. "You've spoken to them about your misgivings, then?"

"Until I ran out of things to say and started repeating myself. Not one of them listened, though." He looked at his knees. "I can't do anything as things stand, but if there's even a slight chance that he might be innocent, I have to investigate."

"Then I think you and I are on the same side."

***

He was never going to get Reverend Roberts' desk fixed at the rate he was going. But, he reasoned, the sun was quickly setting, and unless he wanted to use the expensive oil in the lanterns, the work would have to wait until daylight, and there was no reason to leave off the investigation. Bowe had stayed through the day and, when dusk began to fall, he and Elmore went off to find answers. When they left for the *Blue Dog Inn*, Jacob was left at home with a loaded pistol under his bed, Daisy at the foot of his bed and Harold sleeping comfortably at the top of the stairs.

"Is it wise to leave the boy with a gun?" Bowe asked after Elmore had closed the front door behind them. "He's just a child."

"Wiser than leaving him unprotected, and he's sensible enough. Besides, I'm not about to take him out to a tavern."

They walked slowly, talking softly of Gabe's trouble as they went.

Bowe said, "Let's see if we have all the events in order. Mister Scratch came to your home with a friend, and he brought a gift of the stolen spyglass for his son. He left in a temper and went off to get drunk, then returned hours later and fell asleep. You saw him, still asleep, the next morning before you left your home. When you returned, your house had been robbed and he was gone. The next morning, Lieutenant Passy was found dead. We know Passy had only been dead a few hours, which means that the spyglass was taken before Passy was killed. Captain LeBeau is looking for the spyglass, too; he searched Officer Passy's room and then he interrogated Mister Scratch to find it and, as far as I know, he's still out there looking for it. I think he may be a dangerous person to be against. It's entirely possible that the spyglass has nothing to do with Passy's murder, but it seems highly unlikely. We need to find the spyglass. We need to find who stole it from your home and then where it went after that. Did Passy steal it from you and then his killer took it from him? Did someone else steal it from you, and Passy was killed trying to get it from him? We need the thief." He paused. "Is it possible that Mister Scratch took the spyglass? That could explain why he wants to see you so urgently, if he wants to give it to you." He paused a moment. "No. He asked you to bring it to him, so that wouldn't make sense."

"And he wouldn't take it after giving it to his boy. He wouldn't risk falling out of Jacob's good graces for anything, let alone that piece of junk."

"It's possible that he didn't know it was valuable until after he'd given it up, and then he decided that he wanted it back. He could have staged the theft and, so, he would have what he wanted without the risk of Master Jacob thinking badly of him."

Elmore fingered the circle of glass in his pocket. "Valuable? I saw it. It wasn't even working. The metal wasn't gold or silver. No. That wasn't worth a thing as a spyglass. If I weren't so sure that it had something to do with Passy's death, I'd say the spyglass was altogether worthless. That captain wouldn't be so eager for it without a reason. If Passy was supposed to have the spyglass—his captain thought it would be with him, didn't he?—and now it's gone, then either Passy took it from my home and his killer took it from him or someone else robbed me and killed

Passy when he tried to get it from them."

Bowe shook his head. "Or, the third option, Lieutenant Passy could have been killed for his boots and the spyglass might have been taken from your home by a common burglar who didn't know it was broken and didn't have time to test it, as your Harold is so enthusiastic about guarding the house. It might have been tossed into the sea, by now."

"Maybe. But it would be a heck of a coincidence. What I want is a witness to keep Gabe well away from the rope."

That was why they went to *The Blue Dog* and sat near the door, watching the crowd. It was a dirty, stinking place. The stench of ale, smoke, and the unwashed patrons was so heavy that it was almost choking. A dozen men crowded the few tables in the common room while predatory women stalked around the room and were friendly with everyone. *The Blue Dog* was Gabe's customary drinking place, and it seemed reasonable to think he would have latched onto one of the loose girls who frequented the tavern. The woman Elmore had his eye out for wasn't there, though.

He watched for a time, but there was no sign of her. He tried to look at every face, at each person who came in and each person already milling about the room, and he was so focused on his task that he ignored Bowe completely until he said, "I asked around the barracks about Mister Fa's grandson."

Elmore frowned, then, for the first time since they'd arrived, looked at Bowe. He sat with both hands wrapped around the tankard he'd ordered, but he didn't drink from it, only looked into his ale. "The young man, Bingbang, was a busy fellow. Seems after he was found dead, a short investigation was done. They didn't find out much, only that he lived on the island and frequently set out to sea. He would be gone for weeks, then return for a short while before he went out on a different ship. They never found his killer. We may have no more luck finding the killer of this seaman."

Elmore looked away, again. "Maybe. Don't try and we're sure to never find them. Nothing was learned about his death?"

"Nothing that would give his family any comfort. A friend of his informed an officer about where to find him. They found him on the shore not far from the city."

"That friend say anything else?"

"I couldn't even find that anyone knew the friend's name. The only thing I was told that stood out was that Bingbang had been strangled."

Elmore shook his head. "He were stabbed. I saw that when I put him in his coffin."

"But did you see his throat?"

He hadn't been too keen on taking a good long look at the dead man. Best to do his job and move on, in Elmore's experience. But there were some things that one just couldn't miss, and he had seen something. "He had a bruise. Like a hung man might have, a thin bruise circling his neck."

"And I'm told that it is reasonably certain the young man was strangled and whatever had been used on him left that bruise." He shook his head and took a small drink. "I'll give that trouble more thought later. Let's concentrate on Mister Scratch. You said we're here looking for a woman. What does she look like?"

"Just any other girl. Dark hair and eyes. Taller than me, shorter than you. She was with Gabe the night you said the Frenchman was killed. If she can be found, we'll have a witness to tell where Gabe was that night. He came home well after dark, but before midnight, and stayed there after that. He left there about sunset. If that girl can say she was with him all the time he was away from my home, then he'll have someone to stand up for him court."

"A prostitute may not be the most reliable of ..."

A heavy hand thumped down on Bowe's shoulder, startling him out of his words. The man sitting behind Bowe had turned around in his chair. His face was blotchy and his eyes not quite focused as he sneered at Bowe.

"Slaves ain't allowed in here." His boozy breath wafted across the table, causing Elmore to wrinkle his nose. "Not even bastard slaves." He raised the hand on Bowe's shoulder to pat the top of his head, those fair locks that looked so out of place.

An eruption wouldn't have been unexpected, and Bowe would have been justified in a harsh reaction, but he just turned his head a little and smiled. "I'm no slave." A slap knocked the offending hand off his head. "Mind your own affairs." He started to turn back to Elmore, but the drunk seized his arm and forced him to turn around.

"Affairs? High talk for a dark popinjay. How much will your master pay to have you returned? Or is it a mistress? Was your mother the lady's maid what caught the master's eye? Maybe it were your old man that were a field hand who couldn't get away from the lusty lady of the house?" He snickered while he slurred out his words, either not noticing or caring that drool slid down his chin.

Bowe gave Elmore a look that was frighteningly still. "You should leave, now. Go to the prison. I'll follow in a moment."

There was no point in arguing that the drunk had three friends he'd been sitting with or that Bowe could find himself in a bad way if the rest of the tavern turned against him. No point in saying that his career could be threatened if his superiors got word of him in the middle of such a situation. No point in reminding him that he was unarmed. Bowe was beyond reason, by of the look in his eyes.

At the tavern's door, Elmore paused long enough to see Bowe whirl around and punch the drunkard square on the nose. He left as the brawl fell into full swing and stopped outside to wait it out.

A fool and a cockerel, Bowe was both. Bowe walked out of the tavern not long after with his head held high, despite the thin trail of blood that ran down the side of his face from a gnash on his temple, and calmly walked down the street. He held himself stiffly and didn't hurry. The bit of torn cloth in Bowe's hand was curious, but not alarming. It was the same blue that the drunk had been wearing, and it seemed obvious that it had been torn off during the fight. Elmore hurried to catch up with

Bowe until they walked side-by-side.

"Isn't a man alive that takes kindly to sour words about his mother."

Bowe wiped the blood from the side of his face with the back of his hand and looked at Elmore. His thick eyebrows were drawn together. "My mother and father loved each other very much."

"I didn't say any different."

When they arrived at the Hold, Bowe had gathered himself together enough that he was able to appear as calm as he ever was. In the dim light of the lanterns hanging at the door, it was unlikely that even the guard on duty that Bowe stepped forward to speak with would notice the torn clothes or bruises Bowe had earned in the fight. Bowe smiled and called the guard by name, as if they were old friends, and asked if he might speak with one of the prisoners. It really would be a grand favor, he told the guard. It was all very friendly like and no trouble at all to get in.

Gabe's condition had worsened considerably. He looked as if he'd been locked up for a month rather than less than two days. Of course, he hadn't had an opportunity to shave. His eyes were heavy with dark bags—he couldn't have slept—and were bloodshot. He sat on the cell's bench with his hands resting on his lap and face lowered after he saw who had opened his door. He looked defeated, like an overworked mule. For all that, he seemed to be unharmed, and Bowe's word went up several notches in Elmore's estimation.

Gabe scowled at Elmore. "I told you to bring Jacob."

"And I ignored you. The boy's safe at home; he don't need to see you like this." Elmore sat next to Gabe on the bench while Bowe stood in the open doorway of the cell. "The lieutenant, here, told me you had a visitor."

"Aye, and weren't that a fearsome surprise? Didn't think I'd ever see him again." His mouth tightened. "He wanted the spyglass."

"Why?"

"He didn't say." Gabe looked as if he might have said more,

but stopped and jerked his head towards Bowe. "Does he need to be here? This be family business."

"He's a friend, the only one we've got. Now, you speak up. What did that Frenchman say?"

Gabe looked down, then up and turned a little so he could face Elmore and rested his back against the wall. "Cap'n LeBeau told me that if I gave him the spyglass he'd get me out of here. The only reason I'm here, he says, is his word that I'd gone against his officer. He said that once the spyglass were put in his hand, he'd tell Governor Modyford that it were a mistake—that it weren't me, but someone else, and that he'd just gotten confused 'cause of the heat of battle. All this for that broken piece of nothing."

"Use your head, you ass. It wasn't a bit of nothing. That thing got stolen when the house was robbed. A whole house to go through and the thief took a piece of junk? And it wasn't anywhere obvious, the thief had to hunt for it and nearly turned the house upside down to find it. Someone valued it, aside from that French captain who'd be willing to let you off a murder charge if you'll give it to him. If he thinks you killed his man, then he puts more store in that spyglass than in a life. If he doesn't think you killed his man, then he's willing to put an innocent life on the line to have you tell him where it is. There's something of value about it. Did you tell him it was stolen?"

"I told him I didn't have it, but I think he didn't believe me."

Elmore looked up at the ceiling.

"What are you thinking?" Gabe asked.

"That I like you better sober. Tell me about the battle."

Gabe told him everything he could remember, though he said he didn't see how it could help. He'd argued with Captain Harrington in front of the crew, just as Raynard had said; but it hadn't been anything more than a disagreement. He hadn't thought they ought to take the chance of hunting so far off the trade routes, but Captain Harrington had heard a rumor that a ship would take a lonely course to try to get away from the pirates that haunted the trade routes. In the end, Captain

Harrington won the argument.

No. He didn't think Captain Harrington held anything against him. Gabe was a loyal crewman, and when the crew took a vote and sided with Captain Harrington, he was smart enough to go with the vote.

The attack went well and they hadn't lost a single life, not even from the French crew. He'd taken the spyglass from one of the Frenchmen and they'd left with the booty—meager though it was.

"Why wasn't the French ship taken?"

"Cap'n did think to take it. *Indigo Running* had just made it through a wild storm and taken some damage, so he had thought to abandon *Indigo Running* and just take the French ship, but that was a merchant—too bulky and slow. *Indigo Running* is faster, so he decided to have repairs done and leave the Frenchmen their ship."

"What was the name of that bird you dragged to my doorstep the other night?"

"Dora. Isadora Ratman. What's she got to do with anything?"

"And where might she be found?"

Gabe looked at the tiny window high above his head where there was only darkness. "Working, likely. Could be anywhere. She'll be at her home, come morning. She lives above her father's blacksmith shop on Mayberry. What are you thinking?"

Elmore stood. He almost told. It was Gabe's life and he would want some hope. But that hope could turn so quickly to despair if Elmore was wrong, and it seemed cruel to let him hope only to take it away later. "I'll tell you after I've seen her. Maybe it's nothing."

CHAPTER 11: QUESTIONS

The next morning was spent making the desk leg for Reverend Roberts because, as worried as he was for Gabe, there was work to be done, and Elmore thought better when his hands were busy. He had Jacob dash over to the church and take a quick measurement to see how long the leg needed to be and to be sure that Reverend Roberts wanted it done, for Elmore wasn't going to waste any time on the crafting of it if the good Reverend had gone out and bought himself a new desk. As soon as Jacob returned with the report that Reverend Roberts would, indeed appreciate a new leg for his desk and would happily take off two weeks of Jacob's tuition payment in exchange, Elmore set to work. He found a piece of wood good enough for what was needed and spent a couple of hours sawing and smoothing the leg until it was done and near about perfect.

The fresh smell of cut wood filled the room as Elmore became entirely focused on his work. He loved working with wood: smoothing splinters and drawing something useful out of a bit of wood. He'd loved it since the day his pa had taught him to whittle, and he'd sat by his pa's side and watched the big man bring a doll out of a piece of firewood for the daughter of a neighbor.

Once done, and the length of the leg lay across his lap, Elmore's mind went back to Gabe. Gabe had been locked up for two days and two nights, going on three days, which was plenty of time for whoever had killed Officer Passy to get away. The ships in the harbor kept coming and going, and there was no stopping them simply because one might be carrying a murderer. Even the governor himself couldn't do such a thing without disrupting the entire flow of Port Royal and, the

Good Lord knew he wouldn't do that, as it might endanger his position in the eyes of the king.

Elmore couldn't care less about the dead Frenchman or his cowardly killer, but it would be easier to get Gabe out if he could get a confession from someone.

Through a good breakfast of bread and cheese and sharpening the teeth of his saw while Jacob swept the workshop clean of shavings and wood chips, Elmore kept running over the few facts he knew. He said nothing to Jacob, not even when the boy kept shooting him curious glances.

"Uncle—"

"Get yourself together. I'll walk with you to the school so as I can deliver the leg to Reverend Roberts."

"Please! Did you find anything with the lieutenant? Do you know if Da's going to get out or not?"

"If I can do anything about it, I will. You know I will. Now, let's be off."

The schoolhouse was not a house so much as a room. The church of Saint Peter's was large enough, being the biggest church in Port Royal, that it had room in the back for a generous storage area. Reverend Roberts had deemed the room would be more useful as a schoolroom than as a place where forgotten relics could collect dust, and he had wasted little time converting it.

Immediately upon opening the heavy front door of Saint Peter's, Elmore found himself looking into the cold, black eyes of Reverend Roberts. He stiffened, taken aback, and only just managed to stop himself from stepping away.

"Good morning, Reverend." Jacob smiled up at Reverend Roberts' severe face, which always seemed to be disapproving of something, and slipped passed him, calling out a cheery goodbye to Elmore before he disappeared into the darkness of the church's interior.

Reverend Roberts had barely glanced at Jacob. He stared at Elmore with a calm sort of malevolence that made Elmore feel as if he'd done something unforgivably wrong and was quietly showing his disapproval. But it was no surprise. There was something about Reverend Roberts that had always intimidated Elmore, always made him feel not quite good enough. It had taken time for him to realize that Reverend Roberts made everyone feel that way, and it didn't seem to be deliberate. It was just the way he was.

"Fine morning, isn't it?" Elmore said when he could no longer stand the staring.

"You missed my sermon on Sunday."

"Well," Elmore laughed, uncomfortably. "The Good Lord and me, you know? We're right alike. Work all week, then take a day to rest. Jacob did make sure to carry the sermon home and tell me all that I'm doing wrong. Now, I finished that new leg you need for your desk, and I wanted to see that it fit properly and that you're satisfied with it."

"Oy! You! Coffin maker!"

Elmore turned sharply and saw Gabe's lady-friend, Dora, striding towards him. He pushed the desk leg into Reverend Roberts' hands. . "Good day to you, Reverend." He then started for the woman, thankful that the good reverend didn't call him back.

Isadora Ratman was tall, a good four inches taller than Elmore, and as thin as a corn stalk. She looked no less than thirty-five years old with long, dark brown hair that had been tied into a braid and hung over one shoulder. Her purposeful stride that made her brown skirt rustle on the street around her feet was nearly as off-putting as her handsome face, set like stone.

She came to a stop a few feet in front of Elmore and stood with her hands on her hips. She looked down her long nose at him with her bright green eyes burning, nearly sparking like the embers of a fire. "I saw Gabe being led away by them cursed soldiers. You tell me what's going on. Tell me right now!"

Elmore stepped around her and started walking. Much to his satisfaction, Dora dashed to keep up with him and then stepped in front of him to block his path.

"Tell me. He's your friend, ain't he? What do they say he did? Gabe's a good man."

"You're loud, girl. Put a stopper in that porthole, won't you?" Again, he stepped around her and walked. "Gabe's been taken for murder."

"He wouldn't!"

"Oh? Known him long, have you?"

She flushed. "Couple of years, now. He always visits me when he's in town. I know him good enough to know he wouldn't kill in cold blood."

Regular visits to a particular woman ... that was a surprise. "And does he always visit you when he's in his cups?"

"No." Her heavy eyebrows drew together. "He's normally done with all that when he comes to see me. But I was at *The Blue Dog* when he came in, all fit to be tied. Carrying on about ungrateful brats and useless presents, he was, as loud as thunder."

"You met him there when he was sober, then?"

"Aye, but he didn't stay that way long. Tipsy one moment, then he slid right down to staggering. That's when I took him to you. He said he lived with you."

"'N so he does. When did he get to *The Blue Dog*?"

"Early. It were still full light. Just a bit before the evening bells rung." She shrugged. "Less than an hour before, I'd guess."

Then he would have gone straight to The Blue Dog from home, Elmore thought. "And he were with you 'til you brought him home?"

She nodded. "I'd have stayed the night if you hadn't gotten so uppity."

"You didn't turn your nose up at your pay, did you?" He frowned.

She grinned. "Never once turned down a coin; I've still got a family to feed."

Elmore slowed his step until he'd stopped entirely. "You willing to tell a judge what you told me? 'Cause if you are, Gabe should be out of the Hold in no time."

"'Course I will! Anything. If you can get him out ..." Her mouth trembled. "They won't even let me see him."

"You tried, then?"

Her face was stiff and strong, but her eyes grew a little moist. "As soon as I saw where they took him, I did. 'He don't need no company,' they says. I don't see why not. I can't do no harm. I only wanted to see he wasn't hurt."

"You'll do him more good than anything if you're sure he were with you before the evening bells 'til you dropped him with me. You go to your home and don't leave, I may need you in a few hours. If I don't come for you, a soldier will. Don't look so sour; he's a friend and he's doing his best for our Gabe."

"You know where I live?"

"Gabe told me. I was planning to go find you today."

They parted ways and Elmore hurried as quickly as he could to O'Donnell's. His limp slowed him, but he did his level best to ignore the pain. *Really,* he thought as the pain began to lance up the back of his leg more severely than usual. *It's lucky I can walk at all. Best be thankful for that.* The falling spar could have easily crushed both of his legs, he might have lost them entirely instead of just suffering a bit of pain in one. That understanding didn't help Elmore move any faster, though, and he couldn't help but think that at that rate he was moving, Gabe would be hung before Elmore could get together the evidence to free him.

Once he'd finally made it to the woodcutter's house, Elmore heard O'Donnell before he saw him. Elmore followed the sound of a heavy thumping to the back of O'Donnell's cabin, where he was chopping wood.

"Have you come for more wood?" O'Donnell pulled a large rag from the inside of his sleeve and swiped it across his sweaty forehead. His long-handled ax rested on his shoulder. "You didn't take much when last you'd come here; no wonder you've run out already. I don't think I've seen you out here so often in a month as I have in the past couple of days."

"I don't mean to interrupt your work, but I was curious

about that poor man found here the other day. You get a good look at him? Before you went and ran for the law, that is?"

"I took time to see that he was dead, but I didn't search his pockets if that's what you're thinking."

"I'm not. I never said anything about that. I just want to know if there was anything odd about him that caught your notice."

"Nothing I haven't already told the captain."

"Captain? What captain?"

"He called himself Captain LeBeau. He was a Frenchman and was asking for anything found near the dead man. I let him search the area, but he didn't find anything."

The spyglass.

"Did you happen to remember that bit of glass Jacob found yesterday?"

O'Donnell's eyes widened and he groaned. "Damn it all! I forgot altogether! I suppose I should find him and let him know about it."

"And take all that time to hunt him down? Going down to town, searching the docks looking for his ship? He might not even be at his ship. You can't hunt the whole city for him."

"I suppose ..."

"Now look you here, I'll check his ship and if he's there I'll let him know. I've got to go back at any rate. If he's not there, he should have an officer who can pass the word to him. Can you tell me, when did you last look out there before you found the body?"

"I saw him that morning, just after dawn. Scared the life out of me, I can tell you—what a mess. He wasn't there the night before, I'm sure of that. I'd gone out just before dark to feed the mule and I didn't see a thing out here."

Which meant that Officer Passy had been put where he'd been found while Gabe had been with Dora. So Gabe at least hadn't been guilty of that. Killing the Frenchman, though, that might still have been possible. With his temper, it was certainly possible, but Gabe wasn't a fool and murder was nothing short of stupid. Sober, he wouldn't have sought out Officer Passy, and Miss Ratman had been with him after he'd gotten drunk. Without the excuse of drunkenness, he wouldn't have forgotten a fatal encounter. He wasn't lying about his memory loss—drink always had such an effect on him, and Elmore didn't believe Gabe would lie to him, anyway. Then again, he'd never mentioned having such a close friendship with Miss Ratman. Maybe there were other things he hadn't seen fit to tell Elmore about.

Maybe Elmore didn't know Gabe as well as he'd thought.

That Officer Passy might have chased after Gabe to get the mysterious spyglass was entirely possible. Maybe the confrontation had turned violent and Gabe came out best. Then why not tell Elmore? It wasn't as if Elmore would have turned him into the law and even if he had, it would have clearly been self-defense and not a crime.

"And Captain LeBeau found nothing here?"

"I'm sorry, Finch, but not a blessed thing." O'Donnell gave a helpless shrug. "Nothing but a button." He pulled a slightly muddy button from his pocket and held it out. "Captain LeBeau didn't want it. He said it just came from the dead man's coat." The button was wooden and unpainted. Common enough.

Elmore took the button and left with his thanks to O'Donnell.

***

Bowe, who'd been polishing his boots when Elmore had tracked him down in his room, hadn't been all that interested in the button. "It's hardly an earth-shaking find; anyone might have dropped it. I don't see how it can help us."

Bowe lived in an apartment rather than the soldier's barracks. It was tiny, just one room, with space enough for a bed and a chest of drawers, but little else. He liked his privacy, he'd said, and was willing to pay for it.

"How do you expect to save enough to buy yourself a higher commission if you waste money like this?" Elmore asked, peering around at the remarkably clean room. It was spartan, as was to be expected of a young bachelor, but had the comfort of a rag rug on the floor and woolen blankets on the bed. What impressed Elmore was a pile of six books in a corner. He couldn't read much more than his name and doubted he ever would at his age. Jacob could read splendidly, and on many evenings, when work was done, he was good enough to read to Elmore from whatever it was that Reverend Roberts had him studying, whether it was Shakespeare or some history book about ancient times and far off places.

"Some things are worth the expense. So, you have someone willing to swear that Mister Scratch was with them the night Officer Passy was put in the forest where he was found. He could have worked with someone else who hid the body after he did the deed. That's all a lawyer has to say, and even a bad lawyer knows that much."

"Aye, but it's a start. What we need to do is find out who robbed me of the spyglass. That Captain LeBeau was out to talk to O'Donnell; he was looking for something. The spyglass would be my guess. He wants it that bad and someone has it. He thought his man had it, but it wasn't on him or at his rented room or where he'd been found. Someone took it from us and, mark me, if we find who has it, we'll find the killer. Do you still have the body?"

"He's being kept until the trial. Then Captain LeBeau wants to give him a sea burial."

"Can I see it?"

Bowe blinked. "Why would you want to?"

"To see if anything were missed. I need more information. This just doesn't make any sense. This Captain LeBeau seems fairly certain his officer had the spyglass. Maybe he did, though I don't know how he'd know where to get it unless he followed Gabe to my home. If that officer did steal it, then someone else has it, now. Maybe the killer. I want to know why everyone seems to be going to so much trouble for that broken thing. It's even more broken without this." He held out the eyepiece of the spyglass. "Jacob found it at O'Donnell's."

"No," Bowe muttered, taking the eyepiece for a closer look. "It doesn't look as if it was broken off, but deliberately taken off. I didn't think spyglasses came apart like this."

"They don't, as a rule. I wonder what was inside."

"Inside?"

"The spyglass, of course. If it came apart, there must have been something inside. Whatever it was, someone thinks it's worth two men's lives." Elmore plucked the eyepiece out of Bowe's hand and rolled it between his fingers. Whatever it was, it wasn't worth Gabe's life. "Do you know where Officer Passy was staying? His ship?"

"No. His captain said he'd taken a room with an old widow near the glass blower's shop. The Widow Brandwhite. She said he called himself Jean and was a nice, quiet tenant for more than a week before he disappeared. I searched the room but didn't find anything."

"Anything else?"

"The Widow Brandwhite is hard of hearing. Very hard of hearing. Yell if you're going to speak with her. You are going, aren't you? Don't you trust my work?"

"Did you go dressed like that?" Elmore eyed Bowe's uniform. "Some folks don't trust uniforms. She might have forgotten something the moment she saw you."

***

The Widow Brandwhite was so hard of hearing that within just a few moments of meeting her, Elmore's throat hurt from yelling. She spoke slowly and with difficulty, but she did remember the young man, Jean, and was more than happy to let Elmore see the room.

She'd already spoken to a soldier who'd had her identify the body of that poor, nice young man. "Such a shame, but people do get mixed up in all sorts of nonsense, don't they?"

As she led the way upstairs to the room Officer Passy had let, she repeated what she'd told Bowe, that Jean had caused no trouble and paid without complaint.

"When did you see him last?" Elmore shouted.

"Three nights ago. The night his friend came to see him, again."

"What friend?"

"Oh, I didn't catch the name. He was another Frenchman, but didn't have so strong an accent. Now, his other friend, the one who came after poor Jean was killed, after the soldier had left, he had a heavy accent. Could barely speak English at all, but he had manners enough." She turned to smile, approvingly, as they reached the landing. Her smile stretched wrinkled lips over her toothless mouth. "He'd only wanted to pick up a few of his friend's belongings, but couldn't find what he was looking for. I didn't take whatever it was. I'm an honest woman, and I've never put my hand on what wasn't mine. I told him that the soldier, Lieutenant Bowe, might have taken it, though I didn't see him take anything. He only searched the room. He didn't say what he was looking for, but he didn't seem to find anything that interested him."

The room was small and tidy, but had a broken window and the Widow Brandwhite shook her head at it. "It wasn't like that when I rented him the room. I can't think what happened."

She wouldn't have been able to hear the breaking glass or anything else that had happened. It was Captain LeBeau, still searching for the spyglass, who'd paid the visit, after Bowe had left. Elmore was sure of it. But what of the first man who'd come before Passy had been killed? "What about that first friend who visited him?" Elmore asked. "What do you remember about him?"

"Well, he came twice. I remember he was hurt the second time. He bumped into a chair and hit his arm. You'd think he'd seen a ghost, he went that white. He told me it was nothing, that he'd just been bitten by a dog."

And that would have been Harold. So he'd found the thief and it hadn't been Bowe or Captain LeBeau, for if it was, then surely Widow Brandwhite would have recognized them. It also proved, well enough to Elmore's thinking, that Officer Passy himself hadn't been the thief as he hadn't been injured.

"Did you get his name?"

"Eh?"

"I said, did you get his name?"

"Oh. No. They were in a hurry to get to Jean's room so they could talk more privately. What? Did they think I'd overhear if they whispered?" She laughed good-naturedly at herself. "He was a smart-looking young feller. A seaman by his walk; my George walked like that 'til his dying day, God rest his soul. That was the last time I saw Jean. I suppose he left when I wasn't paying attention."

That didn't help much. The visitor could have been one of Officer Passy's crewmates or any of hundreds of men in the city.

"What did he look like? Any scars or anything odd?"

"No. He seemed like an ordinary man. Middle age. Neither tall nor short. Brown hair."

Again, not helpful.

"When did you last see him? What time?"

"Well after dark. I remember because I'd lit a candle to finish my knitting when his friend came calling."

After dark. After Gabe was with Dora! Elmore felt a surge of elation run up his spine like a crisp fall breeze after a muggy summer night. If the mystery man with the dog bite had been the one to steal the spyglass from Elmore's home, then he had surely been the one to put Officer Passy behind O'Donnell's house, as he must have had the spyglass with him at the time and dropped the lens there. If the Widow Brandwhite had seen Officer Passy, albeit by a different name, while Gabe was with Miss Ratman, then it was looking all the better for Gabe's chances.

Elmore took the Widow Brandwhite's hand. "Ma'am, would you be so kind as to tell all this to a soldier?"

She frowned. "I don't know. I don't hold much with soldiers. Rough. Bad manners."

"This soldier isn't like that. This one's a real gentleman. He's the one what came to see you earlier."

She conceded that he hadn't been so bad, but she didn't like soldiers. A soldier had raped her daughter.

"A man's life depends on you," Elmore urged. "Please."

She agreed, but only for the sake of an innocent life.

Innocent was debatable, but Elmore thanked her all the same and promised to bring the soldier with him when he returned.

CHAPTER 12: UNDER THE BED

As fast as he could, Elmore raced to the Hold. He was so excited to finally have evidence—a good woman's word—that Gabe couldn't have been the one to kill the Frenchman, that he did his utmost to ignore the growing throb in his knee, telling himself firmly that pampering himself could easily wait until Gabe was safe at home, again. Bowe wasn't at the Hold and, in all honesty, Elmore didn't know who else he could trust with the information. The soldiers who had been standing guard were the same ones who had refused to let him see Gabe before, so Elmore didn't even bother to confide his information in them. He turned at once and headed back to Bowe's rented room.

Without thinking of courtesy in his haste, Elmore didn't even pause to knock. The door had been locked, but Elmore's first push against it made something crack and the door swung open. Elmore stepped into the room before he really saw Bowe and, once he did, he froze in midstep as he went terribly cold—as if an icy wind rolled over him.

A feather fan in one hand, kneeling in a circle of candles, Bowe stared, wide-eyed and open-mouthed, at Elmore. On the floor before him was a chalk-drawn circle with a star within it and at the center of that star, a scrap of fabric lay. The shuttered windows and the dancing light of the candles … it was enough to have Elmore catch his breath and step backwards.

"What are you doing here?" Bowe's tanned face went nearly white. He raised himself up with one foot planted on the floor, as if he were readying himself to jump up at Elmore. "Get out!"

But Elmore felt frozen. He'd heard stories aplenty—who hadn't?—of wicked people and their hidden, dark practices, and had even known a few such folks aboard ship who'd come from distant islands and refused to give up their ways and their strange gods. But to find such a sight in a civilized place like Port Royal and to find a genial, well-spoken young man like Bowe doing the practicing was shocking, to say the least.

Elmore found his voice at the last. "What's all this, then?"

Bowe seemed beyond reason. He snapped out with his sharp eyes narrowed, "I said, get out! You don't belong here!"

And then, Elmore's own temper flared. "You don't dare to speak like that to me! What are you doing?!"

"I didn't do anything!" Bowe held up his chin and met Elmore's eyes easily. "I didn't! I only... it's not your business so get out!"

"Not my ... no, sir! No. You'll talk. By God, you tell me what's going on. All ... this?" Elmore gestured at the paraphernalia surrounding Bowe. "I let you into my home. Around my boy."

"And I never hurt you or your boy or your friend. I wouldn't. This ... all this ... was for an insult. I told you—my parents loved each other. They don't deserve to have such filth spoken about them."

The cloth laying in the middle of the circle—Elmore remembered. He'd seen Bowe with the torn cloth after the spat with the drunk.

Bowe continued, "But I haven't changed. I'm the same man I was when you wanted help for your friend, and I'm the same man's who's trying to honestly help."

"Aye, but then I didn't know you'd given yourself to such devilry."

At that, Bowe chuckled and his cool mask faded a bit, and he reddened. "I'm no devil worshipper."

"Well, you can't rightly be expecting me to believe you're a Christian."

"No, I wouldn't. My mother was a witch." He said it with absolutely no shame. "I've followed her teachings all of my life and I will continue to do so."

Elmore paled at the confession and stepped backwards, towards the door. He reached blindly for it.

"And if I speak against you, you'll what? Call some demon to silence me?"

Like a volcano, Bowe erupted. "Get out!" He swore violently and did get to his feet, shaking his fist at Elmore. "You barking dog! Get out!"

In the face of such barely contained violence, Elmore stumbled backwards and, when he was in the hall, Bowe slammed the door with a resounding thump. There was the sound of something heavy being dragged across the floor until it was directly in front of the door, and Elmore felt his whole head go cloudy. He turned and walked down the hall, down the stairs, and onto the street, where he kept walking without have any idea where he was going.

He needed to tell someone what the Widow Brandwhite had said. He needed help and there was no one to trust. Would the other guards even bother to listen? If Bowe was correct, then everyone was only concerned with having someone to blame for the murder; they wouldn't care a bit if they had the right man or not, and it was entirely possible that Elmore's words would be altogether ignored.

Fool and fool again! Elmore snorted at himself and shook his head hard enough that he made himself go momentarily dizzy. Then he stiffened his shoulders, tightened his grip on his walking stick, and put some purpose in his step as he started walking again. He may be alone in his work, but to give up before trying? It was shameful. Unthinkable. Gabe was depending on him. He would speak to the other guards at the Hold and, if none of them would listen, he would go straight to Government House and get himself seen by Governor Modyford to plead Gabe's case. Even if none of that worked, he decided as he headed in the direction of the docks, he would find the man whose lie had put Gabe in The Hold and see to it that they were properly dealt with.

It was a pity to lose Bowe's help. Who would have thought

he'd rely on the law so fully that he regretted the loss of it? But it really couldn't be said that he'd been relying on law, but rather that he'd been relying on a good man.

But that chalk circle … witchcraft …

Elmore gave himself another shake. For good or ill, he'd lost that help. Bowe's anger upon being discovered was proof enough of that, and there was no sense wasting time with regrets. He did his best to pull his thoughts from that chalk star drawn on Bowe's floor and set his mind to puzzling out the other aspects of the situation as he walked.

At the *Indigo Running*, he was hailed aboard by a man who still remembered him. A few men yelled greetings as Elmore limped up the gangplank. Most of the crew seemed to be away, no doubt enjoying their leave, but those left onboard were working. Two men sat on the deck with big needles, sewing up tears in the sails that had, unquestionably, been torn by the hurricane Gabe had spoken about. Some men sweated their day away swabbing the deck, while others carried things here and there. The rigger hung like a spider in the rope riggings, undoubtedly checking their soundness, and a boy with a scar across his nose was playing a tune on a little wooden pipe.

Elmore watched them, but his eyes fell especially on the men repairing the sail and he remembered his own times spent mending, whether it had been sails, or, more commonly, clothes. He missed it. He still did his own mending and had taught Jacob to do his own, but as he stood on the deck, he realized how much he missed his life at sea. It hadn't been all that long ago that he'd sat with his mates, laughing about this or that until some argument would break out. It had been a tough life, but the freedom had been breathtaking. Free, but not happy. Not nice. There had been also been killing, battle, hunger, sickness, and two dozen other nightmares that Elmore did not miss—nightmares he wished he had never lived through—and made him everlasting thankful to be finished with that life. He had done what had been necessary at the time, Elmore hadn't been sorry to leave the life behind, though he had been sorry to walk away from Gabe.

The ship bobbed gently on the water that, in the harbor, was little more than a soft echo of what the rolling sea was truly like. A gray gull stood boldly on the deck's railing, watching the sailors with eyes as black and endless as the depths of the sea.

He ached for the companionship that he had lost. Though many of the men he'd known on his days about *Indigo Running* hadn't been the type of men he ever wanted as friends, there had been good folks, there, too. He missed being part of a crew, missed it every day that he walked the docks and watched the fishermen as they repaired their nets and the full white sails of tall masts coming or going. He missed it when he listened to the rousing shanties as men got their ships ready for a few days in dock. Sometimes he missed it all so much that it was an ache, and all he could do was stand on the docks, lean against a pier and stare out at the sea. He could almost feel the waves in his blood. He missed climbing above the world in the spiderweb that the riggings were, and the smell of gunpowder as the powder monkey ran it to the master gunner.

Of course, on the fishing ship he'd first set to sea on with Gabe leading the way, there had been no gunner. There had been no killing or terrible sea battles, but there had been the constant stench of fish and endless nights preparing the haul that would be taken into port. There had been nights when he'd be so sore and so exhausted that he hadn't bothered to snap at Gabe for some offensive joke, and Gabe had, at those times, shaken his head at the "lazy boy" and tossed a blanket over Elmore as he fell asleep.

It had been on one of those bone-weary nights that Elmore had been startled awake by something like thunder. The ship had rocked violently, and there was suddenly yelling and calls for all hands on deck. Elmore had rushed up with others, staggering with lingering sleep up the short flight of stairs to the deck. Dawn had just broken, and its coming had brought cannonballs and terror. They were a fishing ship—nothing worth attacking. But the other ship did attack, and they had no weapons.

"Keep down!" Gabe was at his side and shoved him to the deck only moments before grapeshot flew where he'd been standing. "Pirates!" He'd shouted to Elmore with a wide, frightening grin. There had been an awful glitter in his eyes that had shown how very excited he was. "We're done for."

"Will we fight?" Elmore yelled back.

"How? We've no weapons, unless you want to toss some cod at them, and this old boat can't outrun that trim lady."

He'd been quite right. The captain had given up without any fight at all and, though bitter, had handed over everything the pirates demanded. The ship was raided thoroughly and at the end, when the pirates seemed ready to leave, their captain had looked over the crew of the fishing ship.

"Any man here who wants a voice in his life and a share of spoils, join us." He was handsome and smiled at his captives. "No more slaving for a living and gutting fish 'til your hands bleed."

Almost before he'd stopped speaking, Gabe had seized hold of Elmore's hand and dragged him forward. "We'll join up!"

"What are you doing?" Elmore hissed as he looked wildly between Gabe and the pirate.

"Fortune and freedom, my friend. What else could a man want?" Gabe was nearly bouncing on his toes like an excited child. Elmore had to wonder if Gabe had been waiting for such a happenstance, or if the attack had simply triggered an unthinking impulse. Gabe often did things without thinking, but this ... and pulling Elmore along ... "You will come with me." He grinned at Elmore.

It hadn't been a question, and Elmore had been almost ashamed of how well Gabe knew him. Yes. He would go. Why not? What should stop him? Respect for law that had never done him any good? Respect for humanity that had only ever given him grief? No. Even if he had wanted to turn his back on Gabe, the crew of the fishing ship wouldn't trust him after Gabe had volunteered him, and then he'd be alone and penniless, again. So he licked his lips and nodded at Gabe with as much confidence as he could muster, and the path was chosen.

"Glad to have you, gentlemen." The pirate captain bowed his head to them. "I am Captain Raynard Passy." He'd always been a cool, well-controlled man. Even when he'd stood on the deck of the captured ship with irate fishermen and desperately clutched the wooden box of the scant medicinal supplies the fishing ship had carried as if they were as dear as his own life, he hadn't trembled or sweated or shown any sign of nerves at all. His confidence had seemed so unshakable that any hesitation that might have lingered in Elmore fled. He followed Gabe to the pirate's ship quite willingly, content in knowing that whatever was to be would be, and that nothing he did was really any worse than what the rest of humanity did with the blessing of the law. Didn't everyone steal? Whether it was the farmer who overcharged for his apples or the wealthy money lender who would throw a good family from their home for one late payment—everyone was a thief. He was under no delusion about the darkest side of a pirate's life. Death. But even that couldn't bring him too much guilt. After all, was it not legal to own another's life? How was that different than a pirate who would, inevitably, take a life?

A cheery call interrupted his thoughts. "Mister Finch!"

Elmore smiled and held a hand out to the other man. "Good to see you, Cap'n Harrington."

Captain Odell Harrington was a big, jolly-looking man. He smiled broadly, and the two rings he wore in one ear gleamed in the sunlight. He had the beginnings of a paunch, but it did nothing to make him look weak or lazy. He strode across the deck and stretched out his hand for Elmore's. "It's been a good long while, hasn't it? Come in and sit with me."

"You know I don't drink."

"The result of a deprived youth. You sit while I drink, then."

They went to the captain's cabin and sat at the square table that had been bolted to the floor. The cabin hadn't changed much since Elmore had left the crew. There was a new quilt on the bed—the only bed on the ship, rather than the hammocks below deck—and a framed painting of some fair-eyed girl. There was a pile of four books in a corner that Elmore doubted Captain Harrington had ever opened. If he remembered correctly, the man couldn't read any more than Elmore himself could.

"I just thought I'd catch up with old mates. I see you haven't been voted back before the mast, yet."

Captain Harrington laughed. "Now why would they do that? I rarely ever bring them back to port without a haul to give them all a few merry days."

"I heard you and Gabe had a bit of a row before that French ship was taken."

Captain Harrington set his tankard on the table and leaned back, crossing his arms over his chest. "Gabe? Nay. No more so than usual. What's this about?"

"Just what I heard."

Captain Harrington wasn't happy, but nor was he afraid or angry or any other sign of guilt. "Gabe say something to you? He's my quartermaster. Of course we argue. You know we've both got tempers like wet hornets. We'd argue if it were day or night given half a chance. I never thought he held any of it against me."

Elmore believed him. Nothing about his demeanor made Elmore at all suspicious. "He doesn't, I suppose. He's in the Hold."

"What for?"

"Murder. The victim was one of those French sailors you attacked. Someone went and told a soldier that Gabe and this feller fought on that French ship."

"And you think it were me?" Captain Harrington's face turned red. He pushed his chair away from the table. "Gabe's my friend, same as he's yours. We argued, but that's the end of it. It's never even come to blows with us. I didn't point the law at him, and I'll stand by that, on my honor."

Elmore believed him. Captain Harrington seemed entirely sincere.

"It must have been someone from this ship. They named

him and Gabe was certain no one said his name during the attack, so it couldn't have been anyone from the French ship that accused him."

The red faded from Captain Harrington's face, but he still glowered. "If you're right, then the rat will answer to me." He refilled his tankard with bumbo. "Ship's articles don't allow any breaking of the company 'til everyone's had a fair share of one thousand pieces of eight. Selling out a mate so he wouldn't be able to sail counts as breaking that code, if you ask me." He stood abruptly and started pacing, crossing the room in four strides, then started back. He swung his drink with every step, but didn't spill a single drop. "Besides what he did to Gabe, seems to me that whoever you've been talking to is trying to set my good name in a poor light. You thought I spoke against Gabe, didn't you? If the crew thinks that, too, then I'll be voted out."

Maybe that was the objective.

Captain Harrington asked, "Who was it that told these lies? Who's spreading tales about me?"

"Ah, no one. Calm down. What am I going to do but cause trouble by giving you a name? All I was told was that you two had had a row, and you've admitted as much—the whole crew must have seen you. I've got proof that he didn't kill anyone, I've just got to tell the right person and Gabe will be free, but I don't even rightly know who to tell. Is Raynard aboard? I'd like to tell him the news."

"No," Captain Harrington answered. "He generally takes a room at the *Anchor's Chain* when we're ashore. I haven't seen him in days."

***

The Anchor's Chain wasn't only a tavern, but also an inn. It was reasonably clean and catered not to the local tradesmen or sailors, but to the higher-class merchants. It wasn't as busy as *The Blue Dog*, but there were curtains in the windows and the tables looked as if they'd been recently scrubbed. Obviously, it was of a finer quality than most of Port Royal's taverns. The bucktoothed barman told Elmore which room Raynard was staying in and, before Elmore started up the stairs, told him that Raynard wasn't in. No matter, Elmore had said. He would wait.

The room was empty but for a bed, a small table, and a chair. Raynard's distinctive purple coat had been laid on the bed. It had gold buttons, and while it was worn and just a bit patched on one sleeve, Raynard had always been proud of it. He'd acquired it from a gentleman during an attack back when Raynard had been captain. He'd crowed and preened over that coat more than he had over the sixteen barrels of sugar they'd taken.

Elmore sat in the chair, resolved to wait, but he had only sat a few moments before he'd grown impatient. Men who spent near every day of their lives working didn't often take to idleness. He stood and took a few steps around the little room. He'd almost given up waiting entirely when he caught sight of a rolled-up paper under the bed. Curious, he picked it up and unrolled it. The paper was new and clean but for a brown stain on one end.

It was a navigational chart. He'd seen enough of them to recognize one, even if he'd never had to use one. He recognized different places such as Britain, Africa, America, and, of course, Jamaica. There, at the far right of the chart, were the chain of Japanese islands. There were lines marked on the chart showing the usual routes for trade, including the Gulf Stream from the Caribbean to northern Europe. There was another line drawn from South America, going near Jamaica, then to France and Spain.

Elmore tapped a finger on his knee. He'd never seen that route on any chart before.

A realization dawned on him. It was a gradual, subtle thing—like the blossoming of a flower.

He slowly rolled the chart up and when he did, he knew that it would fit inside the broken spyglass. The spyglass with one end that screwed on and off.

The door opened and, looking surprised, Raynard walked in. He looked from Elmore to the chart, then back to Elmore. His expression grew hard as he stepped into the room and closed the door behind him.

CHAPTER 13: TREASURE MAP

The air felt too heavy and the room too dark as Raynard stepped closer to Elmore. He didn't like it. He'd never feared a friend, before, but Raynard … there was something cold about him that Elmore had never seen before, not once in all the years he'd known Raynard, and that coldness made him fear Raynard. Elmore had known many, many dangerous people, from his life at sea to living in Port Royal, people that he knew very well had no compunction about killing for the sheer thrill of seeing the life fade out of another human's eyes, people who would hurt another person just because they could, and people who would do such evil for their own wants. But that he should see such a person in his friend, such a look focused on him, was … it was simply disappointing. Not to say that Elmore himself was clean; he had done his share of evil, and would not be so hypocritical as to deny his own vile history, but he had trusted Raynard, and it hurt to see that Raynard clearly didn't see Elmore as any better than the enemy they had fought side by side, that he considered both Elmore and Gabe to be worth sacrificing.

Raynard said, "Fancy seeing you here."

"Fancy." Elmore, still holding the chart, stood and wished his leg didn't feel like it was on fire from all the running around he'd been doing.

"You should have told me you were coming. Poor manners to barge into someone's room."

"Worse manners to let a mate get hung for a murder he had nothing to do with. No wonder you were happy to let me think Cap'n Harrington were speaking against Gabe." Elmore was shaking as his fear and disappointment began to boil into fury and he had never felt such a burn—not even in the heat of battle. "What the Hell is this?" He shook the chart at Raynard. "Why'd you kill your own kin for it?"

Raynard's eyes widened. "You mean Leo? Why would I kill my own cousin?"

"Leave off the acting! Do you think I've gone soft in the head? You'd have killed him for whatever was in the spyglass! This, I reckon!" He shook the scroll, again.

"That?" Raynard laughed. "Don't be daft. That's just a navigational chart. Nothing worth killing a cat over, let alone family. I was seeing about learning to read it, make myself more valuable to the crew. I wouldn't hurt Gabe or my dear cousin."

"Bah!" Elmore waved his hand, sharply. "You barely knew your cousin—said so yourself. Hadn't seen him in years. And you wouldn't have hurt Gabe? Do you take me for a complete fool? I was there when you ordered Martin Hopspool sweated to death. He dropped dead and you went for rum before the body was cold."

"He'd stolen from the company! It was justified."

"Aye, but you'd known him two years and you felt nothing at his death. Not a thing. I don't believe you'd shed a single tear if Gabe died so long as you got what you wanted in the end. You'd let him hang. He didn't kill that man, and whoever did is the same who took the spyglass from my home. That person went and set the law on Gabe and don't you spit garbage at me about it being all Cap'n Harrington's doing! I parlayed with him and I don't believe it. They argued, but the sun rises, too. What of it? They always do and always have. Even I remember Gabe arguing with you when the *Indigo Running* was under your command. Cap'n Harrington didn't have cause to do Gabe any harm. It would do him poorly to lose his quartermaster."

"And me? Why would I do anything to Gabe? What cause do you think I have?"

"The soldier came asking about the Frenchman, didn't he? Must have seemed like a golden chance, eh? An unsolved killing somehow tied to *Indigo Running*. You let rumor start running wild that it were Cap'n Harrington that went and got one of his own hands hung and then he gets voted down. That would be handy for you. Never mind getting voted down, Cap'n Harrington would be killed if everyone thinks he went and turned on the company, and that's just what everyone would think if I come to the ship, screaming for justice because you planted the idea in my head that it were Cap'n's doing. Gabe'll get hung for your deed, but there'll be no soldiers sniffing at your tracks and no one ever the wiser to what you did, so you're all the better in the end. *Indigo Running* would need a new captain. You hoping to be voted up, again?"

Raynard grew red, but his voice was calm. "Who better? It was only luck that gave Harrington my position. My ship. I was a good captain 'til that last voyage."

"You never did take it as easy as I thought you had, did you? Cap'n Harrington didn't steal from my home. My dog went and bit the thief, and Cap'n Harrington wasn't in any pain that I saw. My dog caught the thief going out. If he'd found him going in, the thief wouldn't have had time to search as he did before the dog ripped into him." He shot a hand out and grabbed Raynard by the right arm and, without squeezing, caused Raynard to swear and flinch away. Elmore did squeeze, then, and held on tightly. "Officer Passy's landlady said the last time she saw him, the night he was killed, he went off with a visitor who had a soft French accent and an injured arm. He'd bumped into a chair and showed his pain." He squeezed hard enough to make Raynard go pale. "You run from my dog?"

"Bastard! I told you, I've done nothing to Leo or Gabe. That chart's nothing!"

Elmore let go of Raynard and stepped towards the door. "Fine, then. I'll take this worthless chart off your hands."

"It's mine!"

"But it's nothing." Elmore stepped away from Raynard, towards the door. "I'll get you a new one, one without a stain."

Raynard lunged at Elmore, who took his hand and, dropping the chart, he shoved Raynard's sleeve up to his elbow. The bite mark was clear, scabbed over, and bruised dark purple.

"You foul—"

Raynard shoved Elmore with such force that he stumbled backwards and his lame leg hit the wooden post of the bed. A bolt of pain, like fire, shot up and down his leg and right up his back, so fierce and sudden that he fell to floor.

Like a hungry hawk, Raynard dove, not at Elmore, but for the chart. It lay on the floor near Elmore's feet, and Raynard's eagerness to get his hands on the chart made him thoughtless enough to get too close to Elmore's feet. Elmore kicked at Raynard's head, and when Raynard jerked out of reach, Elmore snatched up the chart and started to get to his feet.

Raynard swung his fist and caught Elmore across the jaw, then in the side of the head. Stars flashed and danced before his eyes. He lost his senses for just a moment before he came to himself and felt Raynard pulling at the chart in Elmore's clenched hand. "Let go, poxed dog!"

Elmore raised his knee and caught Raynard's. He yelled and let go of the chart only to put one hand on Elmore's throat and shove him back down to the floor. He pulled a knife from his belt and jabbed it fiercely downward, only to have Elmore reach up with his one free hand and grabbed Raynard by the wrist, halting the blade a mere few inches from Elmore's face. For several heartbeats they stayed like that, frozen and staring at each other. Finally, Elmore released his hold on the chart and let it fall to the floor, flicking it just enough that it rolled several feet away.

Raynard's eyes followed the chart and that moment of distraction was enough to loosen the pressure he had on Elmore's throat. With a triumphant, unintelligible cry, Raynard reached for the chart and, at the same time, Elmore yanked Raynard's hand to the side, taking the knife away from his face, and grabbed Raynard by the hair. He ignored Raynard's snarl and slammed Raynard's head against the wooden leg of the bed.

Raynard's face went still, then slack as his eyes rolled. He slumped insensibly to the floor, half sprawled on Elmore.

Elmore pushed the dead weight of that body off himself

and turned over. The chart had rolled under the bed, again. He reached for it, but before his hand could even touch it, the door swung open, and Elmore almost wilted as two more men walked in.

One of the men was large and gray-haired, the other smaller, younger and nervous to the point of fear. The older of the two men held a pistol and stepped into the room. He cast a look at Raynard, then at Elmore, before he said something softly in French to his companion. The smaller of the two men replied to the first, then slid by Elmore to kneel at Raynard's side. He pressed his fingers against Raynard's throat. He waited a moment or two, then nodded to the bigger man and stood up. He quickly moved to stand behind the other man.

The pistol never wavered from Elmore. He wanted to run. Every instinct he had pushed at him to run. His own pistol hung loaded in its holster under his jacket, where it was completely useless. The gray-haired man seemed calm, but tense enough that Elmore didn't dare risk reaching for his weapon. So he kept still and quiet while the little man stared at him intently as he spoke to the gray-haired man, hissing like a frightened rat.

Whatever he said seemed to have little impact on the more severe-looking, older man who continued to stare at Elmore with an unshakable calm, a stern determination that made Elmore wary. *Danger,* a soft voice whispered in Elmore's mind. *He's dangerous. Be cautious. Be patient.* It was so clear that the man didn't belong in the parts of Port Royal that Elmore lived in that the very sight of him standing in Raynard's room, even though it was one of the better inns in the city, seemed altogether wrong. The man was well-dressed and wore a neatly trimmed beard and moustache. He was clean. There was steel in his eyes, but it wasn't nearly so intimidating as the steel in his hand. He snapped at the other man, something that made the little man fall silent. Then he jerked his head towards Elmore. "Your name?"

There was no point in lying, Elmore realized. He'd know everything once Raynard woke up, anyway. "Finch. Yours?"

The gray-haired man nodded his head. "Captain Donatien LeBeau. What has happened?" He used a free hand to gesture towards Raynard and spoke with a deep, gravely sort of voice.

Elmore didn't have time to answer as, just then, Raynard woke with a long, drawn out groan. He pushed himself up and took a moment to see what was going on. He rubbed the top of his head while he spoke with Captain LeBeau in French.

They weren't friends, that much was plain as day. Captain LeBeau didn't try to hide the disdain on his face and Raynard showed the captain no more respect than he would have anyone else. Captain LeBeau looked at Elmore, then said something. Raynard shook his head emphatically. There was more shaking of heads, and obviously controlled voices that were only just barely on the friendly side of arguing.

At last, with a disturbingly calculating look at Elmore, Raynard said, "You're coming along. Be wise and walk. Don't cause extra trouble for yourself. I told Captain LeBeau that you came for the spyglass, that it had come into your hands only briefly, but that you wanted it back, as it had been a gift. I also told him that you saw the chart when you came here. He can't let you go, now."

"I didn't read it. I don't even know what it's for."

"That is good." Captain LeBeau spoke for himself. "But I am sorry to say that I can't take any chances with your silence, and silence is of utmost importance. I am not cruel, and I would never wish to harm you simply because you happened to fall into my business. You will be well-treated so long as you are able to mind your conduct. Stand up. You'll come with us, now. To France." His English was just as heavily accented as the Widow Brandwhite had suggested, but he spoke with confidence, like a gentleman.

Raynard disarmed Elmore, taking both his pistols and his knife, then retrieved the chart and stuffed it in his coat pocket. Captain LeBeau tucked his hand holding the pistol under his coat, but he didn't take his hand off it. The second, still nameless man and Raynard walked on either side of Elmore while Captain

LeBeau walked behind as they left the inn and headed towards the harbor.

He had to get away. He couldn't go to France. What would Jacob do without him? The boy didn't know about the hidden treasure in his bedroom's wall, and Gabe would hang after all because Elmore had stupidly let his shock over Bowe's secret get in the way of talking to the man about what actually mattered. Gabe would swing on Gallow's Hill, where so many others had ended their lives with a jerk and a snap. He had to get Bowe to talk to the witnesses. There was no other choice; he had to speak to Bowe. He just couldn't stand thinking of Jacob, starving on the streets, suffering. At best, he would step into his father's shoes and sign aboard a ship, or maybe choose a safer life and join the church, but he surely wouldn't be able to even dream of school in England.

As they neared the harbor and the tall masts of dozens of ships spiked over rooftops, the urge to run grew until it was unbearable. His leg hurt all the more at the thought of running, but he swallowed hard and tried to convince himself that it was only pain, and there were things more important than his comfort. He couldn't get on that ship—he wouldn't! If he did, there would be no going back.

God, he prayed. *Please help me. Help me for the boy and for Gabe. Help this old sinner.*

They started onto the docks and Elmore's desperation grew with every step until, very suddenly, the threat of pistols and knives his captors would undoubtedly turn on him meant nothing. If he were taken from Port Royal, then he would never again see his family, and if he never saw them, then he was as good as dead. *Better to fight than to give in.*

Elmore turned and kicked Captain LeBeau's left foot. He grab hold of Captain LeBeau's pistol and held on tight as he pushed the man on the chest as hard as he could. Captain LeBeau fell backwards, wide-eyed, off the docks and into the sea with a yelp and a splash.

The small Frenchman went to the edge of the dock to

help his struggling captain, and Elmore kicked him in the rump, sending him into the sea, also. Elmore turned, with the pistol raised, just in time to freeze Raynard in place, when he was only steps away from Elmore. Elmore pulled back the hammer on the pistol and held out his empty hand. "Don't you make a move to that pistol of yours, or I'll put a shot clean through your face. Give me the chart."

From the water, the two Frenchmen shouted, but Elmore's entire focus was on Raynard. Elmore could guess at the thoughts going through Raynard's head—wondering if he could draw his pistol before Elmore could fire, if Elmore had it in him to kill an old friend, what he would do to stop Elmore. "I'll shoot you if you don't hand it over before your friends get themselves out of the water."

Slowly, with a carefully blank expression, he took the chart out of his pocket and held it out. He made as if to toss at Elmore's feet.

"Don't you think of it! We both know I couldn't get it fast enough to stop you from going at me. You hand it over like a gentleman." Shifting his eyes from the two men clinging onto the wooden boards of the docks and Raynard, Elmore was all too aware that the pistol had only one shot—one chance at a slim hope of turning the whole mess around.

"You won't shoot."

Elmore almost laughed at Raynard. "And 'til an hour ago, I would have said you'd never turn on me. I suppose we both learned something today. Hand it over afore you learn how good a friend I think Gabe is, and what I'll do to save him."

Raynard held out the chart and Elmore took it. It was dangerous; he hated the damned thing. Still, he tightened his grip on it and began to walk backwards, away from Raynard and making sure to keep out of reach of the other two, for fear they would try to trip him as he walked by. For as long as he could, he kept his eyes on them. He discreetly tucked the pistol under his coat to prevent unwanted attention, but it seemed Raynard knew not to try Elmore's temper, because he kept still as a statue as Elmore crept away. He went down the length of the slip and onto the long, wide wooden walkway of the docks that ran the length of the harbor. As he couldn't go down the busy road backwards to keep Raynard in sight, he would have to turn around.

An awkward bump and a hurried "Pardon!" as some nameless passerby happened to knock against Elmore and nearly push him off balance, was just enough distraction for Raynard to take his chance. His own pistol was in his hand by the time Elmore looked back at him. One terrible blast when Raynard's shot made everyone on the street run for cover. Elmore stumbled and started moving, but he wasn't fast on even the best of days. He turned to run, but he knew very well that Raynard wouldn't have only one pistol, so as soon as he reached the street, Elmore raised Captain LeBeau's pistol and hopped on his good leg to turn back towards Raynard.

He was too slow. Even in his desperation, he just couldn't move well enough. There was no time to aim his shot as Raynard's second pistol was drawn and steady. Elmore fired, forcing Raynard to ground when the shot, gone wide, blew off a chunk of the wooden pier Raynard stood near. It would have been more of a surprise if Elmore had hit his mark. With his teeth gritted and desperation and fear helping him to fight against the pain, Elmore surged forward before Raynard could get to his feet, and he bashed his fist against the side of Raynard's head. Elmore was no weak man, and years of toil at his trade—lugging heavy wood, using a saw, and swinging a hammer—had given him respectable strength. Raynard went down in a flash. Elmore hoped he'd broken the dog's head. He took a look up to see Captain LeBeau getting to his feet on the slip, drenched and furious. With the chart clutched in his hand as preciously as a holy man might hold his rosary, Elmore started running as best as he could, moving through the city and the market like a mad man.

Despite his head start, he'd be caught any time with how slow his faltering run was. He needed an advantage. He needed power. The chart, so coveted by everyone, was the most powerful thing around, and Elmore needed to find a way to use it. To use it, he had to understand it. Sadly, Elmore knew as much about navigation as did a blind newt.

He stepped down on his weak leg, and the pain very suddenly spiked. He saw starbursts of light in front of his eyes, and his leg was no longer just paining him, but it felt weak, as if it would give way on him, despite his will to push on. He kept moving. His eyes burned with tears; he didn't dare let fall. On and on, he kept going, but he felt himself slowing down. He needed his walking stick, needed to reload the pistol, needed some advantage. Elmore's breath came faster as he kept moving, fighting to keep himself calm and clear-headed, fighting against fear and building panic.

Round a corner, he turned and nearly ran straight over little Mei. He stopped so abruptly to avoid hurting her that he nearly fell.

They stood outside the little house her grandfather had let. She looked up at Elmore with wide, surprised eyes as she held a large basket filled with so much fabric that it was almost bigger than she was. He grabbed Mei's arm and tugged her back inside her house. There, he closed the door and put his back against it. Then, panting for breath, suddenly so exhausted that he was shaking, his knee finally gave way and he collapsed on the floor.

He waited.

And waited.

No one tried to force the door. There was no furious yelling, no threats, or any other sign that his pursuers had found him. Elmore closed his eyes and took a deep breath. He held that breath for a moment before he finally opened his eyes. Little Mei sat on her knees next to him. Her basket of clothes had been set down, and she watched him with intense concern.

"Scared?"

Elmore managed a smile for the girl. "Nothing for you to worry about. Won't let you get hurt."

She lightly patted his knee. "Hurt?"

"I'll be right as rain, little bird." He wasn't sure he could walk with help. The pain was almost enough to make him sick. "Where's your grandfather, eh?"

She frowned and hesitated, and it seemed clear she was trying to think of the right words to use. "Grandfather went to the church to speak to … to …" She frowned again and put one finger to her nose, then pulled it away, as if she were running her finger over an immense, imaginary nose. It was almost enough to make Elmore laugh.

"That would be Reverend Roberts." And it was a good idea. He couldn't go to him at home, as Raynard was sure to go there, but he could go to Saint Peter's church. Reverend Roberts was as bright as any man could hope to be, and he'd surely have some idea of what to do. Elmore strained and fought to get himself to his feet, but, in the end, he only got there when Mei gave him a helping hand. He tried to put weight on his hurting leg, but it was so weak, he doubted he'd make to Saint Peter's, despite how close it was.

"I need a stick. Something to lean on." He looked at Mei. "Got something I can use? Anything?"

A broom was the only thing Mei had, but Elmore took it with gratitude. He gave her a pat on the head and took a careful look outside. When he saw no one suspicious, he took a deep breath and put a hand on the door, but before he could even open it, Mei slipped under his arm and smiled up at him.

"I will help."

Elmore was honestly touched. "That's good of you, little bird. But it's too dangerous." But even as he said it, Elmore scowled. If Raynard or his friends were out there, if they saw him leaving Mei's home, then it was possible that they might think he had some sort of weakness for little Mei and go after her to get to him. He looked again at her bright eyes looking up at him, and he couldn't leave her behind when she didn't even have her grandfather to protect her. Taking her to Saint Peter's was a far safer option. At least if she was with him and danger came upon them, he could tell her to run while he dealt with it.

"Look here, you got any weapons in the house? Something to ward off the enemy?"

She looked confused for a time, and he guessed she was trying to understand, but she rushed to one of the many boxes that had yet to be unpacked. After rummaging around it, she proudly brought back to him a kitchen knife. It wasn't what he'd hoped for, but a blade was a blade, and he tucked it into his belt. He took another look out the door.

"You see here," he told Mei. "Stay with me. If I tell you to run, you run. Understand?"

She nodded, and he hoped she really did understand.

Saint Peter's wasn't far, but the pain made it seem like it took hours to get there. He leaned heavily on both the broomstick and Mei's shoulder, all the while trying to watch everywhere around them because he knew Raynard, and he knew that Raynard wouldn't give up without a Hell of a fight.

Eventually, they arrived at the steps of Saint Peter's. Each step he climbed up to the door was agony, no easier than having a thousand needles being jammed into his knee. There were only half-a-dozen stone steps leading up to the heavy wooden door with its long iron hinges, and at every step Elmore cast a desperate glance over his shoulder to catch any glimpse of Raynard or the Frenchmen in pursuit.

Mei stepped forward and pulled open the door for Elmore. He shoved it quickly closed the minute Mei had walked in. He could feel his heart beating, and his breathing was harsh enough that he had to take a minute and lean his back against the door to get control of himself. He closed his eyes and worked to breathe easy, waited until his heart quieted. He couldn't remember the last time he'd had to move so quickly or with such a fire burning at his heels.

"Reverend! Reverend Roberts!" He shouted, pushing away from the door. He yelled again, as he made his way down the aisle between the two rows of empty pews, holding onto them to keep himself from falling, moving towards the raised pulpit. Mei followed at his feet, fretfully, her hands raised just a little, as if she thought she could catch him if he fell, and stayed there until, at the other end of the church's main room, the schoolroom's door opened and Reverend Roberts, followed by Mister Fa, came into the main church.

Elmore took his hand off Mei's shoulder and gave her a pat on the back, which encouraged her to go her grandfather.

"And it seems I have a walrus bellowing in here." Reverend Roberts gave him a sour look as he strode towards Elmore, walking away from Mister Fa and Mei who spoke quietly together. Reverend Roberts looked Elmore up and down before he took Elmore's arm. Those long, thin hands were surprisingly strong. "Sit down. Rest. I was having a meeting and, honestly, a knock on the door is rather more polite than such a din, don't you think?" He helped Elmore to sit on one of the pews, and the sudden relief almost made him want to cry. "What happened? You need a doctor."

"No time. I'm mighty sorry for this, but I'm in a hurry, you see? Reverend, my Jacob, he told me you'd once been a seaman. Any chance you might be able to read a chart?"

Reverend Roberts nodded, sharply. "Easily. I don't see how that can be considered an emergency, though."

"You just take my word on it, Reverend." Elmore gingerly stood and took the chart from his pocket. He spread the chart out on the seat of the pew he'd been sitting on. "Tell me what you make of this."

Reverend Roberts' curious look grew more intense the longer he studied the chart. His eyebrows drew together and his eyes widened. A frantic sort of glimmer flashed into his eyes. He didn't even appear to notice when Mei crept close enough to look down at the chart, or when she darted back to her grandfather's side at his call. Reverend Roberts took a deep, shuddering breath and closed his eyes. He put a hand over his eyes and rubbed them. When he was calm again, he looked at Elmore. "Where did you get this?"

"What is it?"

Reverend Roberts hesitated. "I would very much appreciate knowing why you have this and where you got it."

Elmore quickly told him the story, right from finding Gabe and Raynard in his shop to escaping Captain LeBeau and stealing the chart back from Raynard. There was no reason not to tell, and if he didn't, Elmore believed that Reverend Roberts might get stubborn just to get the information he wanted.

Reverend Roberts stared at the chart as Elmore spoke and, after Elmore had finished, he continued staring. "You do realize that you were likely followed here, don't you?"

"I didn't see anyone."

"Doesn't matter. Are you armed?"

Elmore patted the knife Mei had given him. "All else that I had was taken."

Reverend Roberts muttered a word that was more in fitting with his past as a seaman rather than the holy life he currently led. "I must have a pistol around here you can have. This is a very valuable treasure map."

"Treasure? What manner?"

Reverend Roberts looked up with a delighted smile that seemed out of place on his dour face. "A paper treasure that's far more valuable than gold or rubies or coffee. It's speed. Here. See, here?" He pointed to a line on the chart. "This is the Gulf Stream. Nearly every ship uses it to go from the West Indies to Europe. It cuts weeks off the journey. This," he moved his finger to another line. "Is a similar stream, but going from Brazil to Jamaica, then to France and down to Africa."

It was staggering. "That's ... that's not possible. Someone would have found it before now."

"Why? Everything has to be discovered sometime. This is its time. It's a priceless parchment you've run across. If it works. What do you think greedy merchants or ambitious governments would do for this?"

"I think one man might be murdered and another might be hung for a crime he had no hand in. How much time would this cut off a journey, do you think?"

Reverend Roberts considered. "If a ship were to sail from Brazil with gold to France, then to Africa to get slaves to bring back to the plantations ... I think it could be done saving at least a month, if whoever drew this chart knew what he was doing, anyway. I can read the map, but the words," he ran a finger over the symbols on the paper, "I have never seen the like. It's not Latin or Greek. Not Russian, either. The chart is priceless by itself, but if we could read the words we would know more, perhaps exactly how fast this route is. No wonder someone's died for this. Imagine! If one country could keep this secret, they could run back and forth across the sea while others are only half-done with a single trip. This paper is worth more than an entire, full Spanish treasure galleon." He paused and his nostrils flared. "Be careful. There's blood on this." He rolled up the chart and handed it back to Elmore. "I don't doubt there will be more before this business is done."

Mister Fa reached out and put a hand on Elmore's arm. He held himself very stiffly and his mouth was tight. "May I look at it?"

Elmore obligingly laid out the chart on the church pew, again, and let Mister Fa take a gander at. He said nothing while Mister Fa stared at the chart for a good long while, not even when the old man's eyes grew misty.

"My grandson drew this."

Elmore exchanged a look with Reverend Roberts. "What?"

"This is his art. His sign." He pointed a narrow finger to a small mark on the bottom right corner of the chart. "That is my grandson's name." He swallowed, hard. "This is what he must have meant when he told me that he would make his fortune in this part of the world. He had planned to gain great wealth from this."

The whole church seemed unnaturally quiet, too still. Elmore rubbed a hand across his forehead and felt his heart bleed when Mei clutched at her grandfather's arm and stared intently at the chart. The pain for them only grew when Mister Fa turned his face away as he obviously tried to hide how teary his eyes grew.

Bingbang had been killed for that chart. Elmore had no doubt. How tragic. He'd found something so valuable, had thought he'd be able to provide for his small family for the rest of his life, and it all ended in one of Elmore's coffins. If Fa Bingbang had been hoping to get rich by selling his chart, he'd have had to go showing it to people who might buy it. Clearly, someone had wanted it, but not enough to pay for it. That poor lad Elmore had helped laid to rest ... dead for a piece of paper.

Elmore took the chart back from Mister Fa and politely ignored the man's upset when he went to comfort Mei.

Reverend Roberts asked, "What are you going to do with it? Do you have a plan?"

Elmore shook his head. "I don't rightly know what to do with this wretched thing. I want to be rid of it. I want to have never seen it! It strikes me that there should be a way to use it that would keep everyone safe, but I can't think how. If you're right about what it is, I can't just burn it. They'll be that angry, I'll get killed. Can't give it to them; they'd already tried to take me away."

"You could give it to the governor."

"That would leave me in the same boat as now. That Captain LeBeau wants me a prisoner in France, so I can't tell what I saw. I got no reason to think Governor Modyford wouldn't do the same and keep me under guard here, in my own home."

Reverend Roberts made a peevish face. "Yes, and now you've put me in that same position. How can I ever thank you?" He rubbed a hand over his face and shrugged. "No use bemoaning what's done. Your knee's bothering you, again, isn't it? You're pale as sea froth." Reverend Roberts put a hand on Elmore's arm in a rare show of concern. "Won't you sit?"

He would have loved a rest, but his knee hurt so badly he thought he might not be able to get up if he sat again. He wanted a week or so of rest after such a day and, without thinking much of it, rubbed his knee. "I'm not pale. I just need my breath back. I just need to think."

"And I think," Mister Fa put both hands on Elmore's shoulders and pushed. It was a gentle push, to be sure, but Elmore's knee couldn't take it and he toppled onto the pew, beside the chart. "You need attention. You expect to do any good by crippling yourself?"

"I'm already—"

"Exhausted. Now be still." Mister Fa knelt in front of Elmore and put both hands on the tender knee. "This injury is old?"

"Years old, now. Just leave it be." He gave Mister Fa a pat on the shoulder. "You look after yourself and your girl."

"Give me some chore to occupy my mind." His eyes were dark, imploring. "Please. At my home there is a syrup that will do wonders to dull your pain. If you wish it, I will be happy to bring it here as thanks for your kindness to us." He looked at the chart. "I don't know why Bingbang was involved in people who would kill for a map he made, but even to see him name upon his work one more time is a gift I can't explain."

It seemed altogether wrong to make a man work when he was grieving, when he had a little child to care for, in a new land where they were alone and near penniless. On top of that, it wasn't as if Elmore had time to be lounging around like he was some sort of lord at his leisure. But the helplessness so clear and open on Mister Fa's face was too familiar. How Elmore hated being helpless! So he told Mister Fa, "Damnation, man! I'd take a hammer to the head about now if I thought it would take me away from this ache! You go fetch whatever it is you have, and I'll build you a dozen more boxes free of cost!"

He waited until Mister Fa and Mei left before he said to Reverend Roberts, "If this all ends up poorly, I'll be needing you to look after Jacob. If I … go missing and Gabe does get hung, I need someone to do right by the boy, and there's no one I'd trust more than you. He speaks highly of you, and I'd guess that means a lot. In the wall of Jacob's room, there's a treasure. Everything I've been able to save for years. It's all for Jacob. I want him to go to school and make something of himself."

Reverend Roberts nodded. "I understand, but let's not dwell on that over much. Let's find a plan to keep you from going missing. You can't just run."

"First thing's first: I've got to get Gabe out of the Hold. Then, maybe ... a ... a copy. Yes. Yes! You can write, can't you?"

"I taught Jacob to read, didn't I? It's a fair assumption that I can both read and write."

"You think you can draw a map? A copy of this?"

Reverend Roberts looked speculatively at the chart. "No. This would take days to do properly. All the art—"

"I don't need it fancy, just the information. A rough chart with the longitudes and latitudes."

"I have someone who may be able to do a quick, credible job. I can do the writing. What's your idea?"

"Safety. I think if I tell them that I made a copy and hid it with someone with orders that if I disappear they were to give it to the governor, then there won't be any point in taking me. With luck, they'll go on their way. I'll find some way to thank the church. I'll sell my soul, if need be."

Reverend Roberts glared. He shook the rolled-up chart at Elmore. "You mind your words!" His dark eyes flashed. "Don't risk your immortal soul so carelessly! Have you no fear? It's all you are, and God owns it. You risk everything for this!" He shook the chart, again.

"Enough! Reverend, it were just a manner of speaking. And I don't know that God hasn't got more troubles to worry him than my poor words."

The church's door slammed open and Mei, with panicked eyes, dashed in, not bothering to close the door behind her. She ran straight to Elmore and took his arm, babbling at him and tugging on his sleeve.

"Here, now! What's all this?" Elmore had never thought of himself as a soft touch, but the girl had tears in her eyes and spoke with such desperation that he put his big hand on the top of her head and softened his voice. "Easy, little bird. Take it calmly."

"Come!" The word burst out of Mei as she ignored Elmore's soothing attempts. "Come! Come quick! Jacob!"

That was enough for both Elmore and Reverend Roberts. Mei led the way with Reverend Roberts just behind and Elmore in the rear, but when they reached the doorway of Saint Peter's Reverend Roberts stopped, blocking the open doorway and forcing Elmore to a stop.

"Elmore, keep your temper." It was said so coolly, so completely devoid of emotion, that Elmore felt his throat tighten as he stared at Reverend Roberts' back. "I'm going to move aside for you, but you keep in mind that you're a gentleman and need to be in control." All the time that he spoke he didn't turn to look at Elmore and his even tone didn't change a bit, despite the obvious stiffness of his neck and that Mei was openly crying.

"Move yourself, man."

Reverend Roberts stepped aside, his hand on Mei's shoulder to take her out of the way. At the bottom of the steps leading up to Saint Peter's, Mister Fa stood staring across the street. What Elmore saw when he followed Mister Fa's line of sight was enough to make his blood roll to a boil.

Across the street, Jacob stood with Raynard. Raynard had one hand clamped on Jacob's arm while his other hand rested under his coat. Raynard's eyes were colder than anything Elmore had ever seen, but it was the sight of Jacob that made Elmore's head feel light. The boy didn't stand up straight. His sullen face was bruised, and one of his eyes was red and swelling.

Beaten.

That crab!

That pus-filled sore!

He's beaten Jacob!

Elmore started across the street, and with each step, the anger he'd felt before churned into hate, churning and bubbling until he felt he might erupt. He was aware of Raynard at Jacob's side, but he couldn't take his eyes from Jacob.

Good boy, Elmore thought. While Jacob had been roughed

up, he hadn't been broken. His hands were balled into fists and his face was set in a defiant scowl, ready to fight at the first chance.

"That's far enough," Raynard moved his hidden hand and Jacob jumped. Raynard pulled his hand a little out of his jacket, just enough for Elmore to see the pistol he held against Jacob's ribs. "Just you stay out of arm's reach. The boy has been good company, but he's maybe not feeling quite himself. What say we leave him to get to his bed and you and I take a walk?"

"Enough of that nonsense." Elmore held up the chart and his grand scheme to save himself vanished like morning mist. "You take that grimy hook off my boy."

Raynard smirked and told Jacob to take the chart. Jacob did it without a word and handed it over to Raynard. "Stay where you stand, boy, or I'll blast a hole the size of your fist into your uncle." He took his hand from Jacob's arm and took the chart. Despite the threat, he kept his pistol trained on Jacob as he took a look at the chart. After a moment, he rolled up the chart and looked behind Elmore at Reverend Roberts. "Did you show him?"

"What would the good reverend want with something like that?" When Raynard didn't seem convinced, Elmore went on, "A nobody like me disappearing won't raise anything more than eyebrows, but a man of the cloth vanishing right from his church will cause a right uproar. They find out he were taken aboard a French ship, and you'll have a pack in full sail at your back. I don't hardly think your Captain LeBeau would take kindly to that. Asides all that, I don't think any seaman wants the bad fortune of offending God Almighty by putting hands on his holy man."

Raynard, a devout Catholic, was convinced by the last argument. He shook his pistol at Jacob. "Go on, lad. Say your goodbyes."

Jacob went to Elmore without hesitation. "What's going on? Where are you going?"

"Never you mind." He took Jacob by the shoulders and looked right in the boy's eyes. "You go to the good reverend; he'll give you a bed 'til I come for you. Then," Elmore paused.

Jacob took hold of Elmore's arms, tightening his fingers, as if to hold him there.

Elmore continued, "You find Lieutenant Bowe and have him talk to the Widow Brandwhite, again, and with Isadora Ratman at the Blacksmith's shop on Mayberry. It's for your da. Think you can remember?"

"Yes, sir."

"Then go on, now. Don't you argue!" He snapped the last when Jacob opened his mouth. "You backtalk me and I'll give you such a lickin'!"

Jacob closed his mouth and let go of Elmore's arms. He nodded and silently went to Reverend Roberts.

"Get walking," Raynard said. He roughly prodded Elmore in the back with the barrel of his pistol. "You know the way."

They walked to the French ship with Elmore leading the way, and Raynard behind. There wasn't another chance for escape. They didn't go by the *Indigo Running,* so there wasn't even the faint hope that one of Raynard's crewmates would call out to him. Even if there had been a distraction that would have given Elmore a chance to run, he could only imagine Raynard going to find Jacob, again. He couldn't let that happen.

Aboard the French ship, Elmore was taken immediately below deck and locked in the brig. When the heavy wooden door was locked behind him and the footsteps of the sailors who'd escorted him down faded into nothing, Elmore knew he was alone.

He went to a corner and leaned against the wall. There was nowhere to sit. His leg hurt so much.

He'd never set foot in his shop, again.

Never see Gabe.

Never see Jacob.

A ripping, burning pain tore at his chest. So many nevers. He hung his head and closed his eyes. The darkness was a pinch of comfort. He wished Gabe had never set eyes on that cursed spyglass, or that he'd sold it at Tortuga, or just tossed it away into the sea. He wished that anything had happened, so long as it would have kept that damned thing away from his family.

The ship lurched. A great many shouts went up, and Elmore, still hiding his face, desperately tried not to fall to pieces.

CHAPTER 14: CHOICE

When the door closed behind Mister Finch, Jeremiah stared at it for a long moment, his heart racing painfully. He panted hard and his heart pounded against his ribs like the hoofbeats of a horse. The fear was like a spike in his gut. He couldn't breathe.

He wanted to run.

He's gonna tell. Word will spread. Everyone will know. Stupid! How stupid!

Jeremiah wasn't ashamed of his faith, but he was afraid. Afraid of everything he would lose if Mister Finch let his secret be known. Everything. He would lose everything. His throat clenched shut and he had to force himself to take a breath. He waited and listened. The silence was oppressive; a weight that made the blood rush in his ears.

Should have known. Damned well should have known it was all bound to come out sooner or later.

There was no yelling from the main floor below. No furious landlord barging in, demanding that Jeremiah leave his respectable establishment and no crashing of soldiers rushing to take him to prison. It was more than he'd expected. Still, he couldn't relax and became so tense with the waiting that he doubted he'd be able to move when the danger did come. But, it didn't come at all.

Minutes passed. Nothing happened. Jeremiah let out a breath. He slowly breathed in. When enough time had passed that Jeremiah was fairly certain Mister Finch had said nothing—at least for the moment—his eyes traveled from the closed doors to the circle he'd drawn so carefully on the floor, the candles he'd smilingly borrowed from the good lady wife of the landlord, and the scrap of fabric, the cloth he'd torn from that insulting, drunken dog during their short scrap at *The Blue Dog*.

In that moment, with the heat of his fury having been washed away by the fear of being caught, his mind felt clear for the first time since the brawl. Regret flooded through Jeremiah. He hadn't really thought before, he'd just acted, just wanted to punish the swine who'd insulted his parents. To see all his tools laid out before him ... guilt swamped him. It settled uncomfortably in his stomach, a swirling sort of sickness like the writhing of an angry serpent. "Oh ... mama." The words came out in an awful moan. "What have I done?"

He'd meant such harm to that pig; he'd wanted that dog to forever regret ever mentioning Jeremiah's parents. While wanting something was no great sin, he had acted upon that want. In his rage, he had set up the whole ceremony, and he'd come so close to ... He could feel his mother's disapproval and shame from even beyond life. How horrified she would have been if she'd known that he'd even thought about casting so black a spell for vengeance!

***

She sat by the river, singing with words he didn't understand but loved all the same. Her long hair was undone, not proper, but beautiful as it tumbled down her back. He was so proud to sit at her side, to lean his head against her warm arm with his feet dangling in the water. Her fingers carded through his hair and she smiled down at him even as she sang.

***

With the memory of his mother so fresh in his mind that he could almost swear that he heard her singing in that same room, Jeremiah slowly sat up. She wasn't there, of course. She'd been long in the grave, since just after his twelfth birthday, but throughout the years he'd often felt her eyes lingering on him or, as he teetered on the edge of sleep, her hand touching his face. What would she have thought to see him as he was? He picked up the damning cloth he'd taken from the drunkard and held it to one of the candle flames, burning it until there was nothing left but harmless ash. The fabric was gone and could never do that stupid drunk any harm, and the star on the floor was only chalk. A swipe of his hand made that powerless, too.

The power was never to be used to harm.

***

"It will come back to you," Mother warned, staring at him even as she lit the candles. *"Everything is connected, tied together so tightly that it will never come unstrung. Which means that everything you do to someone else is, ultimately, also done to yourself. The power you use must never be used to harm. That is the rule. The most important rule of all—never harm."*

***

He'd never meant to disobey, but anger and pride had robbed him of his sense. *And now we have to deal with the result of that theft.* Because it wasn't just him who had to deal with the situation, but Mister Finch, also.

He extinguished the candles one at a time and, with the faint trails of smoke snaking upward from the blackened wicks, he set them aside and started to wipe away the star. Water from the washbasin and his handkerchief had mopped about half the star away before a knock on the door made Jeremiah jump. On his hands and knees on the floor, he froze, and then turned his head to look at the door.

"Lieutenant Bowe? Are you coming down for dinner?" The landlady's soft, motherly voice came through the door. "Is everything alright in there?"

"Yes." He slid one foot back just far enough to rest it against the door to prevent it from opening. He'd been surprised by one visitor; he wouldn't be surprised again. "Everything's just fine. I'll be down shortly, missus."

"As you will." She didn't sound entirely convinced. "Your friend left in a mighty rush. Didn't even stop for tea or a chat."

That awful sickness eased, if only by a scanty amount. He almost cried. "Ah. He had business that needed to be dealt with." For all the obvious hurry he'd been in to get away from Jeremiah, Mister Finch hadn't been hurrying to spread around what he'd seen Jeremiah so close to doing. Not that it would matter whether he'd actually done it or not. The mere fact that he'd started to do such a thing would mean the end of him, if Mister Finch decided to turn him in. His career would be over, as would his life, most likely. Everything, right down to his good name, would be ruined.

His life depended on secrecy and without it, he had nothing. His mother had taught him that lesson long before she'd begun the songs and stories that had taught him the ways of the world as it should be. He could never regret those lessons—how could he regret knowing the truth?—but it often felt like the heaviest of burdens, the lie he lived.

Still, he would live it and go on. He wouldn't run. There was too much he needed to do in Port Royal, far too much to be thrown away because of fear of what might happen.

Jeremiah listened to her footsteps as the landlady walked away and slowly drew his foot away from the door. Another two wipes across the floor with his handkerchief, and the star was gone.

***

It was less than an hour later that Jeremiah, dressed in his uniform with freshly polished boots, made his way to the soldier's barracks to report in with his superior. The people of Port Royal watched him as he went through the streets, but that was no new thing. He was a soldier, and there were few people —good or otherwise—who welcomed the sight of a soldier. That day, however, he was acutely uncomfortable with all the attention. The looks that he found drawn to him were nothing more than inquisitive or curious, but the fear from earlier made him self-conscious, and it seemed to him that every pair of eyes that turned to look even momentarily at him were those of an enemy, a spy who knew, who had somehow guessed his secret.

He'd seen people who practiced Vandou hung just as readily as any confessed murderer and he was fairly certain that his mother's faith wouldn't be seen in any kinder regard if it were to become known to the people of Port Royal. He still remembered the awful stories his mother had used to warn him into silence when he'd been a child and hadn't understood why he couldn't tell his playmates about the stories and songs his mother had taught him. But, then, he had been young enough that he hadn't understood why his grandfather would have nothing to do with him or why his grandmother cried the first and only time he'd ever met her.

At the barracks, Jeremiah found his thoughts pulled away from the past when he saw Captain Patner in the doorway of the barracks talking to a young boy. He didn't realize until he was almost upon them that the boy was Jacob Scratch. Jacob's skinny arms were tense at his sides and his hands balled into fists, as if he would punch Captain Patner, who stood over him rather like a Great Dane looming over an enraged house cat.

"Sir! Please!" Jacob's nearly wailing voice was easily heard even before Jeremiah came to a stop right behind the boy. "If he's not here, can't you just tell me where he is?"

"Easily now that I know, myself." Captain Patner gestured over Jacob's shoulder. "He's standing at your back."

Jacob whipped around, and Jeremiah was taken aback by the bruised and bloodied face in front of him. He felt a deep stirring of something dark and burning. "Whatever happened to you, lad?"

"Nothing. It's nothing. I need some help with Uncle. Can you come? He's drunk as a fish, yelling and throwing things."

"Easy, now." Captain Patner patted Jacob's shoulder with one of his huge hands. "Is that all this is about? Just you let him work it out of his blood. He do this to you?" He took hold of Jacob's chin and tilted his face upwards so he could get a better look at the pitiful looking injuries. "Threw you around a bit, did he?"

Jacob nodded as much as he could, considering that Captain Patner didn't release his face. "Yes, but he knows the lieutenant. I think he might calm down if Officer Bowe talks to him. Uncle really respects him."

Captain Patner frowned at Jeremiah. "Got children of my own. I can't abide a man who'd do this to his own flesh and blood." Captain Patner gently told Jacob, "Just take yourself for a walk. Go fishing for a few hours. Best thing to do is get yourself out of harm's way and let him calm himself down."

"But he might hurt himself or someone else. He does get awful angry after a few. I don't want him to get in trouble. Please?"

After a few minutes of consideration and a fatherly pat on the shoulder, Captain Patner nodded. "As you like, then. Lieutenant, go see if you can talk some sense into the man. If he won't listen to sense, then let him sit out his rage in a cell." He smiled genially down at Jacob. "That would be safest for everyone, I think."

Jeremiah waited until Captain Patner had gone back into the barracks and he was alone with Jacob before he narrowed his eyes at the boy. "Your uncle doesn't drink."

Jacob rolled his eyes and started walking. "'Course he doesn't. Come on!" He walked with a limp, favoring his left foot, and with one arm held against his stomach. "Uncle told me to get you. He said you're supposed to talk to the Widow Brandwhite and Isadora Ratman at the Blacksmith's shop on Mayberry. He said it's for Da, but we've got to hurry. There's no time!"

"Then we go." Jeremiah quickened his pace, but stopped when Jacob, who'd tried to keep up, was breathing too hard. "Your uncle never beat you."

"He'd never hurt me."

"Then who did?"

Jacob told him all that had happened in the past afternoon. He told Jeremiah about going home after his lessons and finding the stranger outside the front door. The man had introduced himself as Raynard Passy, a friend of his da's. Raynard had battered him, right in broad daylight on the doorstep, demanding to know where his Uncle Elmore was. Jacob had kept his peace. Proudly, he held up his chin when he'd told Jeremiah how he'd kept silent while being thrashed. His efforts had been futile, in the end. Raynard had known how often Jacob went to the church and had simply dragged him there. "He said Da talked about Uncle Elmore aboard ship. They must be mates. Reverend Roberts followed him after he took Uncle Elmore away and sent me to find you to give you uncle's message."

"Why didn't you want to say any of this in front of Captain Patner?"

Jacob gave him a scathing look. "I'm not stupid. They all think Da's guilty. I come up and ask for help for him, and I'll be chased away with a boot to the rump!"

It was a good point.

It was also a good point that Jeremiah couldn't help but linger his mind on the fact that if Mister Finch were no longer about, whether he was being held captive somewhere or dead, it would mean a good deal less worry for Jeremiah. It was a horrible, evil thought that made his insides squirm, but he couldn't deny the appeal. Like some insidious creeping vine worming its way through his mind, the thought of just ignoring the boy grew until it was nearly overwhelming. It was a dark idea, and surely doing nothing would have been as wicked and vile as if he'd put a knife in Mister Scratch's chest with his own hand. There was so much good he could do in Port Royal, so many plans he was determined to see through to the end. He hadn't a single doubt that he could accomplish all of his goals —he would make Port Royal a city without rival. It would still be the grand commerce center that it was, but it would be safer. Laws would be enforced and no one, no matter who they were, would fear walking down any street in the city. He knew it could be done, but if he were forced to run from Port Royal, then all of his grand plans would end up as nothing but dreams.

His plans aside, it all came down to a choice—to save himself or Mister Finch. Was Mister Finch's life worth more than the welfare of Port Royal?

"Jacob, tell me about your uncle."

"What about him?"

"Anything. I've only known him for a few days."

"He's wonderful." Jacob fell silent and kept walking, quite

clearly believing that he'd said all he needed to say on the matter.

"How did you come to live with him? I suppose your father can't be around much, but what about your mother?"

Jacob's step faltered only once and he kept his chin high. "Ma died a few years back. Some sickness that made her weak before it took her. I went to live with Uncle Elmore after that." He shot a cold look at Jeremiah over his shoulder. "The doctor said there wasn't anything to be done to save her, no medicine could cure what she'd had, so don't you go saying it was Da's fault and that he should have been there to help her."

"I wouldn't think such a thing. So, Mister Finch is good to you?"

"Very. Uncle Elmore taught me to ride a horse and how to use a pistol." He grinned a little. "Da thinks I don't know how to use one, yet, but Uncle Elmore said it was important. He's taught me some of his trade and he wants to send me to a really good school."

"So you were lucky to have your uncle take you in. Did Mrs. Scratch have no family to help you out?"

Jacob's shoulders went stiff. "Ma's name was Miss Tanner."

"Ah. My mother and father didn't share a name, either."

No doubt shocked to hear such a confession so easily blurted out, Jacob gave Jeremiah a guarded look, as if he didn't quite believe the calm smile aimed at him. "Ma loved Da. She talked about him all the time and she was so happy every time he came to visit."

How often had Jacob faced censorship because he was a bastard, Jeremiah wondered. Perhaps the contempt he'd felt from everyone around him was the reason why he was so devoted to his uncle—if Mister Finch had been one of the very few who'd treated him with kindness, then it was no surprise that Jacob would regard him so highly. Jeremiah told Jacob, "Just because they haven't stood up before a holy man, doesn't make two folks love any less and it doesn't mean that their love is of no value in the eyes of any god. I can't see that you've got anything to be ashamed of."

"And I'm not." Jacob did hold himself a little straighter, though, and a smile tugged at his mouth. "I'm happy to be here, but ma took great care of me in Plymouth, too. She'd have done anything for me."

"You grew up in Plymouth? In the colonies?"

"Right near the sea. I used to watch the flags of the ships every morning when they'd come into or leave the harbor. Where did you grow up?"

"In a forest far from Plymouth. So, why did your uncle take you in instead of your father? He was very protective of you."

"Da had to go back to his ship. I didn't want to leave him, but," he shrugged, "that's how life is. Uncle Elmore had been hurt in an accident, and he was in an awful lot of pain, so much that he really couldn't work with Da anymore. He came to live here, and we see Da whenever we can. Uncle Elmore would do anything for me. He's really smart, too and he can cook like the best chef!"

There was such love and admiration in the boy's voice when he spoke of his uncle. How could Elmore doubt Mister Finch's worth?

"I'll do everything I can to help your uncle."

"And my da?"

"I'll do what I can for him, too."

"Then stop talking and walk!" Jacob frowned at Jeremiah. "Can't you move faster?"

Jeremiah found himself looking into the boy's expectant gaze and knew that he was trusted. Jacob, for whatever reason, entirely believed that Jeremiah would help him and would set all to right. That, and how highly Jacob thought of Mister Finch, caused the evil temptation brewing within him to be fully pushed aside. No child, he believed, would love someone so devotedly without good reason. His choice made, he smiled at Jacob, completely at ease. "I can move fast as the wind. Let's see if you can keep up with me. No time to waste."

They went first to the Widow Brandwhite, who offered tea and cakes as she repeated what she'd told Elmore earlier. Isadora

Ratman gave her tale, also, and Jeremiah left her home with a bubble of excitement in his chest. While a lawyer might argue that Miss Ratman was of poor moral character and therefore unreliable, there was no reason to doubt the testimony of the Widow Brandwhite. It was good enough for Jeremiah to go to Governor Modyford, and that was straight away where they went.

They stood outside the governor's office and took a moment to straighten his uniform. Government House was, as should be expected, the richest home in Jamaica. Three stories tall, with rooms filled with plush rugs, portraits, and fine pottery, the house had been home to governors since well before Port Royal had even been Port Royal.

Someday, Jeremiah was adamant, it would be his home.

"Remember to stand up tall. Don't fidget or speak unless he speaks to you." Jeremiah used his fingers to comb out Jacob's hair as neatly as was possible. "This shouldn't take long."

Jacob glanced at one of the soldiers posted in the hall and whispered, "Are you sure he's going to let Da go? Da says you can't trust government types."

"I am possibly in the wrong profession to offer an opinion about that. As for releasing your father, we have strong evidence. We just need to present it." But even as he said it, Jeremiah knew that the outcome wasn't entirely certain. Governor Modyford could choose to ignore the evidence. He was governor, and there was no higher authority in all of Jamaica unless the king himself came to visit, and that was about as likely as a man flying to the moon. Despite what could go wrong, Jeremiah smiled for Jacob's sake. After all, there was always hope.

The door of the governor's office opened and a guard stepped out. "His Excellency will see you, now, lieutenant." Even as he said it, though, he closed the office door behind him and moved closer to Bowe. "Something we should know about? The captain didn't say there was any trouble."

"And there isn't. A friend of mine is in some trouble, and

I'm just doing what I can to help. You have my thanks for getting word to the governor for me, Hans."

"As you said, no trouble; just helping a friend. What good is it to have a friend doing duty as the governor's guard if he can't slip you in? Speak quick, though. He's in a foul temper." He gave Bowe a companionable slap on the arm, then stepped out of the way so that Bowe and Jacob could pass. As Jacob made to step by him, though, he put a hand on Jacob's shoulder and stopped him. "Are you sure you want to take the boy in?"

Jacob shot a fierce look at Bowe, as if daring him to leave him behind.

"I think he'll be fine. He's a well-behaved boy."

Jacob grumbled, "I'm not a puppy."

Bowe chuckled. "Let's go. It doesn't do to keep such a man waiting."

Governor Sir Thomas Modyford was as thin and gaunt as a starving scarecrow. For his position, he should have had enough rich foods to give him a respectable gut and at least one extra chin. "Good day. Won't you sit?" He smiled at them, but it was an empty smile, nothing but manners. His eyes were small and set close together, but bright and sharp. He looked from Jeremiah to Jacob, curious but patient.

Jeremiah sat in the chair in front of the governor's desk while Jacob stood behind the chair. The governor listened silently, always smiling, while Jeremiah told what he'd learned and when Jacob told what he knew.

"And the good reverend followed Mister Finch to the ship where he'd been taken?"

"So I have been told, your Excellency, but, much as I would have liked to go after him, we were more concerned about getting Mister Scratch away from the hangman's noose than retrieving Mister Finch. That was Mister Finch's priority."

Governor Modyford tapped his right index finger on his desk before giving a decisive nod. "And it's what he will get; Mister Scratch must be freed. Justice will prevail." He took blank paper from his desk and dipped his quill into his ink pot. "Give this order to the prisoner commander. Mister Scratch will be released." He used wax to seal the note and handed it across the table to Jeremiah. "That done, we can concentrate on the more urgent matter." He leaned forward with his hands folded on top of his desk. "I want that chart. Considering how very desperately it is wanted, I expect it to be of some value."

Jeremiah could only nod in agreement. "Your Excellency, whatever is on that chart must be of great value. From what I have seen, it is valued more than life by some."

"Yes, and I want to know why. I want to know what is on that chart. Bring it to me."

"Your Excellency, I will do all in my power to bring it directly to your hand." And, if there was any justice in the world, Jeremiah would get enough of a reward to buy a higher commission.

CHAPTER 15: SHOT AND CLUBBED

In the darkness of the Hold, Jacob followed closely behind Jeremiah, nearly walking on his heels. Jeremiah could understand the boy's wide-eyed look of fear as they made their way down the narrow passage between the two rows of cells. There were angry, hungry eyes glaring out at them from the tiny windows in the cell doors, eyes that were plenty vicious enough to frighten grown men. The faint light that was available from the lantern Jeremiah carried cast shadows that made everything, even empty corners, seem sinister. They passed one cell with no one looking out at them, but the sound of soul-deep weeping poured out into the hall and a woman's skinny arm stuck out of the door's window, her hand limp and pale.

"Look et the pretty darling visitin'!" One gap-toothed man laughed with his face pressed into the window of his cell as he leered at Jacob. "Come on, puppy. Wee little puppy. Give us a smile."

Jeremiah put a hand on the back of Jacob's neck and pulled him up to walk closer next to him. "Don't look at him. Just walk and stay with me. You're safe."

The inmate started cackling. "Puppy's got a dog sniffing his rear! Won't let any other dogs near!"

With a roll of his eyes, Jeremiah tugged Jacob along until they came to stand at the door of Mister Scratch's cell. A look into the cell showed that Mister Scratch lay on his back on a bench and when he saw Jeremiah, he turned his face away, but that only lasted until Jacob stood on his toes and was just able to peek into the little window and called out, "Da?"

At that, Mister Scratch whipped his head back around and sat up, lightning quick. "Jacob!"

He rushed to the door and pounded on it, swearing at Jeremiah for no particular reason until Jeremiah unlocked and opened the door. Mister Scratch grabbed the boy, pulling him in for a tight hug. Neither seemed willing to release the other for a good long while, but at last, they separated. There was a brief moment of babbling between the two before Mister Scratch suddenly stopped talking and looked hard at Jacob. He put a rough hand on Jacob's bruised cheek. "Lord, boy! You went and got kicked in the head by a horse?" Then he scowled blackly at Jeremiah. "And where's Elmore? I told him to bring the boy, but I thought he might show up, too—not send some lobster in his place."

"He's unavailable. Frankly, I'd have left the boy outside if I wasn't afraid that whoever had done this to him might still be lurking about. He wasn't kicked by a horse." Jeremiah took a deep breath. "I am sorry that your reunion can't be more pleasant, but there is need to hurry. Mister Finch—"

Jacob pushed away from his da's embrace and looked up at him with frantic eyes. "Uncle got kidnapped!"

"What?"

"For that spyglass you brought home, I think. That Frenchman friend of yours kept asking for it. He thought I had it."

"Wait just a minute! Frenchman friend? You mean Raynard? No."

"I'm not lying! That's what Uncle called him. He wanted the spyglass so much that I didn't think he ought to have it." Jacob touched his swollen, purple eye. "He wasn't very happy. He was that set on getting it, he said he'd kill me if Uncle didn't give it to him, but Uncle did, and he still got taken away and he's on a ship, and if we don't save him we'll never see him again! They might kill him. They might have already killed him!"

Mister Scratch closed his eyes and went very still. "And why might you be here, soldier? Come to give me one last cheery thought afore I swing? Let me die knowing my friend's going to die or worse? Let me know that my son's to be orphaned and alone? Did your damned men even try to stop that French ship afore it sailed?"

"I don't have any damned men, Mister Scratch, and I'm here because I have come directly from Government House where I received orders to pursue the French ship. The only reason I'm here and not heading straight for them is that I wanted to give the release papers to the jailers before you were hung. You may thank Mister Finch when we retrieve him, as he is the one who found witnesses to prove you couldn't have murdered Officer Passy. The governor has ordered your release." He made a sweeping gesture towards the hall. "You're a free man. Now that I've delivered the orders, I will see to Mister Finch." He smiled, brightly. "It seemed sensible to make a brief stop here to save your life first, as the Hold is between Government House and the docks and really took no extra time."

Mister Scratch took a deep breath before he nodded and looked at Jeremiah. "Right. Right, then."

They left the prison quickly. The sunlight made Mister Scratch wince and rub his eyes as they walked. He was filthy and smelled worse than he looked, but he paid his own condition no mind. As soon as they were on the street, Mister Scratch told Jacob to go home. Predictably, Jacob objected and said he wanted to help and he wasn't afraid of Raynard.

"Not for a shipload of gold. Off with you." When Jacob opened his mouth, Mister Scratch held up both hands to silence him. "Don't you even think to argue. Not about this, not now! I won't have you stickin' your nose in with this lot." Then his voice softened. "You have my word on it—I'll bring your uncle home."

Jacob clearly wasn't happy with it, but he nodded, obediently. "Tell Uncle Elmore that I'll be at Saint Peter's." He left then, walking away without another word.

Jeremiah had to move fast to keep up with Mister Scratch as he nearly ran through the streets to the harbor. As he moved, he cast a sour look at Jeremiah. "Where are you going?"

"To the docks, of course. Before I set out to sea, is there any chance that, as the kidnapper is one of your shipmates, he might have gone back to your ship?"

"All things are possible, but I wouldn't bet on it. After all that scheming and turning against a mate? No, he'll be with the French, and I'll be getting shipmates to help hunt him down. When I catch him, he'll regret ever seeing the light o' day." His anger was terrible, making his lips draw back from his teeth and his nostrils flare. Mister Scratch shook his head without slowing his pace. "I'll see that dirty frog keelhauled! He'll regret this. Mark me, I'll gut him with me bare hands! And I don't need your help to do it. If Elmore's going to be got, I'll do the getting. I brought Passy to Elmore's home. I brought the spyglass to him. I *will* fix this!"

"Do you doubt? That we can save him, I mean."

"Passy fancies himself a gentleman, but I've sailed with him a good long while and I know what he's done out at sea. None of those bloody deeds trouble his sleep. But had you asked me an hour ago, I'd not have pegged him as a traitor. I'd have sooner thought me own mind had slipped."

"Why would you be a friend of someone like that?"

Mister Scratch didn't look at him as they walked. "That kinda life don't make a saint of any man. I've sins on my own soul, a great many I'm not proud of. I've got no right to judge any man. But he had to go and hurt me boy. He had to take Elmore. I'll send him to the judge, now, and see that he pays what's owing for the deeds he's done." He gave Jeremiah a narrow look. "I said —you're not needed. I'll deal with this."

"Mister Finch is my friend, too, and even if he weren't, as an enforcer of the law, it's my duty to help those in need. We have the same goal. If I can do nothing else, I can undoubtedly make our enemy's life more difficult."

Mister Scratch slapped Jeremiah's arm and smiled. "Don't lock me up again, and we'll get on just fine."

At the *Indigo Running*, Mister Scratch went straight up the gangplank, but when Jeremiah went to follow him, a hand touched his arm. A black-robed reverend with the nose of a hawk and a tense look about the eyes stood at his side.

"I beg your pardon, officer. May I have a word?"

"Forgive me, but—"

The hand on his arm tightened until the grip was almost painful. There was strength under those robes. "It will only take a moment, officer."

Jeremiah started to pull away, but stopped when he happened to see Jacob standing a short distance away. Jacob watched them from where he stood at the corner of a building, half-hidden. Jeremiah stalked over to the boy. "What are you doing here? Your father made it clear you were to stay away."

"Helping. This is Reverend Roberts. Reverend, this is Lieutenant Bowe." Then he looked at Bowe. "Where's Da?"

"He just went aboard, looking for help to save your uncle."

Reverend Roberts said, "Then get him off. Now. That Raynard blaggard just went aboard!"

"What?" Jeremiah burst out.

The warning was too late.

There was a sudden uproar from the *Indigo Running*, shouts and the blast of gunfire. Jeremiah remembered Raynard Passy from their brief meeting in Mister Finch's home, he'd been friendly and polite, but when he scrambled down the gangplank and ran straight towards them, he had such a terrible look on his face! Fear and anger and desperation made him seem little more than a wild animal.

Mister Scratch was hot after Passy, swearing blue lightning. He held his cutlass tight at his side as he ran and he didn't run alone, as two of his shipmates ran after him.

Reverend Roberts pushed Jacob behind him and Jeremiah, thinking that Passy might do violence to the two defenseless people behind him, pulled his pistol from the holster at his side and aimed. He pulled back the flint and drew his mark.

Passy didn't hesitate. His pistol was already in his hand. He raised it and shot. The shot missed Jeremiah.

Jeremiah fired in return, but his pistol jammed and was entirely useless. A gasp from behind made him turn. Reverend

Roberts clutched at his stomach with both hands. His face drained of blood, bleaching him to the frightening color of seafoam. His eyes met Jeremiah's as he fell to his knees. He took a hand away from the wound and gaped at the blood on it—bright as a poppy. The front of his black robe grew shiny from the spreading blood, even as Jeremiah ran to him and tried to help him lay down.

Passy took the opening as Jeremiah was distracted and unarmed and bolted by them, but little Jacob, snarling like a wounded beast, tried to tackle him and might have done a well-enough job of slowing Passy down had Passy not seen the move and clubbed Jacob on the head with his pistol. Jacob instantly fell and Passy ran on.

Mister Scratch abandoned the chase and went to his son's side. He pulled Jacob's head onto his lap and spoke softly to him.

With both hands pressed against Reverend Roberts' wound, Jeremiah watched, relieved, as Jacob stirred and Mister Scratch hauled him to his feet. "Up you get. Come along, steady now. You're fine. It's just a bit of a lump." Mister Scratch went on like that, muttering reassurances to the slightly swaying boy as he tried to get Jacob to stand on his own. He looked up at the ship to where more men were hurrying down the gangplank. "Poet! Get yourself here!"

Poet, as it turned out, was a huge man with arms twice the size of Jeremiah's and a week's worth of stubble. The ship's surgeon, Mister Scratch told Jeremiah. Poet poked roughly at the lump on Jacob's forehead before he wordlessly moved to Reverend Roberts. He took a quick glance at the wound before he told Jeremiah to keep pressing on it. He shouted for someone to help carry the reverend. Poet took the reverend's shoulders while another man took his legs, and together they managed to haul him aboard the *Indigo Running*, where they gingerly lay him down on the deck. All the while, Reverend Roberts had stayed awake, but dazed and moaning from pain, clearly not really aware.

Indigo Running was in an uproar, the loudest of the roarers being a tall man who stomped furiously around the deck. "Thundering squid! Get that man on a bed, Byron. A holy man will be respected on this ship!"

Poet, who was obviously Byron, shook his head and drew out a knife which he used to cut open Reverend Roberts' habit. "The fresh air will do him more good than the lamp smoke I'd need to see in there."

Tools were retrieved from below deck, a nightmarish assortment of knives and metal instruments dull with rust and old blood caked into every crevice. Byron had Jeremiah move his hands and used his knife to cut away at the rest of Reverend Roberts' habit.

The wound was small, no bigger around than the cork of a wine bottle, but Jeremiah had seen smaller wounds kill. Byron called for rum and, after ordering Jeremiah to press on the wound, again, he started pouring the rum into the reverend's mouth.

Reverend Roberts coughed and jerked on the liquor, but Byron forced him to drink until he was satisfied. The blood had stopped pouring, but still seeped and Jeremiah feared that it was because there was not enough blood left to flow. The round bullet was extracted after some messy digging that had Jacob turning his face away. Reverend Roberts blacked out. Then, with a needle and thread, Byron stitched up his work with the ease of a tailor sewing on a button. A bandage was wrapped on with a long length of fabric.

When all was done, Byron sat back on his heels and looked at Mister Scratch. "If he's going to live, he'll have to fight. Pray for him."

Reverend Roberts was moved into the captain's cabin and laid down on the narrow bed. On deck, Mister Scratch introduced Jeremiah to Captain Harrington.

"And what of our traitorous rat?" Captain Harrington demanded.

"Ran. Cooper and Woodson kept up the chase."

"And chased him right to that French ship." The two who'd

gone after Passy came back aboard, winded, and reported how they'd run Passy to the same ship they'd boarded a few weeks ago. "They knew him well enough that he ran on without any trouble."

Out of reach.

"Uncle Elmore's there," Jacob said, desolate. His eyes were red and his face blotchy. "That's why Reverend Roberts came here. He wanted to tell you that that's where Raynard took Uncle Elmore. A ship called *Juliet*. I came with him because he didn't know you, Da. He said Raynard took Uncle aboard *Juliet* then left. He followed Raynard here. When I pointed you out to Reverend Roberts, Da, he wanted to warn you."

The crew of the *Indigo Running* seemed oddly subdued. Not that Jeremiah had much experience with ships or their crews. He didn't like the bobbling of the ship. He also couldn't escape the idea that there were only a few wooden boards between his dry feet and the cold water. The men still worked, but Jeremiah caught the somber looks and uneasy whispering.

"It's the good reverend that sets them on edge. They don't take such things lightly, and they shouldn't." Captain Harrington stepped up to Jeremiah's side. He watched Mister Scratch put a hand on Jacob's shoulder as they went into the cabin together to see the reverend. "Trying to kill a holy man ... that can't bode well for our crew. Bad luck. Well." He put both hands on the ship's railing and leaned on it. "We'll have to put it to rights."

Jeremiah nodded. "I'll get a contingent from the barracks to get aboard that ship."

"I think you'll find that harder than you guess." Captain Harrington pointed out into the harbor, where the *Juliet* was well on its way out to sea.

"Damn it!" Jeremiah hissed. "Raynard is wanted for murder, and I've got reasonable evidence to bring him to trial. I have orders to arrest him." To call together and get another ship and crew ready to sail would take time, but the *Juliet* was, by the looks of her, a swift craft. He shot a look at Captain Harrington.

"You're setting after her, then?"

"As I said, we've got to set all to rights, haven't we? Can't let bad luck stand."

"Right." Jeremiah turned fully to Captain Harrington, set and settled with his decision. "Captain, I'd like to accompany you in the chase."

"You're most welcome if you're willing to sign articles." He looked at the closed cabin door. "That one of my crew would come near to killing a holy man ... the good reverend might yet die. I can't let that lay. The ship and all of us would be cursed."

They stood together and spoke of what they knew of Raynard, and the result was that Captain Harrington turned red as a cherry with anger and slapped the palm of his hand on the ship's railing.

"I'll keelhaul that leech." The growled words were spoken in a deathly quiet tone. "That treacherous coward. He's not only brought God's wrath down around us, but he's broken ship's articles." He turned darkly passionate eyes to Jeremiah. "He'd have seen me painted as a traitor! I'll see him done for this!" The slapping hand became a pounding fist before he got control of himself and strode away from the railing and Jeremiah.

CHAPTER 16: THE FIRST BREATH

It had been years since Jeremiah had been aboard a ship, but he found that he disliked it just as much as he had the first time. Even the gentle bobbing of the ship on the waves as it was safely docked made him feel sick. But he stayed and he would go to sea.

He watched somberly as he stood at the aft side of the *Indigo Running* and watched while two fishermen who'd happened to be working on the docks nearby carefully carried Reverend Roberts away on a plank held between the two of them while Jacob walked silently at the good reverend's side. As was to be expected, the reverend hadn't woken since the bullet had been removed, and Poet had predicted that he would sleep on for hours, yet. They'd take him to a city doctor, the fishermen had promised.

Jacob, of course, had wanted to go along with Jeremiah and Mister Scratch to rescue his uncle, but Mister Scratch would have none of it and snorted at the idea. "I already told you—not for all the fish in the sea, urchin, would I let you come. You'll go back home and you'll stay there 'til you're fetched."

Before Jacob could argue, as he seemed to want to, Jeremiah added, "I do believe that your safety is what Mister Finch would want, don't you?"

Reluctantly, Jacob nodded.

The articles had to be signed before they set off, and as there was no way Jeremiah could give up the opportunity to hand the chart to the governor himself, he signed ship's articles to stay aboard for the single voyage, meaning that he didn't have to stay until the minimum booty was taken as the rest of the crew did. The ship's articles was an amazing document, Jeremiah concluded when he'd finished reading it. He'd never seen anything like it. A vote. He was given a vote about what happened on the ship. He could question the captain's word. He felt, as he scrawled his name at the bottom of the parchment with the names and marks of the rest of the crew, as if he were a lord in parliament.

Granted, the rest of the parliament were rather unwashed and some almost seemed more animal than man, but, still …

A vote.

Once Reverend Robert's party had gone, a slow procession to avoid jostling the reverend, Captain Harrington ordered five men ashore to fetch provisions as well as crew still not returned from their leave. Orders were barked and preparations were begun to set sail. There was rushing from here to there, up in the riggings and around the deck. Through it all, Jeremiah very carefully kept himself near the railing of the ship and out of the way as best as he could. The missing crew came running within minutes, and as soon as they did, Mister Scratch was at Jeremiah's side and slapped his arm. "Lend a hand, then!"

He led Jeremiah to the capstan, and together they pushed against the rungs with several other men to raise the anchor and Mister Scratch, though still worse for wear by his stay in the Hold, had thrown his all into the job. Once done, Mister Scratch rushed off to another job and Jeremiah, left on his own and without direction, looked back at the docks. He couldn't spot the group with Reverend Roberts, but he did see two queer folks staring intently at the *Indigo Running*: a man and a young girl, both wearing robes that stood out amongst the general milling people like torches on a dark night.

At that moment, a strong, favorable wind caught their sails, and they were away like a shot.

Everyone set to work. Mister Scratch went up into the rigging even before Captain Harrington called for the sails to be lowered. He climbed like a spider in a web along with a half-a-dozen other men and, in a flash, was at the cross-section of the tall mizzen mast untying the ropes holding the sails up.

A smack on the arm made Jeremiah turn from watching

Mister Scratch to a bald, fat-faced man. He had one odd eye that stared off to the side at nothing while the other focused on Jeremiah. "You. Come along." He spoke with a strong accent that Jeremiah couldn't place.

"Why?"

The man scowled and let out a long-suffering sigh before he seized hold of Jeremiah's arm, pulling him along. "You're crew, but idle. Idle do no good. Me boy's busy." He gestured carelessly to a skinny boy who was on his hands and knees, scrubbing the deck. "You'll do, youngin'."

Jeremiah found himself led down into the belly of the ship and through an area crowded with hammocks. Just beyond the hammocks was the galley where, at a stern order from the ship's cook (as the man leading him must have been), he started chopping potatoes.

He heard the calls of the captain on the deck above his head and felt a lurch when the ship turned. His stomach lurched right along with it.

The cook laughed. "Yer' white as snow, youngin'. This boat's sturdy enough and been through fire 'n storm 'n still she floats. Nothing to fear. Just you keep chopping."

Hours passed in the dim light, cooking and cleaning while the cook sang in a deep, surprisingly pleasant, voice.

When they came in sight of the *Juliet*, Jeremiah was called up to the deck by Mister Scratch, who pointed out two spots on the horizon.

"Ever fought a battle at sea?"

Jeremiah shook his head.

Mister Scratch surprisingly laughed and looked back at the ship they chased. "It'll be fun. Just you see."

"I hardly think any battle can be considered fun."

Mister Scratch's good humor didn't fade. "I can think of very little that is better able to set a man's blood boiling with life. And you'll see one 'afore you get to be in one. Looks like some action out there between those two ships."

Captain Harrington prowled from port to starboard, his

face barely turning from their target, and his single-mindedness was so great that Jeremiah worried for his mission, as such single-mindedness too often led to recklessness. He approached the captain.

"Governor Modyford wants Raynard Passy alive, Captain. He's strongly suspected of murder and must stand trial." Although why he would murder a member of the French crew, then take refuge there, Jeremiah couldn't guess. "I hope you won't get carried away when we catch him."

Captain Harrington smiled. "Then you do your best to get that traitor back to His Excellency. If you get him to port alive, he's all yours."

And Jeremiah knew then that there was little chance of Raynard ever seeing Port Royal, again. He wanted to argue; Raynard should be put to trail, not face whatever Captain Harrington had in mind. To just kill him outright and never have the world know who Lieutenant Passy's killer was seemed a terrible offense to the dead.

But he didn't have much choice in the matter. He was only aboard by the goodwill of Captain Harrington and nothing else. He had no power to do anything but wait unless he wanted to try the rights he was assured in the ship's articles and, given how eager the rest of the crew seemed to be for battle, he didn't think he'd get very far trying to change anyone's mind at that point.

As they drew nearer, it became apparent by the thundering noise of firing guns and a plume of smoke rising from the unknown ship that it and the *Juliet* were not allies. Mister Scratch had been entirely correct. Another volley of cannonballs and shot from the *Juliet*, then return fire from her enemy. The crew of the *Indigo Running* fell momentarily silent as more cannon shots were exchanged.

Mister Scratch turned and shouted up at the man in the crow's nest, "What flags are flying?"

"French and Dutch!" Came the reply.

Captain Harrington gleefully slapped the railing. "Stand by the cannons. Be ready. Count their guns. I want a count!"

A cry of, "Twelve French and ten Dutch!" hailed down from the crow's nest.

"Then we wait. Oh, luck! What luck!" The grin Captain Harrington wore was wolfish, a patient predator who knew his prey would shortly make a mistake. "I think we'll hang back a while and let them use up their shot on each other rather than us."

And so they waited while the two ships faced off. Cannonballs were exchanged. A blast from one gun sent, not a cannonball, but long chains flying through the air where they tangled in and tore down the *Juliet's* sails. One final cannon blast from the *Juliet* ended the battle as it bashed through the hull of the Dutch ship low enough that water began to pour in.

"Damn," Captain Harrington scowled. "Waste of a fine ship. That's the second ship lost. Move in, then! We take her while she's tired. Full sail!"

It was no fight. Calling the engagement that followed a battle would have been a joke.

The Dutch ship was half sunk by the time they came upon the ocean battlefield and terrified men plunged into the sea in a desperate attempt to escape the sinking disaster. Jeremiah watched as one man bobbed on the waves twice, then sunk and didn't resurface. The ship soon followed, slipping below the water in a manner that was almost mockingly peaceful considering the still-floundering sailors who'd abandoned her and their desperate screams that faded one-by-one as lives were taken by the sea. He turned away from the pitiful sight and found Mister Scratch watching him. Without a word, Mister Scratch silently went back to his work.

Jeremiah felt sick.

They were dying. They would all die. "Can't we save them?" Jeremiah muttered to himself.

He hadn't realized Captain Harrington was close enough to hear. "We've a battle to fight. We take time to help those men and it'll be us who's drowning, next. We're still too far off to help, anyway. By the time a dinghy could get to anyone, it would be too late." He paused, still looking at where the Dutch ship had gone down, then said, "It's too late, now. Look." He pointed back to the water. There wasn't a single man to be seen. They'd all drowned. "It's over, now."

Indigo Running's crew had hardly looked at the drowning men as they prepared for their own onslaught. Cannons were aimed and firearms readied. The attack began in a cloud of horror in Jeremiah's mind, in which all sound and sight seemed to be in a slow haze until a little hand shook his arm.

"Wake up, won't you!" The cabin boy, the cook's helper who'd been busy holystoning the deck, shook his arm with a scolding look. "Don't just stand there. Move."

And the haze was gone.

There was nothing to be done for the Dutch crew. Best to put that out of mind.

The battle was very short. The *Juliet*, after the earlier fierce battle, had very little left to fight the *Indigo Running*. *Indigo Running* pulled up close to the side of the *Juliet*. Jeremiah made certain his pistol was loaded and ready before he went to the side where men were readying to board the *Juliet*.

The French crew put up little resistance after the boarding. They were tired, and a great many had been wounded by the ferocious, now defeated, Dutch. Still, they didn't simply surrender. Jeremiah shot no one but did draw his sword to fight off one man who tried to attack. Mister Scratch had no hesitation about swinging his cutlass at the enemy. Every crewman of the *Indigo Running* proved willing and eager to fight, but they didn't appear to be aiming to kill. They herded the French crew to the bow and disarmed them.

"Can't I get away from you?" The French captain, with gunpowder burns on his white gloves, demanded when Captain Harrington went to stand in front of him.

Captain Harrington shook his head and smiled. "Not so long as you've got my man. And weren't that just rude of you? To take a man who's not yet finished his contract? He's got a shipful o' mates to answer to." He seized the French captain by the coat, but only to push him aside so he could get at the man who'd been hiding behind him. With both hands, Captain Harrington yanked him by the front of his shirt, hauling him away from the crowd of Frenchmen and in amongst *Indigo Running's* crew.

"You rat. How's our simpering dog?" He shook Raynard. "You put—"

"Please! Odell, you know—"

"Please?" Captain Harrington mocked with disbelief and outrage. "You beg? Coward! Can't challenge me to my face, so you send your own mate to the gallows and try to pin that filthy crime on my chest? You killed your own flesh and blood, and don't that just put you straight away in God's sights? He don't take kindly to the Cains of this world, now do he?"

Raynard spat in Harrington's face. "My ship! You took my ship."

"Loony toad. I were voted in, as is right by ship's articles." Captain Harrington was big and used that to look down on Raynard. "You broke articles, plain as plain, and you'll stand trial, as is right."

Mister Scratch thumped Raynard hard on the side of the head, making Raynard jerk in Harrington's iron grip. He barked, "Trial's too good for you! I ought to rip you in half right where you stand!"

"And you'll wish he had when I've done with you," Captain Harrington sneered.

"A moment, please." Raynard held onto Harrington's wrists with both hands. "You misunderstand. I only did this to benefit the crew—for all of us."

"By setting me for the end of a rope?" Mister Scratch snorted. "Fine thing to say about a shipmate; you think the crew would do better without me?"

"Short-sighted fool! I knew you'd not hang." Raynard lurched away as far as he was able to from Mister Scratch's enraged growl. "I swear! On my life I swear it!"

Jeremiah moved away from them and looked quickly around the deck. The French were all captured. *Indigo Running's* crew were either guarding the prisoners or prowling the deck. The hatch leading below deck stood open, and Jeremiah went down.

It was dark except for a single lantern mounted at the bottom of the steps, but there was light enough for him to see a solid wooden door at the end of a path that led beyond the crew's sleeping area. It looked little different than below decks of *Indigo Running*. Quietly, he crept forward. The sounds and voices from the deck dulled to a murmur the further into the darkness he ventured.

"Mister Finch? Elmore?" He called out. There was no answer, but he went to the door, regardless. There was nowhere else for him to be, and Reverend Roberts surely wouldn't have had any reason to lie about Mister Finch being brought onboard. He thumped on the closed door, but it was tightly locked. "Elmore!"

"Get me out!"

Jeremiah smiled and his head sagged with momentary relief. "The captain must have the key. I'll be back." He got back on deck to see Raynard still begging. Worryingly, Captain Harrington was listening. Jeremiah began walking towards Captain Harrington and his pleading captive.

"Treasure? We took what was worth anything, and there hadn't been so much as a single wagon of hay moving on the docks since they arrived."

"Not hay or gold or coffee." Raynard told him, his voice lowering to a near whisper. "This treasure is paper."

"Silence!" the French captain bellowed.

Captain Harrington didn't so much as look at him. "What paper?"

A sudden scuffle broke out as one of the French men dashed away from his companions and between the pirate guards. He ran like a rabbit for the hatch Jeremiah had just come from and jumped down.

Jeremiah rushed after him and was just in time to see the rabbit grab for the lantern as he staggered to a stop. There was a wrench, and the lantern broke away from the wall. He and the lamp fell to the floor, where the glass shattered and the oil fueling the fire spilled onto the floor. The lantern's flame spread quickly, throwing awful shadows on the walls and ceiling and floor. The rabbit thrust a folded paper into the flames and screamed when the fire burned his hands.

"Fire!" Jeremiah screamed it as loudly as he could.

The rabbit got to his feet and started up the stairs. With the fire spreading quickly behind him, he shouted, "France's treasure won't be taken!"

He was hauled onto deck to make way for men to go down to put out the blaze, but the fire was ravenously hungry and quickly began to devour the canvas hammocks and heavy blankets all around the sleeping area.

A panic broke out. Men charged back up to the deck and to the wide wooden boards that, like bridges connecting two banks of a river, connected the two ships and, privateer and Frenchman alike, they all scrambled for the safety of the *Indigo Running*.

Smoke surged out of the hatch as the fire gained strength.

Mister Scratch had Raynard by the arm and twisted, forcing the arm behind him. "Where the Hell's Elmore? You'll burn if I don't get him back!"

"Below! He's locked up!" Jeremiah shouted over the noise. He could feel his heart pounding in his throat. "He can't get out!" Jeremiah drew his sword and charged down into the smoke. He made it to the fire then jumped right though the flames and the billowing, choking smoke. The whole of below deck was so clogged with the heavy blackness of smoke that Jeremiah's eyes began to water. He stumbled and fell, coughing with every breath. The fire roared, deafening him. It seemed the whole world was ablaze. Hell. It was Hell. He felt like he was being crushed, but he managed to yell, "Elmore!"

"Hurry!"

Jeremiah hacked at the cell door twice with his sword before he was shoved out of the way. He was struck by the sight of Mister Scratch—the fire behind him and the smoke all around gave him an unearthly glow. He raised his arm holding not a cutlass, but a savage-looking boarding ax. Four strikes and the door was battered and splintered enough to be pulled apart.

Mister Finch staggered out of the cell and Mister Scratch caught his arm. Jeremiah let the other two go back through the fire first. He took a running start and held up his arms to protect his face as he jumped through the fire. The floor creaked and complained when he landed. Sparks and cinders fell from the ceiling. He fell to his knees at the steps leading up to the deck and heard something crack as his hand caught the edge of a step. His hand didn't feel broken, though. The crack came from above and Jeremiah looked up to see the wood above him afire, drifting sparks down on his face and into his eyes.

Jeremiah couldn't see. His eyes were burning. He pawed at his face, but it only made the pain worse until tears started washing them out. He was grabbed roughly on the shoulder.

"Get up, you damned fool!" Mister Scratch shouted at him. "We're going down!'

Another crack from the beams above shoved Jeremiah out of his fear and pain. He scrambled up to the fresh air on deck, where Mister Scratch and Mister Finch each took him by an arm, pulled him roughly to the ship's balustrade and didn't let go until Jeremiah yelled above the thunderous fire that he could see, again.

The deck was littered with dead men from the battle with the Dutch ship. Everything creaked and groaned around them. The ship began to tilt. *Indigo Running* had begun to move away from the *Juliet* but was still close enough that a jump to safety was a possibility. On *Indigo Running*, men from both crews stood, watching and shouting for them to jump.

Mister Finch shouted, "Go! It's the only hope. Jump!" He thumped Mister Scratch on the back. "You have to jump!"

With a running start, Mister Scratch made the leap easily enough and as soon as Mister Finch saw him land, he looked at Jeremiah. "You next. Go on!"

"You first." Jeremiah, insisted. "I won't leave you behind."

Elmore looked at the distance between the two ships and hesitated.

"Come on!" Mister Scratch shouted.

Elmore shook his head. "My leg... I can't."

"You have to," Jeremiah grabbed for the balustrade when the ship groaned and rocked. "Try!"

Elmore stepped back. His lips tightened.

"Think about Jacob!" Jeremiah urged. "He needs you."

"You jump. I'll be after you."

"You die and he'll take after his father. He'll be a fine specimen of a pirate, but you can never expect schooling for him. He'll be a drunk with syphilis before he's fifteen. Jump for him!"

Elmore did jump ... and he fell.

He plunged down between the two ships and into the sea, and vanished into the depths.

Elmore:

A yard.

One piddling yard, and he'd missed.

Gabe had reached out, but it wasn't enough. The water was bitterly cold, and Elmore felt as if the sea had swallowed him. Striking the water was hard, like hitting the ground after falling off a roof. He swallowed water and flailed. He broke surface for a moment and saw the smoke and growing flames, along with figures made dark by the sunlight shining behind them, looking down at him. He sank again and couldn't get back to the surface. The distorted light from above grew dim. Sound was muted and then faded to nothing.

Then he was grabbed and pulled up. He didn't fight the pull or struggle. Finally, there was light and he coughed up seawater. The air tasted sweet, like he imagined the first breath of life must have been.

Jeremiah had an arm wrapped around him. "Be still. Just breathe."

Elmore choked on a mouthful of water, but forced himself not to move, to let Jeremiah hold his head above the water. When he calmed enough to breathe properly, he said, "You swim?"

"Grew up on a farm. Pa taught me in the duck pond." His breathing was quick. His eyes were wide with barely suppressed panic. "This is a bit different than a duck pond." He fought with the sea to pull them away from the burning ship.

Laying on his back, helpless and terrified, Elmore was dragged, floating, across the sea, bobbing up and down with the movement of the water.

Indigo Running was still moving away, but upside down, he saw a dinghy being lowered. They were picked up after a moment, pulled into the little boat by rough hands. Gabe hauled Elmore into the boat while another man pulled Jeremiah in.

Gabe laughed, somewhat unsteadily, and slapped Elmore's chest. "You're a lot of trouble, you are."

"Aye. But if I drown, you know I'm going to haunt you. You're a right good mate, Gabe." He pushed himself to sit up and still felt no pain from the burns, but he was cold and unbelievably tired. He looked over at Bowe, sprawled on the boat amongst the legs of rowers, breathing heavily with his eyes closed. He lay like that a moment, then struggled to sit up. Gabe, too, took an oar and started rowing for *Indigo Running*. They cut through the water as quickly as possible, not talking or even looking at anything other than the ship ahead of them.

Bowe was shaking and staring at his knees. He moved his hands under his armpits.

"We're safe, now. Relax and breathe," Elmore told him.

Bowe looked up with unfocused eyes. "The chart's gone. All this for nothing."

"Not for nothing," Elmore disagreed. "We found a traitor." He stared at Bowe and the burns on his face and hands. His uniform was beyond salvation. "And all this showed the true colors of a good man." He bowed his head solemnly. "You risked yourself for me, nearly died in the effort. I thank you, Jeremiah

Bowe."

CHAPTER 17: TRIAL

Elmore leaned over the railing of *Indigo Running* with his arms resting on it. Water dripped from his nose onto his hands. He was cold and miserable and he felt like he couldn't breathe, but all that aside, he was grateful to be out of the stinking hole Raynard's friends had locked him in, and to be breathing good, clean sea air. So he stood there and watched the *Juliet* burn like a monstrous bonfire on the water. There wasn't a trace of anyone in the water, but for a single, lonely shoe floating near the wreckage of the *Juliet*. As Elmore watched, the shoe sunk. Soon, the *Juliet*, too, would slip beneath the water's surface, and there would be no evidence at all that anything had happened to disturb the peace of the sea.

Elmore was well pleased to be done with all of it. He grimaced when the throbbing pain in his leg began to creep upwards towards his hip. The way his leg was feeling, he would be laid up in bed for a week just resting it to ease the pain.

"What a nightmare." Bowe coughed, a harsh sound.

Elmore looked down at his left to where Bowe, looking like a half-drowned kitten, sat on the deck with his knees drawn up to his chest and did not look at the doomed *Juliet*. It was altogether an unsuitable way for a soldier to present himself, but considering he'd just risked his own life to pull Elmore from fire and water, Elmore could be charitable and not mention that Bowe looked more like a miserable child than a grown man in that moment. Elmore didn't move from where he stood with his lame leg gingerly held up to keep his weight off it. "It could have been much worse. Don't think too much on it." He kept his voice mild, and it was no hardship. He didn't say that Bowe would move past it or that he would forget in time. He'd known too many who'd lived through something hard and it nearly haunted them. The sad, unhappy look in Bowe's eyes hinted that he, too, might relive the nightmare of the fire for a great long time. Nothing good would come from dwelling on it, but, at the same time, no good would come of telling the man to forget it. "The Dutch crew weren't nearly so lucky as we were. It's just as well that they drowned before sharks came along."

"There should have been a way to help them."

"Unless you're planning to start walking on water, I think you ought to be putting such thoughts out of your head. The Good Lord calls folks home when He's good and ready—not when it's handy for you or me."

A heavy weight landed on Elmore's shoulders and he turned a little to find Gabe at his side. He'd draped his coat over Elmore's shoulders. "What's this?"

"I don't need it, and you look half frozen in the wind." Gabe looked Elmore straight in the eyes. "I'm mighty relieved you made it through all this with nothing but a wet hide. Don't know what I'd have done if …"

"Don't go getting soppy." Elmore saw the men gathering together in the middle of the deck when he looked over Gabe's shoulder. "It's about to start. Luck to you."

Gabe walked away to join his shipmates, and Elmore turned away from the sea to watch the proceedings. Gabe spoke briefly to Captain Harrington, then went below decks. The crew of the *Juliet* had been safely stored away below decks and, as Elmore had been expecting, Captain Harrington called out for all hands on deck, and everyone but the man at the wheel gathered together in front of Captain Harrington.

"What's happening?" Bowe asked as he stood up.

"Trial. Just keep quiet."

Gabe emerged from the hold with a swearing, fighting Raynard held firmly by one arm and the hair. Gabe yanked and pulled, probably more than necessary, until he had Raynard on deck and standing in the center of the crowd of men. The men were loud, too, hooting and hollering at their shipmate, yelling the worst sort of invectives, when Gabe released his hold on

Raynard and sent him tumbling to his knees with a shove. Red-faced and snarling, Raynard got back to his feet and glared around him, raking his eyes over everyone, but staring at no one more hatefully than he did at Captain Harrington.

How had Elmore missed it? Had not a single man noticed the hate that was so very apparent in Raynard's wide, shining eyes? If Captain Harrington cared about the venom, he hid it well with a roar for silence. "We've got us a runner, my gentlemen." Captain Harrington rumbled without taking his eyes away from Raynard. "A dog what thinks our signed contract means nothing. Worse, yet, he's a traitor, and a traitor to one is a traitor to all."

Raynard lunged at Captain Harrington, but Captain Harrington was faster and had his oak-handled pistol drawn, the hammer cocked back. Raynard froze, with the pistol's muzzle at his face, and then drew himself up straight with his head raised, proudly.

"Mister Passy," Captain Harrington drawled. "You will remember that you are standing trial. Compose yourself."

"Trial?" Raynard snorted and turned to face the crew. "If I'm to stand trial, then I say this crew should reconsider their choice of captain!"

Captain Harrington almost looked as if he would smile, but a twitch just under his eye showed his displeasure. "Hardly a time for you to take an interest in my career. Time to think of your own hide."

"This is my hide!" Raynard thumped his chest with his fist. "I say you deserve the black spot and are unfit to even declare that I have to stand trial!"

A murmur rose among the crew and Elmore knew they wondered if Raynard might have a point. Elmore stared at the rat, enraged. Red mist seemed to close in on his vision, like looking down a red tunnel. "Crawling snake. Yer just trying to get—"

"And that one!" Raynard pointed at Gabe, completely ignoring Elmore. "Our quartermaster! Our judge. He's involved.

He's the one I'm supposed to have betrayed, isn't he? How can he judge fairly if he already thinks me guilty? Is that fair or just? My name is still on the articles, same as all of you!" Raynard looked around at the crew and showed the fire and command that had once made him such a fine captain. "Is this how you want to be treated? No promised fair trial? Just a farce and a bullet in the face? Is that what you all want?" The roar that went up spoke clearly enough, and he swung his head rapidly to and fro, trying to look every hand in the eye.

The sound appeared to energize Raynard. "I was deposed for losing a target. I say Captain Harrington lost a treasure and a great bounty there!" He shot a finger out at the burning *Juliet*.

"You think I could have saved that inferno?" Captain Harrington's eyes widened and he laughed, as if he couldn't stop himself, regardless of the gravity of the situation.

"It started small enough. A bucket of water might have extinguished it. Did you try? No! You ran like a frightened child, and you lost whatever might have been on that ship as well as the ship itself. That's two ships lost, now! How those could have filled everyone's pockets! All for revenge. I'd not have done something so selfish if I'd still been captain of my own ship."

"Your ship?" Elmore blurted out. He grabbed hold of Bowe's arm and used him to balance himself. "This here's an equal crew. You were voted down fair. If you'd any trouble with that arrangement, you should have stuck to selling slaves to the plantations."

"My ship," Raynard insisted, baring his teeth at Elmore. "I sold my family's manor for this ship. Every nail and rope is rightfully mine!" He took a deep breath. "Putting that aside, I say Captain Harrington is not worthy of passing any judgment, not only because he lost the ship, but also because he abandoned a crewmate—Gabriel! I did nothing but run from people threatening me." He looked around, speaking to the crew. "Who wouldn't do the same? Who hasn't? I'm blamed for Gabe's imprisonment. Why would I do it? When I was chased, I ran to my cousin's ship for safety. It was the only option I had."

"Liar!" Gabe thundered. "You think I didn't see my son? See what you did to him? You beat a child, coward! You took Elmore and gave him to the French."

Raynard looked so cold, so still, when he said, "He's not crew. Not anymore. No matter what I did to any townsman, it hasn't got anything to do with here and now."

There was no way to put into words the utter rage that burned within Elmore. It wasn't so much Raynard's impassioned self-defense that stoked his ire—that was only to be expected—but that he actually seemed to be winning over the crew! Elmore stayed very still, for if he moved at all he feared he would attack, and that just wouldn't do at the moment, not when Raynard was so close to getting the crew worked up. So he kept his voice steady and even when he said, "You're not standing trial for anything but setting the law on Gabe. You killed your cousin for the chart tucked away in that spyglass. I've got two witnesses. Then, you told me that it were Cap'n Harrington that put Gabe in the sight of the law. That's your crime."

Bowe spoke up. "I can swear to it, too. You came to me to give me a lead to the murderer of Leopold Passy and told me—"

Raynard snapped, "This is your evidence? The word of a soldier? He's a friend to Elmore and Gabriel. He'll say whatever needs to be said to help them." He spoke to the crew, looking around at them, raising his voice so he could be heard by everyone. "I did kill Leopold, and I'll admit it, but that's my affair. Got nothing to do with any of this crew. I don't know anything about any map and I say, again, I didn't point the law at Gabriel."

"Will you swear to it?" Elmore asked, sharply. "Swear with your hand on the Good Book?"

The color drained from Raynard's face. He touched the cross he wore on a chain around his neck. "Show your evidence."

"You're looking at the evidence." He gestured at Bowe. "Friend or not, the lieutenant knows what you did. And if you are guiltless, if you've nothing to hide, you'll swear before God. Come along!" Elmore called out. "Who's got a Bible?"

"Only a prayer book." One of the men handed over a tiny book with a black leather cover. "It's just as good as a Bible, I reckon. Got holy words in it."

Elmore made a show of brushing the prayer book off and holding it out towards Raynard. "You were my friend 'til you turned on Gabe and you beat the boy. I would have stood up for you, and I'd have had your back. Put your hand on the words of the Lord and swear to Him of your innocence. We might be lied to, but He won't. We'll see if He truly does strike down liars."

Sweat had broken out on Raynard's upper lip. He shook his head. "And if nothing happens, you'll still think me guilty. You're bound to have my neck!" He turned away from Elmore and the prayer book without touching it.

"Got to have a trial." Everyone turned to the man who'd spoken—the one armed cook. He stood near the back of the crowd and frowned at Raynard. "I'll do. Scratch can't do it fairly, so I will. I'll judge." No one argued, and when Raynard opened his mouth, the cook simply said, "Someone got to. You got someone else to do it?" When Raynard looked around, helplessly, at the crew and couldn't find anyone to recommend, the cook nodded, decisively. He walked forward until he stood next to Captain Harrington. "Then we start."

There was no objection from the crew or Raynard, though he clearly didn't like it. Captain Harrington called all to order and all but the helmsman, who had to pilot the ship, were on deck, sitting or standing, and the cook, sitting on the capstan, called the trial to begin.

The silence of the crew showed how seriously they took the event.

Elmore spoke loudly, so everyone could hear, and, as calmly as he could, told about Raynard's visit with Gabe, then Gabe's gift to Jacob. He told about the intruder and the blood on Harold's muzzle. "Show your arm." He challenged Raynard. "I'm betting it'll match Harold's teeth near perfect." He sneered when Raynard didn't move, then went on to say how Bowe had arrested Gabe. He told about his own prowl around Port Royal and the people he'd spoken to until he'd finally been captured by Raynard and Captain LeBeau. He told about the navigational chart he'd found hidden under Raynard's bed.

"Proves nothing." Raynard raised his face, confidently. "What I did to you is nothing against articles."

"But," Bowe said. "I—"

"No, youngin'." Cook waved a hand. "Wait yer turn. There are rules, ya know."

Elmore continued, going through his imprisonment on the *Juliet,* and when he'd finished the cook looked at Bowe. "Now's yer turn."

"He," Bowe pointed at Raynard, "told me that Mister Gabriel Scratch, who was staying at the home of the coffin maker, Elmore Finch, was the one most likely to have murdered Leopold Passy as they'd fought during a raid. I arrested Gabriel Scratch on that accusation and on the testimony of several people who'd seen Mister Scratch violently drunk on the night of the murder. Further investigation proved he couldn't have committed the crime, pointing instead at a Frenchman, thinly built with a wounded arm." He focused on Raynard. "Should you be found innocent here, you will still face another trial at Port Royal. Actually, I feel safe in saying you'll face the hangman."

"And why would I do any of this?" Raynard demanded.

Bowe smiled serenely. "I haven't got the foggiest idea and, as far as I'm concerned, it doesn't matter in the slightest. It doesn't matter why you killed Lieutenant Passy, only that you did."

Raynard, tight-lipped, looked around at his mates. There was no sympathy to be seen. "How can anyone here trust a soldier's word? He's not one of us. They all hate us. He's likely lying just to see any of us dead."

"If I wanted to have some random man dead, I would have left Mister Scratch in prison and let him swing. I want the guilty man dead. Besides, I've known Mister Finch only a few days, and I arrested Mister Scratch. Not exactly close relationships, and certainly not close enough to make me risk my career and my life by lying for them."

"Seems a good witness," the cook said, rubbing his beefy hand over his head. "Why did you tell him these things?"

"I ..." Raynard licked his lips. His eyes seemed too big, too bright. "I ..."

The cook impatiently slapped his leg. "Damn it, man! Defend yourself!"

"Against these lies? How can I? I don't know why the soldier would say these things, but I didn't turn on Gabriel."

The cabin boy said, "But you did try to shoot Gabe at the harbor. You hit the reverend, instead. We all saw that. And you ran right to the French ship where they had Scratch's friend and sailed off with them."

Captain Harrington's eyes lit up with vicious glee. "Then if you're guilty of nothing else, you're guilty of breaking articles by running off. You admitted that earlier, yourself."

"And I told you why—I was being chased. You think I'd stand there like a lump? Of course I ran."

"Makes sense," the cook said. "And why'd you shoot at Gabe?"

Raynard said nothing.

The cook waited for a bit, then looked around at the crew. "Anyone have anything to say? No? Vote, then."

It was a unanimous—twenty-two votes of guilty.

The cook said, "Guilty of breaking the articles. The articles tell plain the sentence. Keelhauling."

Raynard's composure broke. Yelling and fighting, Raynard was taken and pinned face-down on the deck with one man kneeling on his back. Raynard let out a guttural scream. He begged. "God! No!" He looked at Bowe even as his wrists were bound with rope. "Take me to Port Royal! I'll face the judge there, don't let them kill me!"

Bowe made to step forward, but Elmore held him back with a firm hand on the arm. "Don't you interfere."

"Governor Modyford wants him alive."

"Governor Modyford isn't here. Under the ship or at the

end of a rope, he's dead. The only difference is that if you take him back to port, he'll have a chance to escape."

Raynard fought all the way as they dragged him to the stern. "Don't do this, please! Anything! I'll do anything!" He lapsed into French as he continued to beg.

The ropes that bound his wrists were pulled taut, stretching his arms until he couldn't move any more than an ineffective wiggle.

Gabe started towards Raynard with a vile sparkle in his eyes and a grim set to his face, like that of an unhappy bear. He got within four feet before Captain Harrington stepped in his path. Gabe glared up at Captain Harrington. "Move."

"He's got to serve his sentence."

"He beat my boy. I might not have a chance after this."

Captain Harrington shook his head. "Right's right. You think you can play with the articles as you please? Be careful. You'll find yourself facing trial, as well." He put an affable arm over Gabe's shoulders. "Join your mates, then. Pick up a rope."

CHAPTER 18: LEGACY

On the deck there was a carefully formed coil of rope, which was the perfect height for Elmore to sit on without disturbing his leg any more than necessary. He did his utmost to ignore his leg. It hurt, but it had been hurting horribly since he'd run from Raynard, and there was nothing that could be done but ignore it. His throat burned mightily and his chest hurt from the smoke he'd taken in on the *Juliet*; it hurt as badly as if someone had wrapped a chain around him and pulled it tighter and tighter with every breath he took. More than anything, he wanted to be in his own bed, and he wanted to sleep. He felt numb, and even the anger and fear and downright hate he'd been swimming in since that ruddy spyglass had fallen into his lap had been swamped under the thick tide of nothing that had settled over him. He felt numb right from head to foot.

Bowe sat down next to Elmore on the deck. "It's cold."

Elmore nodded. "You'll dry soon enough. For now, just sit."

"Why?"

"Just sit. Be still." Bowe wouldn't understand, and what was to happen was likely going to upset him. Best not to let him make a scene. He'd never served before the mast and couldn't possibly understand how very seriously the articles that bound the crew were taken. Raynard, on the other hand, had understood and had known full well the chances he took when he'd started this whole mess, and it was time for him to deal with the results of his gamble.

The crew of the *Indigo Running* were like hungry dogs with a lame rabbit trapped amidst their numbers. They even sounded like dogs as they circled Raynard in a thick, angry knot of people. The crew fairly howled their rage at their betrayer. Foul curses and other creative abuse upon him and his ancestors were hurled at Raynard as he thrashed and fought with snarling abandon, his good breeding forgotten in the realization of his plight. Raynard's efforts did no good at all. His wrists were still bound, each one tied with a heavy rope. Still, Raynard kept fighting, like a mad animal. It did no good. He was forced to the stern, nearly carried, passing near to where Elmore sat. He thought Raynard might have called out to him, but there was so much noise from everyone else that Elmore couldn't really hear. Not reliably. Even if he had heard or if he had maybe seen Raynard turn towards him, he ignored it altogether.

It was no surprise at all that Gabe was a part of the mob surrounding Raynard. He, however, wasn't angry or shouting. No ... he was smiling. He was quiet.

Even after all the time that they'd known one another, Gabe still had the ability to frighten Elmore at times.

Two of the bigger men picked Raynard right up off his feet and tossed him overboard. There was a short yell and a splash, and Elmore watched as the crew peered over the side of the ship to see what had happened to Raynard. That lasted only for as long as it took Captain Harrington to shout the order, "Run!"

The men, still holding the two ropes that were bound to Raynard's wrists, pulled the ropes, heaving until some of them had the veins in their necks and arms standing out like cords of rope. They started running to the other end of the ship. The air was heavy with stomping and shouting and swearing and even cheering until they reached the bow of the ship and, as one, they began to haul up the two ropes.

Soon, Raynard was brought up to the deck, and what a nightmare of a fisherman's catch he was. Unconscious, with his head lolling backwards, he was laid out on his back for Poet to look him over. There was blood everywhere from where the barnacles growing on the hull had done a fine job trying to shred him.

"Is he dead, yet?" Captain Harrington asked.

"No." Poet, kneeling next to Raynard, was thunderstruck. "Not sure how, but he's alive."

"Then get the water out of him."

Raynard was rolled onto his side and had his back thumped until he spit up water. He didn't wake up.

Elmore watched it all impassively. He felt strangely far from what was happening in front of him. He was tired and cold enough that he could hardly feel his hands and feet. Beside him, Bowe sat with one leg stretched out in front of him while the other was drawn up close to his chest. His eyes were half-closed, as if he were nearly asleep. His fine uniform was soaked right through, and his hair was dripping and flat against the sides of his face. Bowe looked so young, there. If Elmore had felt more like himself, he would have laughed. As it stood, he just watched when Poet eyed Raynard critically and poked at various wounds.

From where they sat, Elmore couldn't see much of Raynard, and Bowe didn't appear interested in even looking. Justice had been done, and the punishment carried out. It was over, but Elmore knew it was quite likely that Raynard would end up dying, anyhow. Poet did some quick stitches with his needle on the worst of the injuries, and Raynard was carried below deck where he could make an attempt to recover in the darkness and out of the wind. As he was brought by, Elmore stared. What a bloody mess Raynard had been torn to. He twitched and flinched, but his eyes stayed closed and water, the remnants of what he'd inhaled, dripped down his chin and out of his nose. The fine clothes he'd been so fond of had been reduced to nothing more than gruesome ribbons.

Bowe started to cough and kept coughing for several long minutes. When he'd finished, he wiped tears away from his eyes.

"You gonna live?" Elmore asked.

His silent nod wasn't quite convincing. Bowe's eyes were fixed on the deck where Raynard had been, on the puddle of watery blood Raynard had left behind. "That's it? His punishment's over?" His voice was weak. "If he lives …"

"If he lives, you can't have him," Elmore warned. "This was

all because he gave Gabe to you and then abandoned his ship. If we give him to you ... well, it's the same thing, isn't it? You just forget about him."

"He's a murderer."

"He's not your concern." Elmore cast another look at Bowe and noticed a slight trembling to his hands. In that moment, it struck Elmore that Bowe wasn't really all that much older than Jacob. "You don't look so steady. Stay here and take the clean air in."

Bowe shook his head. "It's anything but clean. All I'll do is stare at that." He pointed to the still-burning *Juliet*. "And I'll only think of the other men—the ones who drowned. At least if I'm helping cook, I'll be busy." Bowe didn't move.

Elmore knew it was exhaustion that kept Bowe in his place and said nothing to wound his pride. He turned to watch the crew re-coiling the ropes and the cabin boy scrubbing the blood from the deck on his hands and knees. Elmore wished Raynard had died, God forgive him. He wanted the man dead. He was just too dangerous. Jacob's battered face was proof of that. If Raynard was willing to hurt a defenseless boy, then he was sure to do most anything.

A harsh cough made Elmore double over with pain. He kept coughing, even though Bowe thumped him on the back. His chest felt strangely heavy, even once the coughing eased off. He ran his hand across his mouth to wipe away the spittle.

"Come, you two."

Elmore looked up to find the cook standing over them. The cook pulled Bowe to his feet. "Too cold up here for wet folks. Warm by the fire. Galley plenty warm."

The galley was warmer, and there was nothing more to be done.

***

"It's done, then?" Bowe asked, holding his hands out near the fire where a large pot held stew boiling for the night's meal. "No more chart, no more chase for it." Slowly, Bowe seemed to come back to life. The color came back to his cheeks, and he stopped shaking. The cough stayed with him, as it did with Elmore and would likely linger 'til the last of the smoke had left their lungs.

"Aye," Elmore answered. "Back home we go and none too soon. I've got work to do. It'll be piling up, now."

Bowe looked down at his knees. "Business is that good, then?"

"Good enough."

"Your Jacob must be pleased. He'll have a solid trade when he takes over your shop."

"Only if something goes awful wrong. I'm sending him away to school to see he gets himself a gentleman's life."

"I had thought him to be your apprentice." He fell quiet for a moment, then asked, "Would you consider taking one on?"

Elmore raised an eyebrow. "Thinking of a change of career?"

"It does look like it might be a bit of a necessary change. Governor Modyford is expecting me to deliver the chart into his hands. He's going to be rather unhappy, to say the least. I think I may be unwelcome in the military, yet I have no urge to leave Port Royal. I think I may end up having to rearrange my life a bit. Carpentry seems as good a life as any."

Elmore didn't answer him.

Instead, Cook gave Bowe a hardy slap on the shoulder and laughed. "You come sign articles, if woodworking don't work for you. Life's not so bad before the mast."

When Cook moved away, Elmore frowned at the thoughtful expression on Bowe's face. He muttered, "Don't think you'd take a shine to life at sea."

"I may not have much of a choice."

The return journey to Port Royal was nothing to note. It was only a few hours of travel, and the weather was clear and calm. They encountered not a single other ship, and when they docked all was quiet. The peaceful return was marred by the fact that they returned to the island with no treasure, a dreadful tale, and sunburn. Besides all that, there was no way of ever knowing if the chart had truly been a treasure or if it had been nothing but a fake.

CHAPTER 19: HOME

The *Indigo Running* docked at the harbor of Port Royal the morning after it had left, and Elmore and Bowe said farewell to Gabe on the docks. He would meet up with Elmore later, but had work to do aboard ship. So Elmore borrowed a stick to lean on from the ship and, with Bowe walking beside him, started for home. They were both quiet as they walked. Bowe seemed deep in thought and Elmore didn't see any reason to disturb him. They hadn't gone more than a few dozen paces away from the gangplank of *Indigo Running* when Bowe stopped walking and turned to face Elmore. He was a far cry from his previously immaculate state, as he'd gotten tar stains on his uniform, had missing buttons, and his bright hair was all in disarray. His shoulders were slumped, and he had the look of a desperately tired man. He opened his mouth, then closed it. He looked confused and it was clear as day that Bowe had something to say, but couldn't find his words.

"Come to the shop?" Elmore asked, more than willing to offer a rest and a mug o' something to warm the bones.

The question seemed to give Bowe enough direction to order himself, again, and he said, "Thank you, but no." Despite appearances, Bowe's fine manners hadn't escaped him. "Business first." He nodded his head to the left where, Elmore saw when he followed the direction of the nod, three soldiers were making their way briskly towards them.

"Can I help?"

"Wish me some good luck?"

"I'll raise a noggin' to you. Come 'round to the shop when you know what's going on, yeah?"

"Will do."

Then, he was gone. He walked away from Elmore and met

with the soldiers. They were too far off for Elmore to hear what they said, but after a short moment, Bowe, with his head once again held high, walked briskly away with the other soldiers.

There was nothing Elmore could do for Bowe after that.

Elmore continued home.

His knee hurt in the most unspeakable fashion, and he was so tired that he felt he might easily sleep for a year and then take a nap afterwards. By the time he reached his home, he was ready to cry. He walked in and took a deep breath and, almost at once, felt the stress ease away. The smell of sawdust was as strong as ever and, under the workbench, Daisy slept while Harold watched the door. As soon as he saw Elmore, Harold's tense stance relaxed.

A voice from upstairs called down, "We're closed!"

Elmore ignored Jacob's yell and went into the kitchen, where he nodded a greeting to the reverend, whom he wasn't all that surprised to see sitting at the table. Elmore sat himself down. "Morning."

Reverend Roberts gave him an exasperated look. "Good morning. Glad to see you alive."

"Me, too. How're you holding up, Reverend?"

"As well as can be expected." Reverend Roberts kept his voice low. "Your Jacob rather insisted on me staying while I heal. The boy worries more than a nursemaid."

"He does at that. Means well, though." He didn't mention that Reverend Roberts did look a bit on the pallid side and that there were dark circles around his eyes. He was far from recovered, and Elmore knew that he wouldn't be encouraging the man to leave anytime soon. Still, for all that, he seemed in good shape for a man who'd been shot only a day earlier.

They were silent for a moment before Reverend Roberts, who had waited far longer than Elmore had expected him to, asked, "So? The chart?"

"Gone. Burned to ashes, and those ashes sunk right to Davy Jones' Locker." Daisy ambled in and laid her head on Elmore's lap, contentedly letting her tongue loll out of her mouth when he scratched at her ear. "Good riddance."

"Might be for the best."

A thumping down the stairs preceded Jacob's voice. "I'm heading to the market, sir." Jacob poked his head into the kitchen. "Do you want ... Uncle?" He stared for just a moment before rushing in. He fell to his knees in front of Elmore and hugged him so tightly that it almost felt as if he'd never let go. Elmore could admit, if only to himself, that he didn't mind a bit. He held Jacob and kissed the top of his head. Jacob took a shaky breath. "I thought maybe you wouldn't come home."

"Don't be daft."

"Is Da alright?"

"As good as ever. He'll be by later." They sat there for a time before Elmore cleared his throat and said, "I've been giving it some thought, now, about your schoolin', I mean. When I thought I'd not see you again, the idea of sending you away deliberate like and not seeing you for years ... maybe not see you again ... it just didn't sit too well with me. I won't do it. I won't send you away if'n you're set against it."

Jacob pulled away a little and looked up at Elmore, astonished. He then laughed so hard that Elmore thought he might just fall down. "I think," Jacob said when he'd caught his breath enough to talk, "I'm about to upset you."

"Eh?"

"Fact is, I'm not so dead set against going to university, now."

"And where'd that come from?"

"From Reverend Roberts getting shot." Jacob stood, then, and walked over to stand behind the good reverend, putting both of his hands on the man's shoulders. His eyes grew wide and he whispered, as if afraid to voice his thoughts, "I was so afraid he was gonna die, and there was nothin' I could do. The doctor was sent for, but he didn't come for ages. I went and ran for Mister Fa, instead. He knew what to do straight away and even left medicine in case Reverend Roberts took a fever. I wanted to help, but I couldn't do anything. I just stood there like a fool."

The level of Jacob's obvious feeling on this was enough to make Elmore pause. "You want to be a doctor?"

"Yes, sir. I think I'm smart enough."

"Thunder! I know yer smart enough. You want to be a doctor, then a doctor ye'll be."

Reverend Roberts laughed, softly. "I have been trying to convince him of that since I woke. And, really, I wasn't in so great a danger as he seems to think. Many men have faced far worse injuries and survived perfectly well." He looked up at Jacob and shook his head. "Doctor Tamworthy had other patients and can't abandon them at a moment's notice. You know that. I won't have any hard feelings toward him on my behalf."

"Mister Fa said you could take fever!" Jacob protested. "People die from fever!"

"And they die from being trampled by horses, doesn't mean I'm going to hide indoors the rest of my life. Didn't you have to get to the market for something?"

Reluctantly, Jacob did start to leave. However, he only just turned to the kitchen's door when Gabe stepped around the corner.

He crossed his arms at Jacob, then looked at Elmore with a wry smile. "Now you've got the boy reaching for the sky without any prodding. Guess I'm gonna have to get used to the notion that he's gonna be better, more, than his poor old da."

Like he had with Elmore, Jacob threw himself at Gabe, but he stopped a pace away from him. He shook wildly for a moment before he burst out, "I'm sorry! I didn't mean any of it, honest! I'm happy and right proud you're my da!" He went on like that, in a rush, as if he were afraid that his words would fail if he didn't hurry them along, until Gabe hugged him, then pushed him gently away to hold him at arm's reach.

"Yer sure to be a fine doctor, and I'll be here to see it." He smiled at Elmore. "One more good haul and the company will disband. It's been agreed. New articles will be drawn up, and Cap'n will head out with those who want to sign up, again, and new hands as needed. I won't be one of them."

"You're staying?!" Jacob was nearly bouncing in his excitement.

"If anyone wants me here." Gabe's tone was light, but he looked over Jacob's head and met Elmore's eyes seriously ... nervously.

Did he want Gabe around? With all the trouble that followed in his wake? The drinking would be troublesome. He'd likely be getting himself into fights every other night. Gabe wouldn't settle easily into a quiet life.

Still ...

Elmore nodded. "You've a home here if you want. Haven't I said that often enough?"

Jacob let out a joyous holler and Gabe laughed, hugging Jacob, again.

***

Some days later, Elmore was back to work, crafting a new coffin—a tiny, toy-like thing for poor little Annie Coleman, who'd been taken away by a wracking cough that had been too strong for her to fight.

A rap on the door drew his attention and he turned to the open door momentarily to see Bowe before he turned back to his work. "Lieutenant. Good to see you. What can I do for you? Not looking for new employment by the look of you."

Indeed, Bowe had been restored to the state he'd been in when he'd first introduced himself to Elmore, all bright red uniform and shining buttons. Elmore couldn't help but feel a little disappointed.

Bowe smiled when he walked in. "No. Governor Modyford was satisfied with my report and the fact that the chart is lost to all and not in the hands of an enemy nation. I have returned to my duties with distinction for courageous service. I merely came to visit to see how you and yours are faring."

"Jacob's doing good. He's young and heals fast. Reverend Roberts is doing as well as can be expected. Miracle he's alive, really. God must have been watching out for him. He's not teaching, yet, but Jacob said all the boys are enjoying having Roger Moon as a teacher. He tends to fall asleep during the math lessons."

Bowe laughed. "Yes. That sounds about right for any boy that age. And you?"

There were nightmares.

Darkness and voices he didn't understand.

Fire and choking water.

He saw Jacob, broken and lifeless.

"I'm good. You?"

Bowe kept smiling. "I've killed before; people trying to kill me, mostly, or trying to hurt someone else. I've seen the dead many times. That consumption that ran through the city two years ago? I helped collect the bodies. I sat with my mother while she died. But ..." His smile faltered. "I have never just stood by and watched people die. How many do you think there were? Thirty? Fifty? So many men drowned. We didn't even try to save a single one."

Bowe—Jeremiah—Elmore realized, was so young. Elmore set down his hammer and motioned for Jeremiah to follow him into the kitchen. "Sit. I reckon you're thinking too much. People die. Seamen die all the sooner, and they knew that when they attacked the *Juliet*."

"Maybe they were the ones who were attacked."

"No. The *Juliet* were carrying a treasure. They wouldn't have risked a fight, not after coming so close to losing it here. 'Sides, they aren't pirates. It were the Dutch ship that moved first and, unless I miss my guess, they were the pirates. You got nothing to be feeling guilty about. And what if we had tried to help? You could never have saved them all. Stop flogging yourself. Even if we'd tried to help, we were too far off to do any good. Anyhow, the choice wasn't yours. It was Captain Harrington's. If there's guilt to be suffered, you leave it to him. It's done and over. Tell me, what happened to the *Juliet's* crew?"

"Oh, still in prison. Captain LeBeau's being charged with your kidnapping. You'll need to appear in court."

"I'd sooner not. Can we do without it? They aren't likely to do it again, not now that they've been caught, and there's no treasure to show for all that trouble."

"I thought you might say that. Governor Modyford has agreed to pardon Captain LeBeau if he pays you damages of five hundred doubloons."

Elmore's mouth went dry and he stared at Jeremiah. "Five hundred? That's never right."

"I wouldn't lie to you."

"Aye … well …" Elmore rubbed at the back of his neck. "Tell you what—you tell the governor that I accept, and you take that five hundred and see that it gets to Mister Fa."

Jeremiah stared, wide-eyed, then shook his head. "Well … that's … that's very generous, but are you sure …?"

"Sure as the sun rising in the east. And who more rightfully deserves it? They need that reward a good sight more than I do." It would, if Mister Fa was as careful as Elmore thought he might be, enough money to keep them comfortable for the rest of his life and possibly even for Mei's. Elmore was certain that if Bingbang were as good of a man as his grandfather thought him to be, then he'd rest easier knowing that his family would be taken care of.

Jeremiah flushed and looked down at his lap, momentarily speechless. Then he cleared his throat and turned away before he collected himself. "And Raynard Passy? Do you know his fate?"

"Oh, he's doing well enough, far as I know. Still alive and healing."

"What's going to happen to him?"

"He'll be lucky if they take him to some far-off port and leave him in a forsaken town. Traitors aren't looked kindly upon. Before then, Gabe will find time to be alone with him and demonstrate his unhappiness that Raynard hurt Jacob. Gabe's good at that sort of thing." He poured a couple of mugs of ale and gave one to Jeremiah. "Drink up. It's a good ending. Mystery's solved, and the chart's destroyed."

"You're sure that's good? Think of all the time that could have been saved with it."

"Time saved ain't worth lives, is it? Folks won't die for it, again, until they find the exact route, again—if they ever find it. My guess is that if that route is found again, you'll have more deaths. It'll be a good long while before we see any trouble come about that chart." He chuckled at Bowe's surprised expression. "Oh, trouble will come, mark my word. There was plenty of time for that chart to be studied. Their navigator might be dead, but Captain LeBeau would've been a fool not to look at it himself, and who knows who else had access to it? The French will have another ship outfitted and at sea before the year's out, trying to find that route, and I'll lay wages on the fact that Captain LeBeau remembers at least part of the route. And there's not a thing any of us can do about it unless the governor wants to turn ruthless and kill the whole lot of them in prison and let the route die with them. As the man's trying to turn the city civilized, that don't seem too likely."

Jeremiah held his mug with both hands and stared down at the drink. "But it's not right. Leopold Passy didn't get his justice. No one will ever know how and why he died or who killed him. I can't say anything because if it comes out that I knew anything about Raynard, I'm sure that I'd be tossed in prison for letting him go free. He should be standing in court before the governor."

"Right and wrong ... they don't really mean anything. It's all in how you look at life. Raynard must have thought he was in the right as *Indigo Running* was his ship, he did buy her, and he'd brought together the crew. He'd always done his best for his crew and he was a good captain; I'll give him his dues. I know I was in the right, as I had to protect Gabe and Jacob. Is it right to imprison him on an island or behind bars or to stretch his neck? It doesn't matter."

"What's right and just does matter!" Jeremiah insisted, hotly.

"Raynard knows what he's done, as does God. No one more

fit to judge right and wrong than the Good Lord, so I say we leave justice to him. And if it's so important to you that we do what's right, then I should, by rights, be talking to the law about that chalk circle of yours." He gave Jeremiah a knowing look. "Surprised? No, I've not spoken a word of it and I won't. You went and gave me a shock, more than anything, but there's no doubt that you've done right by my people and that's what matters. I can't see anything truly unchristian in you. Even if I did, I'm no shining example of a God-fearing man, myself, so I don't suppose I ought to be casting stones." He finished his drink in a single gulp. "I've got work to do. If you're just going to hang about, you can give me a hand. Jacob won't be back for another hour or so, and a couple more hands are always welcomed. Come along. We'll teach you a useful trade, yet."

Jeremiah set his drink on the table and followed Elmore back into the workshop.

Elmore was, on the whole, satisfied. Everything had turned out rather well. And his leg, according to the good Mister Fa, would be as good as ever with rest and a little care. Jacob was safe and happy, and had finally settled on a future he was keen enough on to work for. Gabe would join them, soon. He would have to keep an eye on Bowe and see that all of his idealistic visions didn't get him into mischief before he had proven himself to be a good lad. Yes, everything had worked out well enough.

The only thing that still nagged at his mind was the chart.

It was gone, true; but he would have liked to know if it was real or just a fake.

BOOKS BY THIS AUTHOR

This Thing Of Ours

A farm girl smuggling moonshine, a playboy mafia prince, and the murderer who brought them together.

Viola Higglebottom, a young, unwed mother during the Great Depression, was willing to risk everything by selling liquor to provide for her family. That risk ended up bringing her into the path of the local mafia don's young brother, Dominic Moretti, who was cheerfully determined to charm her. As Viola knew very well that she was no great catch and had long ago put thoughts of romance aside, she couldn't take Dominic seriously.

But then there was murder and deception, a careful attack on the Moretti family by an unknown enemy. An employee, a rival, and a servant - all dead because of their association with the Moretti family. Together, Viola and Dominic must face danger and stand against a killer if they were to save their families.

Made in United States
Troutdale, OR
12/06/2023

15425689R00139